O'BRIEN'S
DESK

O'BRIEN'S
DESK

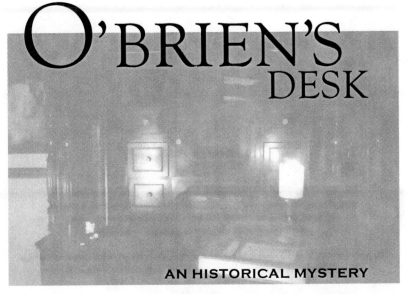

AN HISTORICAL MYSTERY

ONA RUSSELL

To Chris—
So nice to meet
you!

Happy Reading
Ona Russell

SUNSTONE
PRESS

SANTA FE

Sunstone books may be purchased for educational, business, or sales promotional use.
For information please write: Special Markets Department, Sunstone Press,
P.O. Box 2321, Santa Fe, New Mexico 87504-2321.

Library of Congress Cataloging-in-Publication Data:

Russell,Ona,1952–
    O'Brien's desk / by Ona Russell.
    p. cm.
    ISBN 0-86534-416-7 (hardcover) ISBN 978-0-86534-549-2 (softcover)
1. Secrecy—Fiction. I. Title.
    PS3618.U765 O37 2004

    813'.6—dc22

                                                                2003024657

Published in SUNSTONE PRESS
POST OFFICE BOX 2321
SANTA FE, NM 87504-2321 / USA
(505) 988-4418 / ORDERS ONLY (800) 243-5644
FAX (505) 988-1025
WWW.SUNSTONEPRESS.COM

Footfalls echo in the memory
Down the passage which we did not take
Towards the door we never opened
Into the rose garden. My words echo
Thus, in your mind.

—T.S. Eliot

Prologue

Maryville, Tennessee, 1997

Like the cut from a jagged blade. Piercing and dull. Margaret sensed the seriousness of this new pain as she waited for her son to arrive. At seventy, she'd had her share of headaches, but none that couldn't be relieved by an aspirin, or better yet, a cigarette and glass of wine. The sensations she awakened to this morning, however, responded to none of these usual remedies. Nor were they abated by her characteristic attempts to talk herself out of it. So intense, they prevented her from feeding the swans and steeping the tea; so unique, they made even a walk down the hall seem ominously unfamiliar.

Thus, in the brief moments before leaving for the hospital, Margaret regarded what was familiar with fondness. The tongue-and-groove walnut living room walls, her collection of porcelain swans and Delft china, the bay window framing the vast patchwork of lush, Tennessee farmland. As she moved arduously from room to room, it was the tangible things, those that had given her life form and purpose, which drew her attention. The dining room table, solid as ever, appeared immune to the burns and spills that punctuated its history. Crafted from the same rich cherry stood the massive twin book cases. Overflowing with words of the past, they similarly bespoke a permanence that stood in opposition to the harsh temporality of her current physical state. And then the desk. The intricately carved pull-top, which had always been so curiously reassuring.

Frequently seated at its writing table, Margaret had marked the passage of time there; paying monthly bills, filing yearly tax returns, signing birthday, wedding and sympathy cards. A circularity existed in these activities, a predictable order that the desk, with its neat, geometrical openings for pens and pencils, its symmetrical drawers for paper, stamps and tape, its miniature lock and key, embodied. This desk, whose darker purpose she never could have imagined, reminded Margaret of the clearly defined life she had made for herself. With affection she ran her hand over its cool surface.

On this steamy July morning, the car sluggishly made its way to the emergency room of Blount Memorial Hospital. Propped up on a pillow in the passenger seat, Margaret offered her son a reassuring smile, but remained silent for the duration of the ride; in part, to conserve the strength the pain was steadily draining from her, but also because of an inexplicable desire to keep the image of the desk before her. If she lost focus for even a moment, it would somehow lose its materiality. With the coolness of the wood still lingering on her fingers, she began to retrace mentally its shape, countering every incomprehensible bodily sensation with a well-known groove, curve or line. The delicate legs, the sturdy frame, the slightly lopsided top, on which only a few days before she had carefully stacked the scrapbooks.

How strange, the timing of her decision to remove those books from the closet in which they'd been stored undisturbed for so many years. Five of them in all, filled with meticulously ordered newspaper clippings chronicling the life of her father, a judge for twenty-two years who died suddenly when she was eight. Although he occupied a legendary position in the family, she herself had only faint recollection of him.

What made her take the books that day and wipe off forty years of dust? Was it the children? Perhaps. Yes, she remembered thinking that now, as adults, they might very well be interested. But why that moment in particular, when just a month ago she'd casually passed them by? Not a premonition, surely. She simply didn't believe in such things. The mystical was nonsense, an invention of the weak. Life had always been more like the crossword puzzles she daily worked; questions whose clear-cut answers were under her control; empty squares waiting to be filled in by conscientious individuals who believed in the power of human endeavor. Yet, even as the nurse wheeled her into the sterile corridor where she began the process of admission, she thought of those books and their significance.

But not for long. The increasing severity of her pain soon made such vague considerations impossible. Discrete sensations rapidly became indistinguishable, dull and piercing intervals merging into one relentless beat. Despite her distress, however, she remained coherent enough to answer the nurse's official questions; simple questions really, with the exception of one she had dreaded all her life:

"Name?"

"Margaret Louise Russell."

"Maiden name?"

"O'Donnell."

"Date of Birth?"

"March . . . March 4, 19 . . ." She hesitated. No, not this time. It would have to be the right answer now. The response she had practiced for so many years, that she had even convinced herself was the truth, seemed oddly, absurdly inappropriate here. And so Margaret finally spoke what she could never say. The only spaces she had ever left blank would now make themselves known, forcing the past to surface in a present of which she would no longer be a part.

"November 23, 1923."

1

Toledo, Ohio: November 23, 1923

It was getting late, nearly 8:30 and still no sign of him. Sarah glanced furtively down the hall. At least she had managed to restore a semblance of order. With the exception of a few die-hards who would obviously not be satisfied until they could question O'Donnell himself, the reporters had gone—no doubt in search of someone less experienced with their methods.

She closed her door and for the third time this morning reviewed the judge's schedule. Yes, he certainly should have been here by now. With vague apprehension, she reached for the phone and started to dial the familiar number. On the fourth digit she stopped. There, next to her prized, miniature portrait of Susan B. Anthony was her magazine, still opened seductively to where she had left off before attending to the press. No, she told herself. I shouldn't. I can't. There isn't enough time. She reinserted her finger in the circular opening and turned it halfway around. Then again, the trial wasn't until ten. And she had been interrupted at such a critical moment. She deserved just one more column. She hung up the phone, repositioned the wire-framed reading glasses dangling around her neck and, with god-like power, temporarily restored the beckoning characters to life.

> *"All right. Have your way." He sat down at the table and scribbled a check, which he tore from the book, but he refrained from handing it to his companion. "After all, since we are to be on such terms, Mr. Altamont," said he, "I don't see why I should trust you any more than you trust me. Do you understand?" he added, looking back over his shoulder at the American. "There's the check upon the table. I claim the right to examine that parcel before you pick the money up."*
>
> *The American passed it over without a word. A. von Bork undid a winding of string and two wrappers of paper. Then he sat gazing for a moment in silent amazement at a small blue book which lay before him. Across the cover was printed in golden letter Practical*

14

Handbook of Bee Culture. Only for one instant did the master spy glare at this strangely irrelevant inscription. The next he was gripped at the back of his neck by a grasp of iron, and a chloroformed sponge was held in front of his writhing face.

"Another glass, Watson!" said Mr. Sherlock Holmes as he extended the bottle of Imperial Tokay."

"I knew it!" Sarah beamed, although slightly ashamed of her own enthusiasm. Of course. Holmes was the American all along, his brilliant disguise once again halting the progress of evil. A little too predictably, perhaps. Much too tidily, she would have admitted. But in these uncertain times, indeed in the overall uncertainty of life, she found a measure of satisfaction in the mystery so unambiguously solved. She ear-marked the page and returned the tattered copy of the *Strand* to the shelf in the corner of her office. "Until tomorrow," she said. Right now I need to call the judge. Where in the devil is he anyway?"

Seated at his desk, Judge O'Brien O'Donnell gazed through the French doors at the leafless oak tree that in the summer would shade the entire backyard with its thick green foliage. He had always loved autumn, and this year was no exception. The colors of this season were made especially vibrant from the unusual amount of rain in July and August. But the splendor had ended far too abruptly. By the first of November, the limbs were barren, winter convincingly on its way.

It should be spring! O'Brien picked up for the umpteenth time the telegram resting on the desktop. Today of all days buds should be on those branches. The tree's skeleton, sharpened by the early morning sun, possessed its own austere beauty but simply didn't fit the occasion. Glancing down at the rectangular, yellow piece of paper, he read again the message he had already put to memory: "Born to you a healthy, baby girl. Margaret Louise . . . stop . . . 7lbs. 6oz . . . stop . . . mother and child doing fine . . . Congratulations, Judge, Dr. Samuel Lathrop."

Fingering the paper with his sturdy, weathered hands, O'Brien gave silent thanks for what he could only view as a miracle. A healthy, baby girl. An act of God that he vowed he would spend the remainder of his days repaying in any way he could. Inconceivable. He, a father, at fifty-nine. It was too much to hope for, and yet there it was, clearly stated in the certainty of bold Western Union type. The only regret he had was that he could not join Winifred and his new daughter immediately. How he would love to see that newborn face, one that even in its swollen infancy he imagined bore traces of his own. Under normal circumstances, he and his new family would, of course, be together. But theirs were anything but normal, and with the election only a year away, he had decided to wait until Christmas in order to arrange a vacation without arousing too much suspicion.

O'Brien gave the telegram one last look. He would have liked nothing better than to stay home and revel in his news, but he had an exceptionally busy schedule ahead of him and was already running late. Reluctantly, he folded the paper into a neat, small square, and slipped it into an envelope in the top drawer. He knew what he would do with it later.

"Western Union? I'd like to send a telegram. To Mrs. Winifred O'Donnell. Mother's Hospital, Albuquerque, New Mexico. Yes, that's right. Here's the message: 'Well done, my dear . . . stop . . . Very happy . . . stop . . . Will phone on Sunday . . . stop . . . Love, Obee. O-b-e-e-.'

Yes, that's right. The bill? Send to Judge O'Brien O'Donnell. Thirty-four fifty-six Bancroft Street, Toledo, Ohio. Yes. Thank you very much."

O'Brien hung up his new rotary dial telephone and patted it as if it were an obedient pet. Ever since the courthouse had installed this technological marvel a few months ago, he was determined to own one himself. To make a call without the need of an operator, directly from one end of the country to the other. Amazing! And so stylish. The latest model became available in a variety of colors just as the forest green paint was being applied to the hall of his still unfinished new home, which, as he walked toward the stairs, he eyed with immense satisfaction.

The brick and mortar structure, crafted in the Tudor style, befitted someone of O'Brien's stature. How strange the way things worked out. He never thought he would own his own home, let alone have one built from the ground up. Nor did he ever think he would live outside the city, thriving as he had in its pace and energy. But, he'd gotten a good price on the lot in Old Orchard, and had come to believe that a rural setting would be a better place to raise a family. He wasn't alone in this idea. Since he relocated to Toledo from Point Huron in 1906, most of his colleagues had moved to the suburbs, too, lured by subdivisions bearing such nostalgic names as Old Orchard. O'Brien smirked. The pamphlet on the area had promised an escape from escalating urban congestion and crime. So, too, did an accompanying photograph, replete with cows grazing on abundant, sunlit grass. He was suspicious of such advertising ploys, but over time had nevertheless come to agree with the premise underlying them.

Although construction on his home was not complete, most of the work yet to be done was cosmetic, and so O'Brien took early residency. Aesthetic details were important to him, much more so than to his wife. As he started up the stairs, noting the fineness of the darkly stained, oak hand rail, listening carefully for any creaking he may have missed on his way down, he remembered that today the carpenter was coming to install the mantel in the study, the one room that would retain the independent character of his former bachelor's quarters. With his books, desk, and other treasured belongings carefully placed, this would be a refined but cozy, personal retreat, and the Victorian mantel, which he helped design, would be the perfect finishing touch.

The only room left completely to Winifred was the nursery, which he passed on his way to the bedroom. While only mildly interested in the rest of the house, his wife had expressed a strong desire to decorate this room, and O'Brien wanted to honor her wishes. Besides, reserving it for storage for the time being would avoid the inevitable questions of friends and family who would certainly want to take a tour.

O'Brien quickly performed his toilet and began to dress. Normally, he prolonged this latter activity, treating it as a serious study in color and form. Today, he sacrificed art to time and hurriedly selected his grey wool suit and fashionable collarless white cotton shirt. The only item that he pondered with anything approaching his usual scrutiny were his socks, choosing, after limiting the possibilities to three, the dark grey French imports with pink silk thread.

The telephone rang. Heaving a deep sigh, he glanced at the clock on the night stand and hesitated. No, he wasn't going to get it. The ringing continued. It might be a call from the hospital. He ran down the stairs, his left sock still wrinkled around the ankle.

"Hello?" O'Brien answered, with a note of concern.

"Good morning, Obee."

Immediately he relaxed. Though not part of her official duties as Chief Probation Officer of Women, Sarah had taken it upon herself years ago to provide O'Brien regularly with any information she thought would prepare him for his day ahead. She expected in return only the courtesy of being informed of any delays. After all, she was one of his closest friends, and he knew how much she worried about him.

"Morning, Sarah. How are you, my dear?"

"Fine, Obee. I'm a little surprised you're still there, though. I was just taking a chance. Are you all right?"

"Yes, yes, I'm fine, I'm wonderful, in fact. Just overslept a bit."

"Hmm . . ."

"Now, Sarah, don't you worry. I'm not tired in *that* way. I was just up late working on the house, nothing more."

"Nonetheless, I'm glad there's a holiday approaching," Sarah said. "You've had more than your share of tough cases lately. You could use a rest. I'm rather tired myself, you know."

He heard slight irritation in her voice. "Well, perhaps you're right. I, uh, was thinking, in fact, that I might go away this year, maybe down south, look over the new training site for the Mud Hens, or perhaps do some fishing in Michigan, I don't know."

"You're not going to visit Winifred?"

Thankfully Sarah could not see him. She would have recognized his sudden rapid blinking as his characteristic sign of distress.

"No, I don't think so. We've already talked about it. She's so enjoying her time with her family, and I'd like to wait until the baby's born, you know."

"But Obee, that won't be for three months. Surely, you'll want to see her before then?"

O'Brien wished at that moment he could tell Sarah the truth. She, of all people, would have understood. But, even with his trusted confidante, he simply couldn't take the risk.

"Look Sarah, Winifred's even encouraged me to go off by myself. She says I might as well enjoy what's left of my freedom. But, listen," he said, "what's really on your mind this morning?"

"Well, Judge, I've called to warn you that Emanuel Cavender and his attorney are already here. They're both being rather gregarious with the press, too. I tried to fend them off, but Cavender's boasting that you'll give him a light sentence, you know, considering his official status."

"Humph. We'll see about that." O'Brien shook his head in disgust. Cavender was a police officer found guilty of contributing to the delinquency of a minor. That was bad enough. But the man had also been reckless. He knew the police department had been under public scrutiny for months. And, yet, there he was, found with an under-aged girl in the Secor Hotel, the very place several officers were accused of turning a blind eye on mob members holed up there. A relatively minor offense, perhaps, but along with the department's history of criminal collusion—dramatically exacerbated by Volstead, that scourge of legislation O'Brien regretted ever supporting—he knew the public would want him to make an example of Cavender. And he would have to balance that desire against the pressure of his friends on the Force to give their comrade the minimum sentence.

"Is that all?" O'Brien asked, with uncustomary shortness.
"Unfortunately, no. Dr. Miller is also waiting, rather impatiently, I might add. He's interviewed Lulu Carey in jail, and wants to talk to you about the possibility of an insanity commitment."

"I thought he'd come to that conclusion. I told you, Sarah, those letters show extreme mental imbalance. Miss Carey would be much better off in the hospital. Still, there will be those who won't be so easily convinced, even with Miller's recommendation. What else?"

"There's also word this morning that Judge Martin overturned your Ann Arbor Railroad ruling. They might very well lay those tracks on Summit unless Charley Northrup can accomplish something in the Court of Appeals. He'll be here later to talk strategy with you."

O'Brien ran his fingers through his thinning hair. Today there would be no contested wills, no property to settle. *Concurrent Jurisdiction.* He could recite the definition of the term in his sleep. A murky legal category requiring the Probate Court to make judgments along with the Common Pleas Court "in all misdemeanors and all proceedings to prevent crime." *All.* The ruling had turned the Probate Court into a judicial dumping ground. And it was particularly annoying when his decisions in such matters were overturned.

"Judge?"

"Dammit, Sarah, that crossing in the North End will be nothing but a hazard. What's wrong with that idiot Martin anyway? Grade separation's the only guarantee of safety. It's technically out of my hands now, of course, but I'll continue to support Charley's efforts. That's all, I hope?"

"For the time being, Judge."

"Good. As always, I don't know what I would do without you, my dear. You'll be there for the Cavender sentencing?"

"Of course, with the victim's parents by my side. They've been waiting for this day for a long time now, you know."

O'Brien groaned. "Yes, I know. They and everyone else."

CHARGE OF GIRL SENDS CAVENDER TO COUNTY JAIL

Emanual Cavender, former city motorcycle patrolman and dry constable, was sentenced to six months in the county jail by Probate Judge O'Donnell Monday afternoon.

WOMEN ATTACK "SANITY TRIALS"

League Presents Cases To Welfare Director

Characterizing the commitment proceedings to the Toledo State Hospital, as practiced by Probate Judge O'Brien O'Donnell, as "nothing less than a farce," members of the Toledo Housewives League made a plea to State Welfare Director John E. Harper at a meeting in the Secor Hotel on Friday night, for the cessation of what they termed the "railroading of persons into the insane asylum."

Harper pointed out that the probate judge has the authority to appoint a reputable physician or physicians to make proper physical and mental examinations of persons about to be committed to the Toledo

WOMAN HELD AS LETTER WRITER

Annoying Notes Cause Arrest; To Be Examined

Evidence to show that Mrs. Lulu

CROSSING CASE UP TO COURT

Necessity Of R. R. Grade To Be Decided

The question of another grade crossing on lower Summit-st is a necessity to the Ann Arbor R. R.

3 TINY TOTS ORP BY MURDER AND BECOME COUNT

Two Boys Arraigned for Alleged Bootlegger—Another Admits

2

"All rise, the Probate Court of Lucas County is now in session, the Honorable Judge O'Brien O'Donnell presiding."

Sarah exhaled. The judge had made it just in time. She had anticipated a full court room for the Cavender sentencing, but nothing like the standing room only crowd that greeted her boss as the bailiff announced his entrance. Only half as many people attended when Cavender's verdict was read, and then it seemed as if all of Toledo was there. She was afraid that the unexpected sight would rattle his nerves, but, if it did, he didn't show it. Officially cloaked in his immaculately pressed black robe, he took the bench with all the confidence and solemnity the occasion required.

Sarah noticed O'Brien glancing around the room, briefly holding the gaze of a number of individuals in attendance: Chief of Police Martin Dodd; County Commissioner George Hoffman; Democratic party head John O'Dwyer, whose presence here was puzzling to say the least; and, of course, the defendant, who, sitting quietly in the front row with his hands folded on his lap, appeared calm and subdued. The judge's bespeckled grey-blue eyes then drifted further down the same row where they looked encouragingly at the young victim, Marie Harrison, her parents, and at Sarah herself, who nodded at him reassuringly. As usual, Sarah had swept her thick, dark hair into a loose French twist; a style easy for her to manage, but one that also revealed her heart shaped face, deep-set brown eyes, full lips, and clear, olive complexion. Although already in her forties, an age by which most women had long since lost their feminine allure, Sarah was unusual. Neither her figure nor her skin bore more than scant traces of deterioration, and her straight, if slightly gapped teeth, were a brilliant white. Time had been kind to her, adding through a few gentle lines and an occasional grey strand of hair, a depth to her features that while not beautiful in the conventional sense, produced an overall pleasing effect.

It wasn't any of her physical attributes that the judge was currently admiring, however. Of this Sarah was certain. What had captured his attention, she knew, was her dress. He was relieved that she had selected an appropriate outfit, a respectable, if flapper inspired, crepe black frock. She had considered something more modern. In fact, she had come close to eschewing tradition entirely and wearing the bloomers he so violently opposed. But she decided that this was not the day to make a statement. His parting, grateful smile indicated that she had made the right decision.

Silencing the court with one sharp tap of his gavel, O'Brien began by asking the defendant to rise and followed with a few preliminary words of recrimination. "Mr. Cavender, I must tell you that I find your actions particularly deplorable. The youth of today are in desperate need of moral guidance, of role models they can respect and trust. What are they to think when they are victimized by someone whose job it is to protect them?"

Even though the question was clearly rhetorical, an audible reaction came from several people in the room, including the police chief who shifted uncomfortably in his seat and John O'Dwyer who grunted out an epithet louder than he must have intended. Cavender himself didn't budge.

O'Brien continued, "A police officer taking advantage of a young girl is no better than a druggist selling dope, and everyone knows how I feel about that."

This comment also caused a stir, but from exactly where or whom was uncertain.

"Now, Mr. Cavender, I know that this is a first-time offense, and you have said you are remorseful. Do you have anything else to add before I sentence you?"

Cavender looked up at O'Brien and then over at Marie Harrison, who was pressing a handkerchief to her wet eyes. He then cleared his throat. "I only want to state again, your Honor, that I am truly sorry for any pain I have caused Miss Harrison and her family. I take full responsibility for my behavior and promise, that if you would be so kind as to let me return to my job, I will carry it out for the rest of my life with integrity."

The court room was now hushed, waiting to hear O'Brien's response to Cavender's attempt to get off the hook without any real punishment; a hook on which a great deal was hanging. O'Brien glanced around the room again, and then fixed his gaze directly on the defendant.

"Emanuel Cavender, I appreciate your apology. Nevertheless, I cannot in good conscience heed your wishes. You have seriously violated the code to which you swore allegiance and are therefore from here on out barred from serving on the police force. And, and," O'Brien continued, quieting the crowd with a severe look, "pursuant to section ten of the Ohio Criminal Code, you are hereby sentenced to six months in prison, beginning today November twenty-third, nineteen twenty-three."

Gasps and whispers erupted, prompting O'Brien to forcefully tap his gavel once more. "Order . . . I'll have order in this court! I am not quite done yet." O'Brien waited for the noise to settle down before proceeding. "Mr. Cavender, you are furthermore ordered to pay a one hundred dollar fine." This time there was little response from the crowd. "The people must know that there are consequences for any official who abuses the public trust. The defendant is now remanded to the custody of the Ohio Bureau of Prisons. Court is dismissed."

As the bailiff commanded the court to rise, freeing reporters to run to the phones and everyone else to simultaneously voice their opinions, Sarah offered O'Brien an appreciative smile. The sentence, though not undeserved, was a bold move, and she knew that he would take some heat for it. Already she could see the disappointment in Chief Dodd and hear outright anger from several individuals inching out of the room. O'Brien had stood firm today, and she was proud of him for it, especially as she observed the relief on Marie's face. But, as usual, she was also worried about the added strain this could place on him. Her boss didn't take pressure of this sort well, even though he would never admit it.

I must catch him before his next appointment, she thought. After I offer my congratulations to the Harrisons, I'll ask him to lunch. Then I'll really be able to tell how he's doing.

Assuming a much practiced, neutral expression, Sarah approached the formidable set of closed double-doors that led to O'Brien's chambers. She was just about to knock when the judge's secretary, Elaine Marsh, appeared alongside her, balancing three cups of steaming coffee. Having only been on the job for a couple of months, Elaine had already proved herself to be an invaluable employee. Sarah had taken to her immediately, especially because in spite of O'Brien's protests, she had recently cut her hair in the new bob fashion. "A woman after my own heart," Sarah had told her in approval. "I'd do it myself if I were younger."

Elaine shook her head. "He's got visitors, Sarah. Two men."

"Already? Court just let out. Do you know them?"

"Can't say as I do. But then, I don't recognize many faces yet. They followed the judge in here. I don't think either of them had appointments."

Just what he needed, unexpected guests.

"I guess I'll just have to come back later," Sarah said. But instead of leaving, she remained standing next to Elaine, staring at the coffee. "Hmm, tell you what, Miss Marsh. It just occurred to me that you might need some assistance. You look a little unsteady there. How 'bout if I help carry that heavy load?"

"Sure, Miss Kaufman," Elaine replied, with a knowing wink. "So kind of you to offer."

Sarah winked back as Elaine passed her two of the cups, and deferentially pushed open the doors.

Guests indeed. There with O'Brien were two of the most unlikely Sarah could have imagined, engaged in what appeared to be a surprisingly good-humored conversation. First to catch her eye was John Augustus O'Dwyer, Napoleonic leader of the Democratic party whose influence, like that of his Republican counterpart, Walter F. Brown, extended far beyond Toledo. She had spotted the portly, ruddy-faced man in court, but still couldn't fathom why he would be there. Finding him in this room was even more confusing, for, as far as she knew, he and O'Brien were barely on speaking terms. Currently, O'Dwyer was chairman of the Democratic Executive Committee, but for many years he served as president of the Lucas County Board of Elections, and while in that capacity, during the election of 1912, a deep rift between him and O'Brien occurred.

The puzzling incident was never really resolved. In short, O'Dwyer was accused of putting the lean on one of his precinct judges to vote and stuff ballot boxes for, ironically enough, Walter F. Brown. This was particularly strange because O'Dwyer, in addition to being known for his strict allegiance to the Democratic party, had always been notoriously hostile to Brown and all he stood for. Nevertheless, the case went to trial and the presiding judge was O'Brien, who, despite eventually dropping it for insufficient evidence, strongly believed in O'Dwyer's guilt. When O'Dwyer became aware of this, he immediately put into practice the philosophy for which he would eventually become known: "never forget an insult, or never forgive an enemy." Severing all but the most necessary communications with O'Brien, O'Dwyer even went so far as to try through innuendo and rumor to turn fellow

Democrats against him. But now, there he stood, in seemingly excellent spirits, laughing along with the judge as if they were the best of chums.

Joining in the fun was Kenneth Ballard, whose presence was equally baffling. Kenneth, a tallish, slender, and fastidiously well-dressed man, had been O'Brien's roommate at the Monticello, the hotel where the judge lived when Sarah first started working for him and where he continued to live for many years thereafter. She knew Kenneth well, but had not seen him since O'Brien's wedding reception last May. The sight of the three of them together in such a jovial state was simply bizarre. As far as Sarah knew, Kenneth didn't even know O'Dwyer. An engineer who worked for the Ohio Gas Company, Kenneth didn't travel in the same circles as O'Brien. He had never held public office nor had he ever been seriously interested in politics, two of the chief reasons O'Brien had found him so appealing as a roommate. In fact, during the entire ten years they had lived together, Sarah couldn't recall even one visit to the courthouse from Kenneth, something she had always attributed to his lack of interest as well as his confessed uneasiness with, as he had put it, the "unsavory characters" who steadily streamed through its doors.

As Sarah stood contemplating this unlikely trio, O'Brien said, "Sarah, my dear, for goodness sake, you look positively mesmerized. Put those cups down before you drop them."

"Oh, of course . . . certainly, Obee," Sarah said, and placed them carefully on the end table next to the one Elaine had already placed there before leaving the room unnoticed. "Sorry, Judge," she added, apologizing as much for the lapse of formal address as the near disaster. Sarah was among the handful of friends who were close enough to O'Brien to call him Obee, the moniker he had acquired in his youth. The problem being that she was not always successful in remembering to observe his title in an official setting, a *faux pas* that some saw as a consequence of the judge's failure to assert his authority over the weaker sex.

"I was supposed to be helping Elaine, wasn't I? Seems as if she really could've done the job better without me . . . even though, as you know, Judge, a broken cup is a sign of good luck."

"You know better than I that it is a broken glass which is said to have such properties. But, never mind that. Let's have it. You didn't come here just to aid my more than competent secretary. Come on. What are you up to?"

"Well, actually," Sarah admitted, "there are a few things I'd like to discuss with you. I was hoping we might have lunch and go over them, but . . ." she added, turning from one visitor to the other, "I didn't expect you to have company so soon after the trial. Hello, Mr. O'Dwyer. Good to see you, Kenneth."

"Humph, yes, well of course you'd want to talk, Sarah," O'Brien said. "And, I suppose you have a right to wonder. Gentlemen, do you mind if Sarah joins us?"

Neither man objected so Sarah moved closer, reshaping the triangular group into a perfect square.

John O'Dwyer greeted her with a stiff handshake, a gesture befitting his general distrust of women who ventured beyond what he thought to be their rightful sphere. Sarah could never figure out why O'Dwyer was considered a Progressive, for he was certainly not progressive in this sense. Kenneth, on the other hand, gave her an affectionate hug and seemed genuinely happy to see her. "Hello Sarah. How are you, my love? You look wonderful. Really, just wonderful. Not like our friend here, however, I'm afraid," Kenneth said, pointing in O'Brien's direction. "Marriage must be wearing him out. Looks a bit drawn, doesn't he? Yes, I think you better keep a closer eye on him. Winifred doesn't seem to be doing such a good job."

"I try, God knows I try, Kenneth," Sarah answered, "and I'm sure, when Winifred returns—"

"Winifred gone?" Kenneth frowned in mocked concern. "Left him already? Well, where is she, my good man?"

"Winifred is visiting relatives, if you must know, Ken," O'Brien snapped. "But I must say if there's anything I dislike, it's being talked about in the third person. Everyone is so worried about how I look these days, but the truth is I feel great. In fact, I've never felt better. So, please, let's put that topic to rest. Anyway, Sarah, aren't you interested in knowing what these men are doing here? You seemed to be exceptionally so a minute ago."

For the second time today, O'Brien had purposefully steered the conversation away from himself . . . and from his wife. Although she and Kenneth had only been half teasing, Sarah knew better than to push any further. Nevertheless, she registered the move as yet another sign that the judge did indeed bear watching.

"Well, yes, I am a bit curious," she conceded.

"Actually, it's not as mysterious as it seems, at least from my perspective." O'Dwyer's raspy voice startled all of them, but each seemed willing to let him do the explaining.

"I came to see the trial like so many other Toledoans, Miss Kaufman; it's as simple as that. And from what I understand, Mr. Ballard came for the same reason."

Kenneth nodded.

"And, like myself, Ballard sought out the judge after the trial to commend him on the courage of his decision. Of course, I have to admit, I was initially taken aback by it. Uh, perhaps you even heard me in court, uh, express my, uh, surprise," he added with an embarrassed grin.

They all exchanged knowing glances, and O'Dwyer continued. "Well, after court, Ballard and I caught up with O'Brien at the same time, and got to talking about the November election. Now, what I've told the judge is that I'm ready to let bygones be bygones. More than that, I want to work for his campaign. I like what he's done for this city, and I think he has shown himself to be a real man today. And Ballard here said that if someone such as myself can undergo such a radical change, why he might even become more political and do a bit of work for the campaign as well."

Kenneth smiled broadly.

"And, that's where you came in, Sarah," O'Brien said, gently rocking on his stocky legs.

Sarah nodded but was anything but convinced. She would have been delighted if O'Dwyer had really had a change of heart, but she didn't believe it. At the very least, he would want something from Obee in return for his forgiveness and support. And Kenneth would ultimately renege on his offer. He had been inspired to work for Obee's campaign before, but had never followed through because he just didn't have the interest or the personality that such work required. His intentions were good, and he was certainly one of Obee's most devoted friends. But his enthusiasm would soon wane. Furthermore, why had either man come to the sentencing in the first place? Even though it was an important case for the city, O'Dwyer usually only appeared at events of a much grander scale, and Kenneth had just never cared enough. Of course, O'Brien wouldn't be thinking of any of these things now. No, now he would be reveling in the comradery of the moment. Later, he would come to his senses and remember O'Dwyer's cut-throat reputation and Kenneth's fickleness, but for now he would be enjoying the bond between men caught up in a common cause. And the fact that the cause was O'Brien himself would make the experience all the better.

For the time being, Sarah would do nothing to spoil O'Brien's pleasure. A positive attitude would help the judge through the challenging meetings scheduled for the afternoon. Besides, any warning she might offer would pale in comparison to his own eventual self-recriminations. All too aware of his gullible nature, in the light of day O'Brien would realize he had fallen prey to it again. Therefore, during lunch, which he agreed to have with her once his guests took their leave, Sarah restricted the conversation to mostly glowing remarks about his handling of the Cavender case. The only exception came with the topic of Lulu Carey. Initially, Sarah, too, simply thought the woman was mad. All those obscene letters to city and state officials. Including the Governor! But she now thought differently and felt compelled to speak her mind.

"Obee, before you and Dr. Miller decide to commit Miss Carey, I must tell you that if the Housewives League ever discovers your failure to act on the content of some of those letters, you'll never hear the end of it. They'll have your head before the election."

O'Brien blinked and started to respond, but Sarah stopped him. She knew what he was going to say. A few years earlier the League had charged him with railroading persons into the insane asylum, calling his commitment proceedings as "nothing less than a farce." The accusation had deeply wounded him. Occasionally, he might have been a bit overzealous, but nothing was more important to him than improving conditions for the mentally ill. He was the only Progressive—indeed, nearly the only person—in town who advocated the building of a new psychiatric clinic and who tirelessly argued for patient rehabilitation. Still, the League was powerful, and Sarah sensed that the morning's events had put the judge in a receptive mood. She needed to take advantage of it.

"Please Obee, please let me finish."

"All right, Sarah. Go ahead, my dear."

"Thank you. Now, I agree that some of what is in those letters sounds a little crazy. But, the ones where Lulu writes about her husband repeatedly striking her have got to be taken seriously. It may very well be that this abuse she describes has significantly contributed to her illness, if not caused it entirely. At the very least, I think you should find a way to have the husband questioned; this would satisfy the League and perhaps help this young woman more than long walks on the hospital's grounds. I'm not saying she doesn't need help or even confinement, Obee, but wouldn't it be better if you at least investigated these allegations before locking her up?"

O'Brien took the remaining bite of his Roquefort salad. Judging by the agonizingly long time he took to chew it, she surmised that he was probably carefully considering how to phrase a dismissive retort. But, when finally he put down his fork, placed his napkin neatly back on his lap, and slowly raised his large, kindly eyes, his expression told her before he uttered a word that she had made an impression.

"Sarah, Sarah, Sarah. You are certainly getting feisty these days."

O'Brien paused, repositioned his glasses, and stared at her in a somewhat bemused fashion, as would a father who suddenly realized his young daughter had grown up.

"But of course, you're right," he conceded. "I do think you have something there. I sometimes can't see the forest for the trees, you know. Maybe I need a new prescription for these old things," he added with a laugh, removing his glasses altogether. He paused and stared at her again. Drumming softly on the table, he leaned in close. "Listen, Sarah, I'll tell you what. I'll suggest to Miller that we hold off on commitment until we can find out what's going on with that husband of hers. In the meantime, you might want to visit Miss Carey yourself. She could probably use a sympathetic female ear about now, and you may be able to discover something the police can't."

"I'd be happy to" Sarah said, careful not to appear too smug. "It's good that you're taking this seriously, Obee. I really think you're doing the right thing for your career, not to mention Miss Carey and possibly other women like her. Now, let's finish our lunch, shall we? Your meeting with Miller is in twenty minutes."

"Quite right, my dear," he said, checking his pocket watch. "I'm glad one of us is keeping track of the time."

"That's what I'm here for," Sarah said. But as she sliced into her roasted chicken that had long since grown cold, she silently replaced "what" with "all" and was momentarily saddened that the remark was now closer to the truth.

Carrying off his remaining business successfully, O'Brien's spirits remained uplifted throughout the afternoon. Things had gone especially well with Dr. Miller. Once O'Brien brought to Miller's attention Lulu's references to her husband's brutality, the doctor agreed they should delay commitment. Miller was an intelligent man with an impressive list of credentials. But, similar to O'Brien, he had, in his reading of the letters, assumed those passages to be simply the ravings of a mad woman.

"I begin to see your point, Judge," he said, when O'Brien presented him with Sarah's theory. "I thought I examined those letters pretty finely. But I suppose even my well-trained mind has its limits. Cause and effect may very well be at work here. You've got quite a sharp officer there."

"Don't I know it," O'Brien replied, his chest puffing out slightly. "Sarah's an invaluable employee, and a great friend, too, I must tell you. I'd trust her with my life."

As for the railroad case, O'Brien really could do little more then lend his support to Charles Northrop in the legal battle for safer crossing conditions. His own judicial authority had been officially superseded by Judge Martin in the Common Pleas Court, although he really couldn't figure out why Martin would overturn such a rational decision unless, of course, he had incurred political pressure similar to his own. The thought triggered a wave of nausea. He breathed in and out quickly, forcing from his mind a familiar rain-swollen image of the river. No, that was unlikely. In any case, what could he do? His hands were officially tied. Still, with O'Dwyer now apparently on his side, he did feel somewhat emboldened, free to lend his name to the cause without seriously impairing his chances for reelection. And he was happy Charley was counsel in this matter, for he had the utmost respect and liking for the man. Before O'Brien made his bid for the judiciary, he and Charley had practiced law together, and O'Brien had come to know him intimately as a man of principle and integrity. Over the years, his admiration only grew, and the two became good friends as well as trusted colleagues.

Several weeks had passed since O'Brien had talked to Charley, and so after discussing the best approach for taking the case to the Court of Appeals—which was primarily offering testimonies of those whose lives had been tragically affected by the absence of grades—they caught up on some long-neglected personal business and made a promise to see each other more often, a promise Charley attempted to follow up on immediately.

"By the way," he asked, as he was leaving O'Brien's chambers, "you're going to the telepathist performance tonight, aren't you?"

"Well, I don't know about myself, but I sense you'll be there, Charley," O'Brien said, smirking at his own joke.

"No, really, my man, this is supposed to be quite the show. You do have a seat don't you?"

"Yes, of course I do. I'm just not sure I can make it. There's so much to do in the house right now, you know . . . we'll see."

"Do try, Obee, a bit of entertainment would do you good. You look a little tired."

"Perhaps, Charley, perhaps. I'll see how it goes."

"Good, I'll look for you there," Charley said with a nod and closed the doors solidly behind him.

O'Brien stood lost in thought. Despite being slightly vexed that once again someone had criticized his appearance, he thought that all in all it had been an extraordinary day. Beginning with the birth of his daughter, everything that followed was an implicit affirmation of that event. That he should, on this momentous occasion, be reunited with one of his bitterest enemies as well as two of his dearest friends, imbued the event with mystical significance. John O'Dwyer, Ken Ballard, and Charley Northrup; the exchanges he'd had with each of these men would have been special by themselves. Add to that Dr. Miller's approval of Sarah's astute advice as well as his own courageous performance in the Cavender case, and the day was extraordinary indeed, one that perhaps signaled God's forgiveness in those other matters on which O'Brien preferred not to dwell.

Out of habit, he walked over to the full-length mirror that hung in the corner of his chambers. He always gave himself a quick look before heading for home, and despite all the excitement, today was no exception. As usual, he lifted his chin, straightened his tie, and dusted off his coat sleeves. Then he moved closer to the mirror and subjected his face to his own intense scrutiny. Did he look tired? Were there signs of strain? Yes, he had to admit he noticed it, too. The image reflected back at him even appeared older somehow; the lines around the large, grey-blue eyes deeper, the heavy jowls a bit droopier, the thinning hair whiter. He had never been a handsome man, but had always—well, almost always—exuded a vitality of spirit that made him attractive nevertheless, and now that quality seemed somehow diminished. Perhaps the horn-rimmed glasses. He removed them from the end of his nose where they frequently ended up. A new style as well as a new prescription. Or perhaps it was his posture. He should stand more erect. That would make him look taller than his five feet, nine inches and thinner than his one hundred and eighty-six pounds. Now, that was better, wasn't it? Perhaps this was all he needed; some minor adjustments, and he would be back to normal in no time. Why, in just a few weeks, they'd be complimenting him on the improvement.

Having managed to quell his concern, O'Brien turned from the mirror, gathered his belongings and headed down the stairs. If he were going to go to that performance tonight, he needed to hasten his pace; it was already 6 p.m. and the performance was scheduled for 8. Hurrying toward the exit, however, he neglected to carry out his evening ritual of stepping on the frog. An inlaid design on the court's terrazzo, lobby floor, the bespeckled, emerald green creature with bulging black eyes was a reminder to all that encountered it that the site of the courthouse had once been a muddy swamp. To the judge, it had become a symbol of good luck, and he soon regretted having not taken advantage of its power. Because though he had completely forgotten about the press, the vulturous gathering on the courthouse steps told him that they most assuredly had not forgotten about him.

3

August, 1924

Sarah had guessed right. No time remained to go home before the movie. *Ponjola*, a controversial film about a woman whose wearing of men's clothing inspires her to live as a man, was on at the Princess.

38

She had been wanting to see it ever since Obee told her it wasn't worth the bother. As she filed away the last docket, she congratulated herself for bringing her own change of clothes: a tan, silk bloomer outfit she had ordered from the Sears catalog. Just as smart as the one she had seen in the Lion Store window and half the price.

Absent the usual bustle, the building felt a little eerie. Even the judge had gone, unusual for a man who often stayed long enough to greet the cleaning crew at 10. But then again, he was a family man now.

Quiet, still, cold. The Lucas County Courthouse. An imposing structure, built in the Italian Renaissance design when the style was first becoming popular here, it was faced in sandstone, with alternating columns and arches and an intricate frontal fraise. Venturing out of her office into the massive vestibule, the emptiness covered her, the strangeness of seeing a familiar object from a different vantage point. Concrete, wood, and glass, usually fading into the backdrop of human activity, were suddenly brought to the fore, striking in their material indifference. Even the floor beneath her seemed altered. Odd that she had never noticed it before, but in the gleaming, polished marble she could see her reflection clearly. Appropriate perhaps for a place of justice. She envisioned some tortured soul waiting to plead his case. Intending to skirt the truth, he rehearses his lines with downcast eyes. But in the process, he encounters his own image, comes face to face with himself, and changes his mind. Truth prevails. Justice is served.

Truth and justice. Words that Sarah took for granted. Ideas that she breathed in like air. But what of those ideas? Were they eternal principles, outside the bounds of human history, or man's invention and therefore subject to interpretation? In court she had heard convincing arguments for each point of view. But this was one of those questions to which she herself didn't have a definitive answer. What she did have, however, was a remedy for the queasy feeling to which it gave rise: Mr. Sherlock Holmes. Just thinking about the magazine started to settle her stomach, which she also realized was painfully empty. She had never before read about his exploits in the evening. But she had never been here alone before either. One rare event surely deserved another.

Sarah couldn't remember precisely when her flirtation with the master detective had become an habitual affair. She did know that beginning the day with him and the trusty Dr. Watson was good for her. Not only did the practice sharpen her mind, but it made her more empathetic. If the order, the logic, the impeccable deciphering of clues in the story encouraged her to think more analytically, the problems surmounted by the fictional cast made her better understand those faced by the real people she encountered at court. Not that her reading was limited to the works of the popular Arthur Conan Doyle. Not by a long shot. But more demanding literature she saved for the privacy of her living room. There she had tackled everything from Milton to Austen, Dostoevsky to some of the recently published poems by Emily Dickinson. Last month she had even made it through, although not entirely comprehended, the new translation of Emile Proust's *Remembrance of Things Past*. But it was Doyle's larger-than-life, eccentric protagonist who inspired her in the quotidian present.

Over the years she had become fascinated with Doyle, too, a man whose complexity nearly matched that of his most celebrated character. A physician turned writer, Doyle possessed both the logic and imagination necessary for each of those professions. He even claimed to believe in the paranormal, and while Sarah didn't go quite that far herself (her rather embarrassing participation in the telepathist performance last fall notwithstanding), she admired someone of his intelligence admitting that things existed that reason alone could not explain.

It was, however, Doyle's acute sense of justice that Sarah found the most compelling. Like the time he demonstrated that a man convicted of having slashed a number of horses and cows couldn't have committed the crime because of poor eyesight. Or the incident involving Sir Roger Casement. Though adventure fantasy wasn't her type of story, she had read Doyle's *The Lost World* because the character of Lord John Roxton was based on Casement, an Irish diplomat accused of trying to get Germany's support for the Irish independence movement. Casement had previously alerted Doyle to the terrible injustices committed against blacks in the Congo, and when Doyle felt that Casement had become the victim of injustice himself, he offered his support. Convicted of being a traitor in 1916, Casement was eventually put to death, but not before Doyle almost succeeded in sparing his life.

Sarah reached into her emergency candy jar with one hand and turned to the final paragraph of *The Last Bow* with the other. She had read the story once before, and therefore already knew that Holmes averts the death of thousands by infiltrating a German spy ring. But the plot was only part of the pleasure. Words themselves were comforting. As were the familiar characters. If they were interesting enough, what did it matter that they repeated themselves?

> *Good old Watson! You are the one fixed point in a changing age. There's an east wind coming all the same, such wind as never blew on England yet. It will be cold and bitter, Watson, and a good many of us may wither before its blast. But it's God's own wind none the less and a cleaner, better stronger land will lie in the sunshine when the storm has cleared. Start her up, Watson, for it's time that we were on our way. I have a check for five hundred pounds which should be cashed early, for the drawer is quite capable of stopping it if he can.*

"Done." She closed the magazine and sighed with a familiar mixture of satisfaction and loss. Finishing a story was always like a little death, no matter how many times one had read it. Best to begin another immediately. Next on her list, *The Valley of Fear*, the only full-length Holmes novel she hadn't yet read. She would start it bright and early tomorrow.

She slipped on her outfit, exchanged her tortoise shell comb for one with pearl studs, and added a pair of matching drop earrings. She sighed again and frowned. What was bothering her? She couldn't place the feeling. Too much chocolate? The disruption to her pattern? Perhaps the story's not quite-so-happy ending. Generally, of course, it was optimistic. But, as Holmes had rightly predicted through his metaphor of the east wind, bad had to precede the good. For the story was published in 1914, when England's worst days of the Great War still lay ahead.

Sarah walked rapidly down the long corridor that led to the stairs. With the building empty, her Cuban heeled, brown patent leather shoes echoed loudly, drawing her gaze momentarily toward the floor, where once again she saw her reflection. The marble here was duller than upstairs, her image fuzzier, the outline of her more formally attired shape blurred. And that gave her pause. If the same tortured soul she had conjured up earlier had been waiting down here instead, he might have very well decided to stick with his lie, the entire course of his life altered by something as minor as a slight shift in location. She gave a departing look around the court's hallowed halls and exited feeling queasier than ever. Chilled rather than refreshed by the cool breeze that was starting to gather force, she headed quickly for the theater, wondering when the approaching storm would touch ground.

Ironically, it was on a balmy Friday evening, about one week later.

Celebrating a break in the oppressive humidity that lasted nearly the whole month of July, Sarah had decided to walk rather than take the streetcar home. The courthouse gradually disappeared as she strolled past Adams, Monroe and Madison to Summit, where she had an unobstructed view of the Maumee, the deep ribbon of water that wound its way through the industrialized southeast section of Toledo and emptied gracefully into vast Lake Erie. Framing the city skyline— a cluster of domes and uneven box-like structures—the Maumee served as the harbor of Toledo and a major port of the Midwest. In recent years several new draw bridges had been constructed over it, including the steel and concrete Cherry Street Bridge with a lift span to accommodate large ships. As in much of the country, these were booming years in Toledo, and the Maumee, though only navigable for about twelve miles from its mouth on lake Erie, contributed greatly to the city's economic prosperity.

When Sarah looked out and observed the relentless flow northward, she felt a sense of continuity, a belonging to something larger than herself. Gazing out at the water's soft swells she was temporarily transported in time and space. At moments like this, the inner workings of the city, the quest for money, and particularly the corruption that accompanied it faded from view, and she could almost imagine turning around to find the buildings replaced with the lush primeval marshland upon which they were originally built.

She sighed. But, of course, the river had its dark side, too. Flooding had repeatedly occurred during spring thaws, steamers had broken away from their moorings while docked on its shores, and people in despair had used it as their last resort.

Sarah continued walking, past her beloved Madison bookstore with the scandalous new work by F. Scott Fitzgerald in the window, past Steton's Shoe Shop, past the full stock of Victrolas on display in Grinnell's. A Citizen's Ice truck, parked in the street for a delivery and lilting like the Tower of Pisa, halted the elegant glide of a jet black Paige Fairfield "Six-46" and momentarily blocked her own path. After maneuvering around it, she picked up speed. The exercise and fresh air had sparked her appetite for the home-cooked meal she knew would be awaiting her. A relaxing dinner and perhaps a game of cards with her brother and sister with whom she shared a small house on Fulton Street was just what she needed after a long week in court.

First she would light the Sabbath candles, since the sun had already begun to set. Sarah partook in this weekly ritual not because she was devout, but rather to honor her parents who had long ago passed away. God, she felt, was subject to interpretation, Judaism no more or less correct than any other religion. But, as German-Jewish immigrants, her parents had experienced episodes of vicious antisemitism, and Sarah felt that if she abandoned her traditions entirely, their suffering would have been in vain. Besides, the history of her people served as a continual cautionary tale. As someone born a Jew, she could never become complacent. Although she had found a level of acceptance in Toledo, many in the city were vehemently antisemitic. As others had done in the past, they would seize any opportunity to blame the Jews for the ills of the world.

As head of the Women's Probate Court and now probation officer of the Juvenile Court as well, Sarah had followed the lead of other Jews at the time, who, while discouraged from serving in medicine, law, and other professions, were welcomed and often rose to power in local government. For a woman of her background, she had accomplished a great deal, certainly much more than either of her siblings. Her older brother, Harry, was at one time department manager of Lamson Brothers, a retailer of dry goods, clothes, and millinery, but he lost his job several years ago due to illness. Her younger sister, Tillie, never held a job. Lacking Sarah's ambition and burdened with a slight limp from a bout with polio, she was designated the family's domestic, a role with which she was content.

The three appeared to live a rather odd life; none had married, and all were in their forties. But in the main, they functioned as normally as any other family, perhaps even more so because despite variances in personality and intelligence, they enjoyed each other's company immensely. To be sure, they had their conflicts. Harry and Tillie demanded a great deal both financially and emotionally from their sister, and at times Sarah tired of the responsibility, at times she resented her siblings' dependence on her. She always hoped, in fact, that she would one day have a different kind of life, one that would involve a husband and perhaps children of her own. But as the years passed, the suitors who were once plentiful became scarce. Many had been put off by her commitment to her work, especially when she told them that if she ever were to marry, she would want to keep her job. Others found her political activism—her support of suffrage, membership in the NAACP and the like—unfeminine, and still others, even those who considered themselves open-minded, saw her religion as a stumbling block to the development of a long-term relationship. Yet it really wouldn't have mattered anyway, because none of her gentlemen callers had been what she sought either. To be more exact, none had quite matched the fantasy that she had secretly held since the time she had met O'Brien O'Donnell. And when word eventually got around that Miss Sarah Kaufman was too hard to please, they simply stopped trying.

Sarah pushed open the rusty, wrought iron gate. She was happy to be home. Any hope of sharing in domestic pleasures, however, was dashed soon after she entered her front door. For long before the food was served and the cards were dealt, even before the candles were lit, she learned that O'Brien had been admitted to the Toledo State Hospital. Her shorter and fuller-figured sister gave her the news as she was removing her coat and inhaling the rich aroma of stewed beef. Tillie had become a skilled cook since their mother died, and for this Sarah was grateful because she herself could do little more than boil water.

"Sarah, dear, I hate to break this to you before dinner, but the doctor sounded very concerned."

"Doctor? What doctor?" Sarah asked, hanging her coat. It needed a good cleaning.

"The doctor from the hospital, dear ... from the state hospital. Seems the judge has taken ill again, Sarah. It's pretty bad this time; the doctor said he's been asking for you."

Sarah stopped in her tracks. Hunched over, with one shoe perilously perched on the end of her foot, she felt as if she'd been turned to stone.

"The judge? Obee, ill? What do you mean?"

Tillie's dark eyes were troubled. "I mean the doctor just called, Sarah. Obee's very sick."

"I don't believe it," Sarah said, just as gravity got the best of her shoe. "It can't be true, Til. He's been looking so much better lately; everything's been going so well. Why, we just spoke this morning. He was absolutely fine. Tillie, are you sure? This isn't some sort of joke, is it?"

"The doctor's name is on the note pad by the telephone Sarah, along with the hospital phone number. Call him. Maybe it's a mistake." Tillie pursed her thin lips and turned away.

Sarah reached over and touched her sister's arm affectionately. "Tillie, dear, I'm sorry if it sounded like I was accusing you. I know you wouldn't make something like this up. I'm just shocked, that's all. Did the doctor say anything else?"

"No, not really. I think he was hesitant to give me any more details."

"Yes, yes, of course, he would be. I'd better call him immediately. You and Harry go ahead and eat. It sounds as if this may be a long night."

"I knew I should've waited until after dinner to tell you," Tillie said frowning. "If I say so myself, the stew is particularly good tonight."

"Well, just make sure to save some for me then. Your meals are always just as good if not better the next day."

Tillie offered an appreciative smile. "All right, I'll set aside a platter for you. You just better hope Harry doesn't get a hold of it before you return."

Sarah responded with a knowing sigh, straightened her dress and headed toward the telephone.

"Unit two, Dr. Miller's office."

Sarah thought she recognized the voice on the other end of the line.

"Hello . . . Jan?"

"Yes?"

"Hi Jan. This is Sarah Kaufman. May I speak to Dr. Miller, please?"

"Yes, of course, Sarah. The doctor has been waiting for your call. I'll put you right through."

Thank God Dr. Miller was attending Obee. No matter what had happened, the doctor would keep it to himself and would admonish his staff to do the same. Miller was a compassionate man who impressed Sarah during the Lulu Carey case by admitting that he had overlooked crucial evidence. He was also a friend of Obee's, and, fortunately, a Democrat.

"Ah, Miss Kaufman. Good of you to call back so quickly."

The doctor's voice was calm but somber. Sarah took in a deep breath before responding. "What's happened, Doctor? Why is the judge in the hospital?"

"Miss Kaufman . . . Sarah, may I call you Sarah?"

"Certainly."

"Sarah, I don't know quite how to tell you this, so I'll just say it outright. Normally, I would only reveal such sensitive information to the immediate family, but knowing your closeness to O'Brien and seeing as though he seems so desperate to see you. Look, Sarah, here it is. The judge took an overdose of laudanum today. We don't know yet if it was intentional or accidental. His wife found him unconscious on the floor of his library. She'd been calling him, and when he didn't respond, she tried without success to open the door. It was locked and, believe it or not Sarah, she didn't possess a key."

Dr. Miller uttered this last statement with a note of incredulity. He hesitated for a moment. Was he looking for some reaction? When Sarah offered none, he continued. "Fortunately, however, Mrs. O'Donnell remembered that the carpenter who had done some of the work in the house still had a key to the room. She called him, and he immediately came over. It was lucky that he was home, Sarah. An hour longer and the judge would have been gone."

Sarah stood pale and mute. How could this be? Her brain felt numb. In the past such news might have been less perplexing. There were times when she'd almost expected it. Last fall, for instance.

But now, at the height of O'Brien's popularity, with the election in his pocket and Winifred and the baby finally home, it simply didn't make any sense. That he had taken that despicable drug again after all these years was confounding enough. But the possibility that he had tried to take his own life was beyond belief. If true, there must be something wrong, something terribly wrong.

This last thought brought Sarah back to her senses enough to realize that Dr. Miller was speaking to her.

"Sarah, Sarah . . . hello, Sarah, are you all right?"

"No, Doctor. To tell you the truth, I'm not. How could I be?"

"Yes, I imagine this comes as quite a shock. I was stunned myself when the judge was admitted. But then, we must be grateful that he's alive. And I will of course do anything I can to help him. Tell me though, Sarah, do you think you feel strong enough to come to the hospital? As I've said, O'Brien is quite determined to see you. And, Sarah, I would like a few minutes to speak with you privately as well. Mrs. O'Donnell is quite out of her mind over this, and there are, well, some questions you might be able to answer better than she."

Both comfort and alarm ricocheted through her. The doctor certainly made Sarah feel that Obee would pull through. But his desire to involve her in the matter was something else again. Of course, Miller was a psychiatrist; he would need as many personal details as possible to adequately perform his job. But, for her to be the one to provide them would be stepping into dangerous waters. She would divulge anything if it meant saving Obee's life. But what about Winifred? After she recovered from the shock of it all, how would she feel if she learned that Sarah knew more, much more perhaps, about her husband than she did?

"If the judge wants me there, of *course* I'll come," Sarah replied. "And I'll be happy to be of any service to you, just so long as you don't ask me to . . . to . . . well, to betray any unnecessary confidences."

"I guarantee you that whatever I ask of you will only be in O'Brien's best interest."

"I believe you, Doctor Miller."

"Well, then, how long do you think it'll take you to get here?"

Sarah hesitated. Fewer streetcars went out that way this late in the evening.

"I guess about an hour. I live on the other end of town, and the line to the hospital is indirect. I'll have to change cars. It could take a little longer than that, but at any rate I'll be there as soon as I can."

"Fine. I'll be waiting for you. Oh, by the way," Dr. Miller added, "I should warn you. O'Brien has been extremely agitated. We've got him mildly sedated, but his anxiety level is so high that it is overriding the effect of the medication. I'm hoping you'll be able to calm him down, but be prepared, Sarah. He's quite a different man from the one you're used to."

You mean different from the one *you're* used to, Sarah thought. Unfortunately, this is a man I no doubt will recognize all too well.

4

The Toledo State Hospital was located five miles from the business center of Toledo to the south. From a distance, the main two-story colonial brick building situated on five hundred and eighty-eight acres of agricultural land, appeared more like an elegant plantation

51

mansion than an institution for the mentally ill. An additional four hundred and eighty-three surrounding acres of land, leased by the Welfare Department for crop cultivation, six small lakes, more than a thousand trees and shrubs, as well as the small patient cottages that peppered the landscape greatly contributed to that effect. But the pastoral image quickly evaporated as one approached the structure and saw the heavy steel bars fixed immovably over the windows. Especially at night. Then, the mind conjured something more akin to the slaves' quarters that hovered on the margins of the plantation's genteel facade.

Walking briskly across the hospital's dewy, immaculately manicured lawn, breathing heavily as she approached the imposing, front locked doors, Sarah again noted with greater irony than usual the discrepancy between the benign appearance and what she knew to be the reality within. She had been here many times before, mostly to counsel women such as Lulu Carey, who had come through the courts and for one reason or another were sent here for treatment. Similar to the general probate court, the women's division handled a range of cases, from the delegation of property to criminal charges of rape, white slavery, and even murder. Technically, Sarah's job was to oversee officially the filings of all cases involving women, but she often served as confidant and friend.

Sarah knew the routine well. In order to gain entrance, she would have to ring the outside bell and wait for the attendant to escort her into the front office. Then she would sign her name on a guest sheet and specify the reason for her visit. Despite such familiarity, however, she hesitated. Even in the most official of circumstances, one had to prepare for the sights and sounds found behind those doors. But to know that this time it was O'Brien who awaited her there, required a bit more preparation than usual.

On paper, the Toledo State Hospital was a model facility. A pioneer in developing more humane treatment for the insane, it had, in the late 1800s, gained a worldwide reputation for its innovative practices and attempts to make, through the so-called "Cottage Plan," a more habitable living environment for its patients. But, conditions had greatly deteriorated since that time. Though a pioneer in the last century, in this one the hospital was the last frontier of the reform movement. Inside those walls behavior was unpredictable and every human function and frailty brutally exposed. Indeed, the rules that governed the treatment of patients in other medical facilities seem to hold little sway here, allowing for neglect, psychological cruelty, and in some instances, physical abuse. There simply weren't enough professionals like Dr. Miller, who cared deeply enough about the patient's welfare. Every time Sarah was there she witnessed something that convinced her all the more of the urgent need for action, beginning with the building of a new psychiatric clinic.

Ironically, O'Brien himself proposed such a facility, although his reasoning for doing so was something Sarah had questioned. In a recent lecture to the Toledo Chamber of Commerce, O'Brien had argued for the need of "weeding out" humanity, so that the society might be bettered. "Hundreds of citizens," he claimed, "are running at large not knowing that they themselves are mentally ill, a condition which certainly is not known to the average person."

Obee's heart was surely in the right place. He genuinely wanted to provide an environment where these patients would be treated decently and also where they would not pose a threat to others. But, as she told him after the lecture, "when people think of weeds, they think of something that requires permanent removal. Weeds overtake the healthy plants, and there's nothing that can be done to rehabilitate them. Now, I know that's not the kind of analogy you meant to draw, is it Judge?"

He didn't answer her then, but Sarah believed he would eventually see her point, especially considering his own rather ... how should she say it . . . uneven psychological history. And no doubt his current situation would convince him all the more. Yes, I'm sure he would agree with me now, Sarah thought as she rang the bell, now that he very well might be numbered among those who would have to be plucked from the garden.

Dr. Ethan Miller rather than the attendant greeted Sarah on the other side of the entrance. Heavy-bearded, pipe-smoking, and somewhat disheveled, the Freudian-trained Miller looked the part of one who spent his days delving into the hidden recesses of the unconscious. His thickly lensed wire-rimmed glasses completed the image, suggesting the physical consequences of dedicating oneself to such deep psychological labor.

"Hello, Sarah," Dr. Miller said, warmly shaking her hand. "You made it here rather quickly and look none the worse for wear, I might add."

"Thank you," Sarah replied, tucking a loose strand of brown hair behind her ear. "Fortunately, all the connecting cars were on time. The speakeasies must have shut down early tonight!"

Dr. Miller smiled. A soothing smile, despite his crooked, tobacco-stained teeth. "Ha, that's good," he said. "You didn't need that headache this evening."

"No, indeed, perhaps the gods are with us after all."

"I sincerely hope so, my dear. They are certainly needed here."

Dr. Miller smiled again, took Sarah's arm, and swiftly escorted her down the hall, barely permitting her to glimpse the hollow looks and indecipherable gesticulations of those they passed along the way. Ordinarily, she would stop and offer a word of encouragement to as many of these patients as she could, even to those who didn't seemed to desire it. But tonight she was glad not to have the opportunity, for she sensed O'Brien would require all the energy and compassion she had in reserve.

"Sarah, I'd like to take you directly to O'Brien's room. He's in the main building here. No need to sign in since I'm with you. I'll let you speak with him privately first, and then we can talk, all right?"

"All right." Sarah huffed, trying to keep step with Dr. Miller's quick pace. "By the way, Doctor, does the judge have his own room? I mean, I do hope we can be alone."

"Yes, of course. The ward is full, but, you know, we always keep a private space open for patients of O'Brien's stature."

"Good, that's very good indeed." For once Obee's notoriety is a blessing.

***

"The privileges of class!" Sarah said mockingly, as she entered the room. "My, my, look at this place! The epitome of luxury!"

The small eight by ten room was in actuality cramped and dank. The tiny window on the south wall was locked and barred, offering little relief. Aside from the bed, there was no other furniture except a requisite table and lamp, the light from which cast a sickening glow over O'Brien, who responded instantly to the sound of Sarah's voice.

"Sarah, Sarah, oh Sarah, my dear."

Sarah immediately abandoned her meager attempt to lighten his spirits. In truth, she had made those trifling remarks about the room as much to calm herself as to ease his suffering. When Dr. Miller had left her at the threshold of the door, she experienced a surge of anxiety so intense that she worried at her own ability to cope. She even briefly considered turning around to purchase some cigarettes, something she hadn't done in several years. Finding humor in difficult times had helped her before, so why not try it? But she had clearly made a mistake: there was no way to view this as a joking matter.

That became even more evident as she approached the judge and witnessed the physical signs of his torment. The thin, white hair matted with perspiration, the drawn and pale face stained with tears, the usually soft grey-blue eyes dehumanized by frighteningly constricted pupils. Worst of all, although O'Brien was extremely restless, he couldn't really move because his arms and legs were cinched tightly to the bed. *My God, they have him in some kind of strait jacket. Miller said nothing about this.*

"Sarah, Sarah."

"Yes, Obee, it's me."

O'Brien gazed up at her. "Sarah, I'm so ashamed. So ashamed." He began weeping.

"Ashamed? Ashamed of what, Obee? What's happened? Try to calm yourself and tell me what exactly has happened."

Without hesitation, Sarah untied O'Brien's right hand and held it comfortingly in her own. Generous and strong, this was a hand that had reached out to those in need and commanded entire court rooms. Today it was clammy and weak, barely able to return her grasp.

"Obee, now please, you wanted me here. Talk to me."

O'Brien moaned. "Yes, I did want you here. I wanted you here so badly, Sarah. I need your help. All is lost unless you can help me . . . you're the only one who can help me!"

Sarah's heart skipped, but she showed no sign of such a response when she answered. "You know I'll do anything I can. But I first need to know what the problem is, Obee. And, I need to know *now*."

O'Brien stopped crying, stared straight ahead, and in a hoarse, detached voice began.

"This afternoon, after I returned to my office from lunch, I noticed a letter under my door. There was no postmark, no return address, only my name on the envelope. I went to my desk, opened the letter, and in an instant witnessed my entire world coming to an end. The letter was a threat, Sarah, a threat of such magnitude that I thought I might do myself in right then and there."

If Sarah had not witnessed Obee's condition, she would wonder if he had not invented this story. The whole thing sounded like something out of a bad novel. But seeing him . . . she simply said, "go on."

"The letter was typed on plain white paper. The words were few. It stated that if I did not withdraw from the coming election, that everything would be revealed. The person who wrote the letter knows all, Sarah. They know about Winifred, they know about the drugs, and they know about . . . about . . ."

"About what, Obee?"

"My God, Sarah, they know about Westfall, about Frank Westfall!"

This last statement caused O'Brien to weep again, and move his head about so fitfully that Sarah thought he might never regain his composure. Nevertheless, she needed a few questions answered to ever make sense out of any of this.

"Obee, try to hold yourself together. Let's take this slowly. Now first, what does this person claim to know about Winifred?"

"Oh, Sarah, please don't judge me too harshly."

"I won't, you know I won't. Now tell me, what is it?"

"Sarah, my friend, I should have told you long ago." O'Brien's expression became even more pained. His face contorted into deep rivulets. "No, no, I can't!"

"Obee!"

"All right! Winifred was pregnant before we were married! Do you hear me?" he nearly screamed. "I got my wife pregnant before we said our vows, months before! And now someone, someone horribly evil is trying to use it against me!" He reluctantly glanced at Sarah.

Calmly, she nodded. When the idea had first occurred to her months ago, she dismissed it as utterly fanciful, first, because she had what she believed at the time to be convincing evidence to the contrary, and secondly, because she was so hurt by the possibility. Since then, however, circumstances, particularly the hastiness of the wedding and Winifred's extended holiday, had forced her to suspect that Obee had indeed married the young woman out of necessity. But for someone else to actually have proof and use it so viciously was another matter entirely. That this blackmailer—for that was clearly what they were dealing with—also knew about and was willing to expose Obee's drug problem was even more disturbing. As far as Sarah knew, she was the only one, outside of the doctors who attended him, who possessed that information.

There would be time enough to ponder the identity of this dangerous individual, however, let alone figure out what to do if she were to actually discover it. But the ominous reference to Frank Westfall took the air from her lungs. Because according to the extremity of Obee's reaction when he mentioned the former county commissioner, the worst was yet to come.

"All right, Obee, I admit that this situation looks a bit hard. But, really, you must know that you haven't actually done anything that wrong. You've done right by Winifred in marrying her, and people will understand about the drugs. It's not as if you're an addict, and no one can prove that your current lapse is anything more than overwork. I mean, that's what it's always been due to anyway, hasn't it, Obee?"

"Yes, yes my dear. Of course."

Sarah chose for the moment to ignore Obee's unconvincing tone in responding to this question and proceeded on.

"Okay, then, all we need to really be concerned with is Frank Westfall. I hardly remember him, Obee. What could anyone possibly know about him that would be injurious to you?"

Obee looked away with such an odd, far off expression, that Sarah feared he might stop talking altogether. When he remained silent after she repeated the question, she tried a different tact.

"Obee, tell me more about the letter. Do you have it here?"

O'Brien shook his head.

"Where is it?"

O'Brien now did turn to her, but with deranged eyes. "I burned it. I tore the letter up and burned it! I couldn't let anyone see it, Sarah. Not anyone, especially Winifred. She knows nothing of the drugs, nothing of Westfall, and if she thought the pregnancy might be exposed, why, why . . . it would be too horrible to imagine!"

Very foolish, Sarah thought. Very foolish. But of course he wasn't aware of what he was doing.

"Obee, tell me about Frank Westfall. If I'm really the only person who can help you, then I must know what—"

"I can't tell you, Sarah. No, I *refuse* to tell you that!" O'Brien started to weep again.

"Obee, Obee, you're being irrational. How am I supposed to help you if I don't have all the facts? You must tell me. Obee, do you hear me?"

Sarah took O'Brien's face in her hand and tried to force him to look at her. But his eyes were closed now, and even when she shook him a little, he lay there listless and limp.

Frustrated, confused and exhausted, Sarah retied Obee's arm. Perhaps it was just as well. What he had told her so far was disturbing enough. Better to digest these terrible facts first than become surfeited with any more. She stood up, walked toward the door, and turned off the light.

"Sleep well, my friend," she whispered, and headed shakily toward Dr. Miller's office.

5

Scribbling some notes to himself, Mitchell Dobrinski, a lone figure in *The Blade*'s still empty newsroom attempted to map out his coverage of the upcoming election. It was only 5 a.m., but as one of the paper's most dedicated and insomnia-prone reporters, Mitchell was already considering what new angle he could use to breathe life into what was undoubtedly going to be a stale campaign. The fact that he was selected to exclusively cover O'Brien O'Donnell, the Democratic candidate for probate judge, made this task especially difficult. Not because O'Donnell wasn't newsworthy or even interesting. The man was undeniably both. But his reelection was a foregone conclusion. After all, although he was a Democrat, O'Donnell managed in his previous five terms to attract voters from both parties, and there was no reason to believe he wouldn't do the same thing again. He was still known for his unique ability to strike a compromise, still considered one of the most intelligent and eloquent men in Toledo, and he still worked tirelessly for social reform. And, especially important to the majority of Toledo's citizens fed up with the city's corruption, he was still thought to possess the highest moral standards of any public official. Naturally, he had his share of detractors. That movement several years ago by the Housewives League to remove him from office, for example. And John O'Dwyer's failed but nevertheless persistent attempts to defame his character. But even those situations had changed in his favor, making O'Donnell currently one of the most popular and trusted men in the city.

Nevertheless, as a seasoned reporter, Mitchell knew that some careful investigating would bear fruit. Having worked for *The Blade* for over twelve years, the tough forty-five year old had enough experience to know that no one was beyond reproach. There was always a crack, something overlooked, forgotten, or simply not taken far enough. Not that he enjoyed digging up dirt for its own sake. On the contrary, he considered himself a man of journalistic integrity who believed in giving his readers as unbiased and serious an account as possible. This was why he worked for *The Blade* rather than *The Bee*, that noisy gossip rag that passed itself off as a newspaper. But a commitment to objective reporting also meant providing readers with as much information as possible, the good and the bad, and in this case, the possible flaws of a candidate even his own paper was supporting.

Lighting his fifth Lucky Strike of the morning, Mitchell leaned back on his well-worn swivel chair and tried to refocus, a strategy he often employed when faced with a topic that offered no clear point of entry. Once he had ruled out the most obvious approach, his brain seemed to require some brief diversion before a more subtle route would present itself. Drawing on his cigarette deeply, he glanced aimlessly around the room, registering with relative indifference all the objects that signified it as a place where events became news and the "scoop" was a hallowed word. Typewriters, telephones, paper, and pens, of course, but also prize-winning articles hanging on the walls which announced *The Blade*'s rich history and respected place among the country's most notable newspapers. With only slightly more interest, Mitchell recalled how intimately tied to the development of Toledo the paper was, that it was established even before the city was incorporated in 1835. And he remembered too, how it had come to wield a great deal of political influence, as evidenced most strikingly by the fact that almost every candidate it supported not only had won, but done so handily.

But really, the employees made the whole engine work: news creation, execution, and even consumption. Remove them—the reporters, printers, and Newsies—and most of the things that happened in Toledo, not to mention the world at large, would go unnoticed . . . and unprofited by. Mitchell had often taken solace in this idea, especially when his boss was dissatisfied with something he had written or when rumors surfaced of a change in ownership. He and all those who would shortly take their seats at the line of desks next to his own were needed, and would continue to be so until people lost their insatiable appetite to make sense of the world and their place in it.

Adrenalin surging, he looked around again at his surroundings. Those telephones and typewriters were not just the machinery of the news, but the tangible objects that connected him to his fellow workers. Of course they assisted reporters technically in carrying out their tasks, but they also symbolically joined them in a common purpose.

Yet, even as he was reading a kind of brotherly union in the sameness of those objects, Mitchell also noticed just as many items that served to distinguish one employee from another. On each desk sat coffee cups and figurines, flowers, stuffed animals and other such trinkets whose designs reflected something of the distinct personality that occupied the space. What might his own unadorned, functional-looking collection say about him? Frugal, efficient, and undoubtedly a bachelor, for in all of that linearity and absence of color was no sign of the softening influence of a woman. Steady, quiet, and perhaps possessing difficulty with relationships, because unlike nearly everyone else's, Mitchell's desk lacked even a single photograph, an absence made even more striking because he considered himself a serious amateur photographer. One of the most common and yet distinguishing objects of all, with their frames of varying shapes, sizes and materials, the photographs were indeed the most visible marker of individuality. They were also, then, the greatest symbolic intrusion into the utopian work life he had been envisioning, because what they brought into that public setting were the cherished loved ones of private life.

"Private life . . . private life . . . private . . .," Mitchell repeated excitedly, grateful to leave his vaguely disturbing, philosophical musings behind. Yes, of course. How obvious! The place to begin was not with O'Donnell's all too consistent record of public service, but with the recent change in his private status—namely his marriage. Certainly marriage in and of itself was never a political liability, but certain details about this particular union were extremely unusual. First, it was surprising that O'Donnell had married at all, seeing that he was fifty-nine and a self-avowed bachelor. Moreover, his wife was thirty years his junior. Marrying someone so young was shocking to say the least, and certainly out of character. Second, the woman he married, Winifred Jackson, had been a clerk in the hotel in which he had lived for several years, not the sort of intellectual or social match one had imagined for such an esteemed individual. Third, O'Donnell invited only his closest friends to the ceremony and told no one else about the event until it was over, strange for a man who over the years had publicly revealed so much of himself. Finally, and perhaps most intriguing of all, was that although a good deal of private speculation occurred, no one had officially pursued the topic. An implicit agreement seemed to have existed that any real exploration was forbidden. Newspapers reported on the marriage, but, as Mitchell recalled, even *The Bee* treated the subject with kid gloves. Perhaps the time had come to take off those gloves. Yes, this might very well lead to something.

Halfway through another cigarette, he glanced up at one of the room's three disproportionally large clocks. Soon his comrades would steal the silence against whose backdrop he had once again circuitously found the beginnings of a path. Before then, he at least wanted to get to the archives to pull his own paper's articles on the judge's marriage. They would lack any probing commentary, and if a clue existed, he would have to find it by quite literally reading between the lines. But he needed to start somewhere, and this seemed the most logical place. Besides, this sort of challenge revved his blood. It was for him what made life worth living. Adding one more butt onto the ashtray's smoldering heap, he rose with his mind on fire, even though his lanky, unfit body had grown cramped and numb. With a fleeting pang of envy, he took one further quick look around the room and headed for the archives.

A half hour later, he was back at his desk with a thick stack of papers. The articles on O'Donnell's marriage were his chief objective. However, he decided that it might be worthwhile to review the overall coverage of the judge for a few months preceding and following his betrothal. Refreshing his memory on other matters in O'Donnell's life, however clear-cut they might appear, would allow him to see the event in a larger context and thus perhaps provide him with some bit of information he could bring to bear on the marriage, at least as it was represented in his paper. The possibility of turning discrete incidents into dramatic narrative stirred his journalistic juices. Something in him instinctively searched for the general in the particulars, and in the context of a developing story, even the most seemingly extraneous particular had the potential of becoming an important link in the general chain of events.

This kind of literary sensibility in fact prompted Mitchell to save his examination of the marriage articles for last, going so far as to initially read nothing beyond the headlines. This way he would enhance his anticipatory experience, much as an author who has ordered the pages of a book to achieve a maximum, emotional effect. Indeed, in the spirit of a novelist, he began to peruse these other pieces with the certain belief that some intriguing plot would emerge that would ultimately lead him to formulating an equally intriguing denouement.

Starting with January of 1923, six months prior to the marriage, he thus began the task of combing the papers for anything regarding Judge O'Brien O'Donnell. Articles on the judge would be easy to come by, as his activities had been recorded in the papers nearly every day for years. Much of the coverage naturally involved his court cases, but during this specific period, only a couple of these struck Mitchell as having any possible significance for the election. The first was the Ann Arbor Railroad case, which, though opening in February of 1923, only recently was decided in favor of the railroad:

Grade Crossing Case in Court: Ann Arbor Railway Sues City for Right to Lay Tracks. "The case of the Ann Arbor Railroad Company against the city of Toledo, seeking permission to lay a new track in the North End was opened in probate Judge O'Donnell's court yesterday," Mitchell read.

After O'Donnell ruled against the railroad, the case had been relegated to the Court of Appeals where his decision was overturned. This came as a blow to O'Donnell and all those who believed the crossing would be a safety hazard. The potentially interesting aspect of this case, however, was that O'Donnell had remained vocal in his opposition to the railroad, and had received criticism from some members of the business community for being so. Whether those same individuals had forgiven him now that the crossing was a certainty remained to be seen. One thing was for sure, however, the attorney with whom O'Donnell had formed an alliance on this issue, his former law partner Charles Northrop, was seen as an enemy of business. A Progressive's Progressive, Northrop's litigative reform efforts had cost many companies a fortune. Though O'Donnell was also a reformer, he typically stated his cause, the railroad case notwithstanding, in such a way as not to alienate the business community. Mitchell opened a fresh pack of cigarettes. Political grudges could surely rear their ugly heads at any time, and especially during elections. Perhaps, he thought, turning his attention to another set of articles, I have been a bit hasty in my assessment of the judge's base of support.

The articles on which Mitchell now focused, dated several months later, followed a case which came to be known as the "Love Cottage Cult," so-called because it involved groups of young people who regularly rendezvoused in vacant cottages in the Harbor View area. Depending on to whom one listened, what took place there was anything from simple petting to out and out sexual orgies. O'Donnell, the presiding judge, strongly believed in the latter characterization, as the quotation from him that Mitchell now read indicated:

   "I fear that before I complete my investigation the public will be shocked and ashamed by the facts and confessions I now possess . . ." "In many of the cottages there have been found shocking aftermath of all night parties. Cigarette stubs, whiskey bottles, tattered and torn clothing, face powder, underclothing and the like have been left by members of these parties."

   Everyone in Toledo was, of course, morally outraged over the discovery, but what caught Mitchell's eye was that in making his final decision, O'Donnell set a new precedent by blaming and ultimately fining the parents of the youths involved. Justifying this move by invoking the law against contributing to the delinquency of minors, he later, in one of his many talks on the subject, boldly asked: "What right have parents to sleep when their children are out until two and three in the morning? It is the duty of the parents to watch over their children."

   Many in the city agreed with the judge. But most of the parents who were charged not surprisingly felt that he had overstepped his bounds, trying to dictate how they should raise their children. In fact, if Mitchell remembered correctly, some were so incensed that they briefly attempted to join forces with the Housewives League in their efforts to oust the judge from office. Asserting that in both cases O'Donnell was abusing his power, the two groups for a time made quite a noise, providing fodder as well for John O'Dwyer, who had been hell bent on bringing O'Donnell down.

   Since then, O'Dwyer had inexplicably become one of O'Donnell's most ardent supporters. And, the Housewives League had tempered their attacks, somewhat appeased by the judge's inquiry into the allegations by that poor, young woman, Lulu Carey, that her husband had been physically abusing her. Although Mrs. Carey was ultimately committed to the psychiatric hospital, the allegations were proven to be true, and her husband was currently on trial, which the League viewed as a minor victory in their efforts to stiffen commitment criteria. Yet, it was nevertheless becoming clear that any of these individuals might still harbor resentment toward O'Donnell, that these were avenues to explore, and that others may exist about which Mitchell had simply forgotten.

As it turned out, details surfaced about the judge that the articles helped him to remember, but most of them only seemed to confirm O'Donnell's high moral character and commitment to the Toledo citizenry. For instance, the judge's abiding and endearing support for the Toledo Mud Hens. Every year the papers chronicled his trip to spring training, where, sporting a team uniform, he would assess their chances and sometimes even serve as umpire. As a former minor leaguer himself and a close friend of Roger Bresnahan and Casey Stengel, his opinions on this matter were completely trusted. If he said, as he did in the article Mitchell had before him, that the team looked good, then by God the people of Toledo expected a good season. Then there were O'Donnell's continuous contributions to underprivileged groups such as the Newsies. The judge gave an endless amount of time and energy to these young boys, organizing and overseeing the annual picnics among other things.

As Mitchell continued to thumb through the newspapers, he was, in fact, above all else reminded of the outstanding accomplishments of this singular individual. On one page was a description of O'Donnell's efforts to form an intra-wall correspondence course at the Ohio State Penitentiary; on another his proposal for an opportunity farm, a place where homeless boys and girls would learn skills to enable them to enter the workforce. If a social cause that would benefit the city existed, rest assured O'Donnell would be a central figure in the promotion of it. And whether the venue was the Rotary Club, the site of a newly erected building, a lake, ballfield or church, the press would be there to record his every word.

The next paper contained one such example that though highlighting the judge's dedication to social justice, suggested another group perhaps not so eager to reelect him.

Holier Than Thou Reformers Rapped by Probate Judge. "Women of the holier than thou type of reformer are a menace to Toledo, Probate Judge O'Brien O'Donnell told members of the Civics and Philanthropy Department of the Women's Educational Club at a luncheon in the women's building on Thursday noon: 'If you go in for social work in needy homes, as a lot of Toledo women do, treat the people as your equal, or for God's sake stay out of their homes,' he said. 'There is no place in social work for the self-satisfied woman who says to some overworked mother: Your floors must be scrubbed. Why don't you wash your windows?, the minute she enters that house.'"

Mitchell smirked. He knew exactly the kind of self-righteous individuals to whom O'Donnell was referring, and he admired the judge for taking them to task, especially because many of them came from his own social circle. But surely, some of these women would be indignant over the judge's reprimand, so much so that they might very well seek revenge in the ballot box. So too, no doubt, would some members of the community do the same in response to other strong stands O'Brien had taken, such as his support, reported on the following page, of a ban on the showing of a bigoted film entitled *Nigger*. That, as Mitchell himself wrote in a piece last week, would at least cost him the vote of the Ku Klux Klan, which was ominously gaining power in Ohio as well as in other states around the nation.

The slant of light streaming in the office windows, in addition to Mitchell's audible hunger pains, signaled the noon hour. As was his custom, he reached in his desk drawer and retrieved the boxed meal he had packed for himself. Unlike most of the employees at *The Blade* who went out for lunch, Mitchell usually ate quietly at his desk. Although he appreciated a good restaurant as much as anyone else, he long ago realized that he was especially susceptible to the lure of alcohol at that time of day. And Volstead offered little comfort. He had overcome much greater obstacles than a silly law when he really wanted a drink. On more than one occasion early in his career, his propensity for noontime drinking had resulted in his failure to return to work. Years had passed since any of these incidents had occurred, but still he didn't quite trust himself in the congenial atmosphere of Toledo's lunch rooms. So as others made their way to Jake's or Betty's or Reed's Chop House, a particular favorite of the press, Mitchell munched on his ham sandwich, apple, and cookie and continued to read.

When only crumbs remained, he wiped his mouth, tossed the garbage into an already overfull container, and took note of one further point before turning to the articles on the marriage. With few exceptions, O'Donnell's leisure activities were scrupulously, if not obsessively, recorded by the press. Mitchell couldn't recall any other official, or for that matter, any person at all, who received such attention. Fishing trips, hotel stays, even a simple night on the town instantly became public property. Such as the night of November 23rd, when the telepathist, Eugene de Rubini, came to Toledo. Although the pieces on this subject indicated that many of Toledo's elite were in attendance, O'Donnell's participation in the event received top billing. Quoted as saying that he had a "keen interest in the program," it was the judge who was pictured with Rubini, and he whom reporters sycophantically followed both entering and exiting the theater. The only reference to other notables in the crowd that night indirectly related to O'Donnell as well. Charles Northrop, was mentioned, for example, but only with respect to his participation in an act O'Donnell had suggested, asking Rubini to find a hidden coin that ultimately wound up in Mr. Northrop's coat pocket. Sarah Kaufman, the head of the Women's Probate Court and frequently in O'Donnell's company, was likewise mentioned in relationship to a telepathic episode the judge had proposed. O'Donnell asked Rubini to guess what was on Miss Kaufman's mind. When he responded that it was the judge himself who occupied her thoughts, everyone applauded when, as the article reported, "Miss Kaufman somewhat reluctantly confirmed that this was indeed true."

Exactly why everyone was so interested in these activities and why O'Donnell so willingly divulged such information had always been a mystery to Mitchell. But what this long-standing tradition did underscore was the curiousness of the rare instances when the judge resolutely denied the press such access. According to the date of this specific paper, Mitchell determined that one of these times oddly enough occurred on the same day as Rubini's performance.

"After responding to a number of questions about his ruling a few hours earlier on the Emanuel Cavender case, Judge O'Donnell refused for the second time that day to reveal the location of his Christmas holiday."

Stating that the judge was "Sphinx-like" when asked about his plans, the reporter furthermore suggested a willful inscrutability on O'Donnell's part, an attitude so uncharacteristic, that it should have aroused suspicion in any Toledoan who was even remotely familiar with the man.

The obvious answer, the one that everyone avoided and at which even Mitchell himself winced as he finally confronted it was that the Honorable O'Brien O'Donnell was going to visit his wife for the holiday; a woman he had most likely impregnated before the marriage and who was now too visibly with child to be seen. That would indeed explain such secretiveness on the judge's part on that occasion, as well as the absence of Mrs. O'Donnell long thereafter. Everyone knew that his new wife left town shortly after the marriage. O'Donnell had made a public statement on the matter, claiming that she had some family business out west to attend to that he expected would take her quite some time to resolve. Everyone also eventually learned that she was to deliver a child in March, exactly nine months after the marriage. But the trip lasted much longer than even the judge predicted, and, purportedly, due to that same family business, Mrs. O'Donnell gave birth in New Mexico instead of Ohio, where the event was recorded officially in the papers on March 4, 1924. In fact, the new mother only just returned last month, and because of what was described as "excessive fatigue," had remained with her new daughter in seclusion since doing so.

One didn't have to be a genius to realize that the O'Donnells were hiding something; and that something had to be a child who no doubt still looked a bit too old for her age. Mitchell lit a cigarette and nodded. He'd really known it all along. The KKK, the Housewives League, and all the rest aside, this had always been the most compelling angle. He was just reluctant to admit it.

But then, he had been reluctant for good reason. This was a story that needed to be approached with great caution. Possessing the key to it was not enough. One had to know how to use it, how to shape the facts for the public good, rather than for public spectacle. Finding substantiating evidence would pose no problem; if nothing else, a harmless bribe here or there could do wonders. But what was he to do next? First, there was the issue of *The Blade's* endorsement of O'Donnell. He knew from prior experience that the paper had a limited tolerance for internal criticism of their positions. Second, though certainly intrigued by the situation, he didn't tend to categorize such behavior as good or bad, nor did he think of it as having much to do with one's ability to carry out a job. As long as no one was hurt, sex was a private matter. But many in this city felt differently, would wonder how the judge could really have moral authority if he himself had performed an act they considered highly immoral. How, they would ask, could his frequent exhortations to live a "clean" life have any real meaning in the face of his own rather unclean behavior? And, as a journalist, Mitchell had an obligation to those people as much as he did to anyone else. They had a right to the facts, even if they might use them to an end with which he did not agree.

But did the good citizens of Toledo really want to know the truth? All along there seemed to be a kind of willful collective ignorance when it came to this topic, as though if the words weren't spoken, the act didn't occur—an attitude of which, up until this very moment, he himself had been guilty. More than that, even while O'Donnell's trademark was his openness with the public, Mitchell had once before experienced the consequences of delving *too* deeply into the man's personal life. That was the one other time O'Donnell was unusually evasive with the press, so much so that he was simply said to be "unavailable for comment."

Several years ago, O'Donnell suffered what the doctors termed a "nervous breakdown; a combination of extreme dyspepsia and exhaustion," they were quoted as saying, "resulting from overwork." Following the current medical thought, a brief rest was prescribed in addition to some invigorating physical activities in the out of doors. In the model of Teddy Roosevelt, O'Donnell headed to some unspecified location in the wilderness and attempted to recapture his strength through hunting, fishing, and fresh air. When asked to cover this issue, however, Mitchell was never allowed to interview O'Donnell personally. Everything was mediated through his attending physicians, who spoke of his condition as if it were a badge of honor, a rite-of-passage for someone who devoted so much of himself to his career. Even more frustrating, however, Mitchell was implicitly forbidden by his paper to probe any further on this matter . . . and not permitted to ask why. When he tried to do so anyway, he was told in no uncertain terms that if he persisted, he could lose his job, something he simply could not afford to do.

Odd. Here was a man about whom people on the one hand possessed an extraordinary amount of personal information, but on the other didn't really quite know at all. Oh, they could tell you all right about the pink rose he wore in his lapel, his sock collection–said to be the most extensive in the city–and his predilection for fine tweeds. Here's where his own paper *did* overlap with *The Bee*, Mitchell thought with some embarrassment, for it too had frequently carried such stories over the years. But those same individuals did not know—or chose not to know—what might be simmering beneath those endearing surface markers of respectability; descriptions were always welcomed when it came to O'Brien O'Donnell, but analysis was taboo. What focusing on such superficialities did perhaps do, however, was give people an illusion of intimacy, a relationship with the judge that felt as cozy as his softest pair of socks. And with intimacy came trust, trust that their native son, their mascot, their symbol of virtue could never do the thing that was staring them in the face.

Mitchell finally picked up the articles that only barely hinted at the secret he had already discovered.

Toledo Judge Falls Under Cupid's Spell: "O'Brien O'Donnell, for thirteen years judge of probate and juvenile courts, has joined the ranks of the benedicts. Miss Winifred Jackson and the judge were married at 9 Thursday morning by the Reverend Monsignor O'Connell of Saint Francis de Sales Cathedral . . ." "Immediately following the ceremony, they left on a honeymoon which they said would be at ten days duration. Neither would say just what direction the trip lay . . ." "The marriage came as a distinct surprise. Perhaps a few intimate friends suspected the judge was contemplating the step, but few knew when. It was not until Thursday morning, when the marriage license book was thrown open after the Memorial day vacation, and the judge's signature was noticed that the fact became generally known . . ." "Miss Jackson lives at the 2580 Monroe Street with her mother, Mrs. Elizabeth Jackson. She was formerly employed at the Monticello Hotel where Judge O'Donnell lives."

Other than noting the unexpectedness of the event, this first article was as banal as Mitchell had predicted. The second article, however, was, even if unintentionally, a bit more suggestive.

Meet Mrs. O'Brien O'Donnell: "Without the famous 'Here Comes the Bride' music, Judge O'Brien O'Donnell of juvenile and probate courts, at 9:00 a.m. on Thursday married Miss Winifred M. Jackson. In his thirteen years as probate judge, O'Donnell has signed thousands of marriage licenses. His own wedding was quiet. His license was issued on Wednesday night by Common Pleas Judge Harry Lloyd. His bridal party and the only witnesses to the wedding were: Mr. and Mrs. Charles Northrop, Miss Sarah Kaufman, Mr. Kenneth Ballard and Mrs. Elizabeth Jackson, the bride's mother . . ." "The bride wore a tailored suit and small, close fitting hat. Her corsage bouquet was of sweet peas. The judge wore a tweed suit. In his excitement he forgot to wear a rose, a habit he has observed each day for years."

Some emotion quite other than excitement probably caused the good judge to forget his beloved flower that day. For once, the obsession with that ridiculous rose may have some significance. No wedding dress or wedding song either, the article states. And that photograph. They say a picture is worth a thousand words, and no one believed this more than Mitchell. Well, what does it say when a newlywed couple stands apart, gazing in opposite directions?

Even with the affirmation the article seemed to provide, by 5 p.m., twelve hours after he had started his work, Mitchell was not yet clear about what to do. As he packed up his belongings and waited for the day to end, he still wasn't certain whether pursuing this topic was worth it, whether he was prepared to unleash a scandal, the particulars of which nobody really wanted to confront. He wasn't sure if it was right to tell all, and risk further disillusioning a public already cynical about their civic leaders. Such an action could backfire not only with the people, but with his boss, potentially putting his job in jeopardy once again. But there was one thing Mitchell did know. During the course of his search, questions even more troubling than these had begun to occur to him: who or what was behind *The Blade's* perpetuation of the myth that the judge was in this, as in all other instances, beyond reproach? Why was it that issues that deserved closer scrutiny in O'Donnell's life didn't receive it by the press? Why had Mitchell himself been dissuaded from pursuing such issues? And though these questions went dangerously beyond the scope of his duties, Mitchell could not help but admit that in their answers might be something of great import, something against which all the other potential stories about the judge, including the one he had just been contemplating, would pale in comparison.

6

Sarah's customary eight hours passed more soundly and dreamlessly than they had in years. Part of this was due to sheer exhaustion, but mostly it was because of the renewed sense of mission this otherwise horrific situation offered. To be sure, Obee was in trouble, his candidacy mortally threatened, not to mention his mental health. But as Sarah pondered this fact on the way home from the hospital, she also realized that here was an opportunity to help her friend in a way she never had before, to repay him for all that he had done for her.

How to go about such a seemingly insurmountable task was something else again. Certainly, she couldn't tell the police anything, not yet anyway. Because with the police came the press, and that would be the end of that. Fortunately, however, she did have an ally in Dr. Miller. During their conversation after she left Obee's room, she found that she could confide in this man, for not only was he obliged to comply with the doctor-patient privilege agreement, but he was ready to prevent at all costs the Republicans from discovering the true nature of the judge's illness. Moreover, she discovered that Miller had an antipathy toward the newspapers that nearly matched her own. Together, they decided to tell reporters of O'Brien's hospitalization, but simply to characterize it as it always had been before: a nervous breakdown, the result of overwork. There would be no mentioning of a letter, no reference to a threat. They would not tell them that if his condition didn't improve soon, he might need electric shock, the most extreme of a whole host of new treatments for mental illness. They would say that he would be in the hospital for only a couple of weeks, that it would no way affect his ability to campaign or later to carry out his duties on the bench. And if the past was any indication, people would not only accept this explanation but applaud it.

In return for the information Sarah provided, Dr. Miller would keep her abreast of anything relevant in their therapy sessions. He said that O'Brien had told him: "I would trust Sarah with my life." Thus, for her and her alone, the doctor would bend the rules. Thank God.

Unfortunately, after a week's time, neither Sarah nor Dr. Miller could extract anything new from the judge. Since the evening of his admission, O'Brien had retreated into a nearly catatonic state. Sarah continued to question him about Frank Westfall, and the judge continued to respond with silence or agitation. The only clue, if one could call it that, was a vague comment he made about a desk, but it was uttered in such a rambling and incoherent manner that Sarah couldn't make sense of it. Dr. Miller had even worse luck; O'Brien told him that the only one he would speak to was Sarah.

During this time, Sarah and Dr. Miller had managed to keep the press at bay, but they wouldn't be able to for long. It was mid-August, and the election would soon be in full swing. Something had to be done. Thus, on the morning of August 16th, Sarah decided to call upon Winifred O'Donnell who had been bedridden herself since the night her husband had fallen ill. She would have to be cautious; there was much of which the young woman was unaware and Sarah owed it to Obee to keep it that way. She didn't know exactly what she would say or what she hoped to find. All she knew was that something was telling her this might be a place to begin. Going strictly by instinct, she trusted that somehow this nebulous feeling would pay off in concrete terms.

The ride to the Toledo suburb of Old Orchard was one of the loveliest in Lucas county. As the streetcar traveled west, the crowded, urban landscape quickly gave way to open, lush green pastures. The two-story, wood frame and brick homes that were nestled here and there, with their fenceless yards and earthy colors, seemed to inherently belong. Today the lifting of the heat had changed the colorless sky back to a brilliant blue. Marshmallow clouds appeared in seemingly regular intervals. The glistening sun polished the licorice coat of a frolicking mare to a high gloss. Yet, ordinarily this would be a journey Sarah would loathe to take. She closed her eyes and folded her hands as if in prayer. To the home of Mr. and Mrs. O'Brien O'Donnell, a home she had for so long imagined would be hers.

It was, of course, true. For years, Sarah believed that one day the judge would return the affection she had grown to feel for him. At times, he seemed to come very close. At moments, when working late, he had looked at her with what seemed liked romantic desire. Others when he touched her with unusual warmth. Mostly, however, it was that they had shared so much and for the most part saw life through the same lens. Oh, they'd had their minor disagreements, on superficial matters such as food and dress—especially on dress. But on the big things they were in accord. They both had a strong reforming spirit, read anything they could get their hands on, and loved music; particularly the new ragtime. Both creatures of habit, they laughed at the same things and found pleasure in everyday activity. And then, O'Brien was so accepting and respectful; of her ideas, her ambition, and especially of her religion. It had simply never been an issue for him, even though he was a devout Catholic. All of this contributed to an intimacy that Sarah believed . . . or at least hoped . . . would at some point result in a formal decree of love.

But over time, she began to sense her quest was doomed, not because O'Brien didn't care for her, but because he was incapable of returning the kind of love she sought. For a while, she believed this was because of his commitment to his work and the community. He simply didn't have the time. But then, another thought began to creep in, a complicated thought but one she couldn't dismiss. She began to think that perhaps no woman could fulfill his needs. There was nothing in particular she could put her hands on to support this belief, other than the fact that he rarely dated and lived as a bachelor. Other vagaries, such as his heightened aesthetic taste she wrote off as her own succumbing to stereotyping. She refused to believe that his involvement in the Big Brothers, the Newsies, and all other boys organizations was anything less than honorable. And certainly nothing in his everyday behavior was suspicious. O'Brien hunted, fished, played baseball, was in many ways a man's man, and his roommate, Kenneth Ballard, had a steady girlfriend. Still, the thought persisted. In an odd way it even comforted her, making her feel less rejected.

Until Winifred. When O'Brien announced that he was getting married, she was stunned. When she discovered Winifred's age and beauty, she was wounded. Her suspicions about the pregnancy only served to throw salt in that wound. Nevertheless, despite initially distancing herself from him, her friendship with the judge had endured this blow. It was simply too important to give up. But then, she had already given up a great deal, and now she was on her way to the house of the woman who had made that sacrifice an especially bitter pill to swallow.

In contrast to her modest little cottage, the O'Donnell home seemed like a palace. Tudoresque in architecture, it reflected in its furnishings and ornamentation the grandeur of that style. The mixture of rich woods and textures, French doors, tapestries, Impressionistic paintings, Chinese porcelain vases, Persian rugs, all announced that someone of influence and in possession of refined taste lived there. As she waited in the entryway for the housekeeper to take her to Winifred's room, Sarah recognized O'Brien's imprint in all this beauty, and experienced a strange kind of melancholy, not for the life she actually ever had, but for the one she had so often imagined. "What's that cliche?" she said under her breath, "so near yet so far?"

"Excuse me ma'am?"

Sarah jumped. "What!"

"I thought you said something, ma'am."

"Oh, no, I'm sorry, I guess I was just thinking out loud."

The housekeeper, an elderly, wizened woman frowned at Sarah. I suppose she's particularly suspect of someone talking to herself, Sarah thought with amusement, seeing that one of her employers was prostrate in the mental hospital and the other nearly in the same condition.

"Shall we go?" the woman said, and abruptly escorted Sarah past an expansive living room to an ornate winding staircase. The woman led Sarah up the stairs and down a hall still smelling of fresh paint and new wood. Pointing to a closed door along the way, she said tersely that the baby was sleeping and continued walking. So, Sarah would not be permitted to see the child, no doubt a prearranged plan. Winifred kept up appearances in this way at least, and unless it was absolutely necessary to do otherwise, Sarah would not deprive her of her illusion.

The room Winifred currently occupied was not the master bedroom, which Sarah glimpsed from the corner of her eye as the housekeeper marched swiftly past it. Rather it appeared to be a guest room, decorated with lilac floral wallpaper, frilly white lace curtains, and dark, Victorian furniture. The ultra-feminine style was not to Sarah's taste, but it matched perfectly the woman propped up in the huge, overstuffed four poster bed. Looking much better than Sarah had expected, Winifred nevertheless reminded Sarah of one of those heroines in a sentimental novel: beautiful, delicate, ethereal, and sickly. Or perhaps a little like an illustration of *The Princess and the Pea* she had once seen, with her pained expression and dark, wavy hair rippling on her pink chiffon night gown. Like Sarah, Winifred had dark brown eyes, but hers were wider set and outlined with thicker, blacker lashes. Her nose was straighter, her lips fuller and, as Sarah was quick to notice, even without lipstick, exceptionally smooth and pink. An improved and younger model, Sarah mused, immediately chastising herself for such childish jealousy.

"Sarah, so nice of you to come," Winifred said softly. "Sorry I look so dreadful. I've been quite incapacitated you know."

"You look nothing of the sort," Sarah said truthfully, taking the milky white hand that was weakly offered her. "In fact, I'm surprised how well you look, considering all you've been through."

"Yes, it's been quite a shock. I still can't believe it." Winifred's lip quivered slightly. Glancing at the housekeeper who had planted herself in the middle of the room, she turned back to Sarah. "Would you like some tea? I know it's an odd hour for it, but I feel like a cup. It seems to strengthen me."

"I'd love some. After all, we're not British. We can have tea any time we'd like, can't we?"

Winifred replied with more seriousness than the question demanded. "Yes, I suppose so . . . Elizabeth, please bring us some tea, and do try to have it hotter than the last pot."

The housekeeper scowled as she made her exit. Perhaps because doing so would deprive the woman of sitting, or rather standing, in on the conversation. In any case, Winifred's condescending tone would have been reason enough to take anyone, if not the pot of tea, to the boiling point.

Sarah and Winifred chatted about a number of feminine matters. Winifred seemed to crave such conversation, and because of what she'd said about the therapeutic value of the tea, Sarah thought it advisable to wait until she'd been nourished to broach the subject of her husband. During this talk, Winifred did mention Margaret, but only from the perspective of how demanding motherhood was. What she was most interested in discussing was the latest fashion. Did Sarah notice in *The Blade* that the Lion Store was having its sixty-sixth anniversary sale? No? Well, there was a plaid Felice frock in a lovely shade of tan for just nineteen dollars she just had to have. She only hoped that she'd get well before the sale ended. Where did Sarah buy her own light blue chemise? She loved the string of pearls, and especially those brown kid shoes she chose to accompany it—"a Gore pump, isn't it?" Now, Sarah enjoyed clothes as much as the next woman, but she couldn't help but wonder at Winifred's enthusiasm for such superficialities at a time like this. She continued to humor her, however, until Winifred told her that she thought she dressed appropriately stylish *for her age.* Then, tea or not, Sarah was going to change the subject.

The problem was, she didn't exactly know where to start. She'd come on a hunch, not with a clearly developed plan. Winifred seemed in control of her senses enough to withstand some questioning about the day of Obee's overdose; the rainbow of concoctions and pills lined up on the night stand no doubt ironically had helped calm her down. But what good would that do? The young woman didn't know about the letter. She knew even less about Obee's true past. Perhaps it was best just to wish Winifred well and write this off as a friendly visit.

Winifred herself, however, unexpectedly turned the encounter in a more meaningful direction. As Sarah was silently considering her course of action, Winifred gravely asked: "Sarah, why do you think Obee tried to take his own life?"

Sarah stared at her, swallowing her surprise. "We don't know that for certain, my dear," she finally said. "It's likely it was an accident."

Winifred's doe eyes filled with tears. "Yes, well then, why did he take those drugs at all? Perhaps it's me. Perhaps it's the baby, perhaps it's all too much for him at his age."

"I don't think that's it at all. I know for a fact that you are both very important to Obee. More than likely, and this is what the doctor thinks too, it's the pressure of the campaign. You know, there's been a lot of negative remarks made by the Klan; I think they might of gotten to him, Winifred. You know, he *is* subject to nervousness."

"Yes, so I'm told. I've never really seen that part of him. He's always been so strong, so in command. I've been the high-strung one. I love him very much, you know, Sarah. Very much indeed."

"Of course you do," Sarah said. The sincerity in Winifred's voice was at once reassuring and depressing.

"I know that people talk about our age difference, but it's never really bothered me. He's been good to me, and I love him; that's all I care about."

The steaming tea arrived in a blue and white China teapot with a pastoral design. Sliced lemons, heavy cream, and cubes of sugar accompanied the matching cups on a highly polished silver tray. It was a welcome sight to both women.

"Thank you, Elizabeth," Winifred said with a smile.

"You're welcome, ma'am," Elizabeth said, her own smile an acknowledgment of the apology her mistress seemed to be offering.

"Oh, Elizabeth, I see you found the sugar spoon." Winifred turned to Sarah and explained that the tarnished antique resting on the tray belonged to her grandmother and that it had been missing for some time. "Where was it, Elizabeth?"

"On the desk ma'am, your husband's desk. A rather odd place for it, I have to admit. Found it when I was cleaning."

"That is an odd place, you're right," Winifred agreed. "Especially since Obee is so meticulous about such things. Well, perhaps now we know that he's human after all. All too human, I suppose," she added, with a cloud momentarily passing across her eyes.

"Is there anything else you'll be needing, ma'am?" Elizabeth said turning to leave.

"No, not for now, thank you."

"Tea hot enough?"

Winifred hesitated, then answered, "It appears to be."

As the two women quietly sipped their tea, Sarah, too, experienced the healing influence of the delicious liquid, for with each swallow she seemed to feel more sympathetic toward her rival. Perhaps she had misjudged her. True, Winifred was naive, a little silly even. She was, as she herself admitted, obviously high strung and perhaps lacked great intelligence. But she did seem to genuinely care about Obee—the one thing about which Sarah had always wondered. Sarah was no martyr, but she did want the judge to be happy, even if it wasn't going to be with her.

The tea was so tasty that Sarah decided to have another cup. Adding her usual cream and two lumps of sugar, she took the newly recovered teaspoon and began stirring the ingredients slowly. Swirling the mixture around with the spoon produced a spiraling pattern that reminded her of Obee, who, if something wasn't done soon, would surely spiral out of control. Gently tapping the spoon on the lip of the cup, she took her napkin and attempted to dry it off so as not to irreparably moisten the remaining sugar cubes. As she did so, she gazed at the spoon. The utensil was obviously a family heirloom of sorts; not a particularly interesting one, but no doubt meaningful considering how relieved Winifred was to have it back. Elizabeth had found it on the desk. O'Brien's desk. Was this the same illusive piece of furniture Obee had in his bachelor apartment all those years? Although she'd never had the opportunity to examine it up close, she'd always noticed it when she'd come to visit him there, not only because of its beauty, but because it was somewhat hidden from view. Tucked behind a Chinese screen, only its silhouette was visible unless one walked from one end of the room to the other, which Sarah sometimes did just to get a glimpse of it. She had never questioned Obee about his reasons for keeping the object private. Nevertheless, the secrecy surrounding the desk did, she had to admit, make it all the more alluring. She winced with embarrassment.

But this memory sparked another, of something much more recent. Could it also be that this was just the desk Obee babbled about the other day? She hadn't attributed much significance to that seemingly mundane remark. But now . . .

Sarah put her tea down and glanced over at Winifred who smiled meekly. Clearly, she needed to examine that desk. But how to approach the topic? Thinking on her feet had never been her strong suit. Nor did she lie very well. Winifred would surely get suspicious. Then again, all the woman could say was no.

Sarah relaxed her expression, leaned toward Winifred slightly, and addressed her in as ingenuous a tone as she could muster. "Winifred, the desk you referred to, the one where Elizabeth found the spoon. Do you mind if I ask you where it is?"

"In Obee's study, of course. Why do you ask?"

"Oh, I was just wondering if there might be anything there to help the secretaries at court. They've been trying to keep up with Obee's paperwork and . . . and, there are a few dockets that they couldn't find. Obee might have taken them home to review. We'd so like to have everything in order when he returns. Tell me, Winifred, would you mind if I looked the desk over a bit?"

Winifred shuddered, and again appeared as if she might cry. "The desk is in the room where he was found, Sarah. No, I guess I don't mind if you go in there. You'll forgive me if I don't join you, though."

"Certainly, I understand. You probably shouldn't get up anyway."

"I'll have Elizabeth show you to the room. It's open . . . I've kept it open . . . I'll never let Obee lock it again," Winifred said and moaned. "You may look all you want. In fact, this might be a good time for you to leave me, Sarah. In spite of the tea, I'm feeling a bit fatigued."

Winifred put her tea cup down and lay back on the mass of pillows, resuming the dull expression of a helpless invalid. Offering Sarah her hand in the same listless manner as before, she thanked her for coming and rang for Elizabeth. A brief awkward silence filled the room as they awaited the housekeeper's arrival, but suddenly, with renewed animation, Winifred broke it.

"Sarah, before you go, I want to say something to you. That is, I want to ask you a favor."

"Of course."

"I'm not as smart as you are, Sarah, and I know that you and Obee . . . well, I mean I know you care about Obee. So, if there's anything you can do to help him, please promise me that you will. I don't need to know the details; in fact, I don't think I want to know them. But I trust you. Will you promise to try and help my husband?"

"Yes, I can promise you that," Sarah said honestly. Although uncomfortable at Winifred's allusion to her feelings for Obee, she exhaled. Pursuing her task unhampered was vital.

"And please," Winifred added, "come back and visit me soon. Maybe next time the baby will be awake."

"Yes, dear," Sarah said as she followed Elizabeth out of the room, "next time."

7

O'Brien's study was through a door off the far corner of the living room. If Sarah had noticed it when she first arrived, her feeling of melancholy would have certainly been more acute since the room was a near replica of his former apartment where she had been a frequent visitor.

This space bore more than his imprint. It *was* the judge; everything about it bespoke his presence, and if her visit with his wife had made his marriage more real to her than ever, Sarah still felt faint with longing at encountering this tangible reminder of the unrequited past.

Here were all the familiar objects. The worn, burgundy leather chair molded precisely to Obee's stocky dimensions; the ebony Victrola with diverse recordings stacked neatly beside it, the collection of canes to which, she observed, a gold-tipped black one had been added. Even the intoxicating aroma of his cherry pipe tobacco lingered in the air. If his judge's chambers displayed the public servant, this room revealed the private man. The intellectual, the aesthete, the lover of art, music, and books. Especially books. Sturdy floor-to-ceiling shelves had been built into two of the mahogany-paneled walls and books of every kind jammed each available space, just as they had in his apartment. The complete collections of Shakespeare, Flaubert, Montiesque, and Balzac. Volumes of Irish poetry, *Modern Eloquence*, Emma Wheeler Wilcox's *Poems of Power, Passion and Love*. Every genre, every type of author. "One need not read only the high bred to be well read," O'Brien had argued with populist zeal.

Lying open side by side on one of the shelves were two books that seemed to speak directly to that belief, an illustrated edition of Walt Whitman's *Leaves of Grass* and *Between Caesar and Jesus*, a short expository piece by the popular reformer George D. Herron. Obee had marked passages in the margins of both, which Sarah surmised he had been comparing in some way. In Whitman, it was the first stanza of a poem which read: "Whoever you are holding me now in your hand, without one thing all will be useless, I give you fair warning before you attempt me further, I am not what you supposed, but far different."

A curious passage. *I am not what you supposed, but far different.* Then, she turned to the one he had marked in the Herron book: "The laws and customs which govern the relations of individuals to each other, and which make up the collective life, are the larger and ever-increasing part of the life of each individual. The highest right of every man is the right to do right; the right to obey an enlightened conscience; the right to earn his living in such a way as to help the living of every other man; the right to live a guiltless life."

Now, this made sense. These were Obee's guiding philosophical principles; why he was a Democrat, a liberal, an idealist. But, she thought, perhaps his very failure to live up to them also made him so sick.

I am not what you supposed, but far different.

Sarah recited the line again, and looked back at the illustration accompanying the Whitman poem. It was a sketch of a Christ-like figure holding a book and looking sympathetically down at a young boy who was reaching for him in supplication. Not unlike Obee and all of the children he had helped.

The poem on the next page was the often quoted *I Sing the Body Electric*:

"Was it doubted that those who corrupt their own bodies conceal themselves?" That was the line that caught Sarah's eye. Caesar, Jesus, and Whitman, too. *I am not what you supposed, but far different.* Yes, there may be something to this.

From the book shelves she looked to the centerpiece of the room, a brick fireplace with an ample, cozy hearth. On the ornate, wooden mantel rested the onyx clock with the missing second hand, the baseball trophies and other mementos that she remembered from his apartment. Centered on the wall above it was a thickly textured, gilded framed painting of a farmer with two horses tilling a plot of fertile land. Because of the harsh light that streamed in through the room's large bay window, these objects initially appeared faded and flat. But soon the sun fell partially behind a cloud, filtering rays that lent them definition and depth. And, as if by some metaphysical force, one of these rays shone directly on the object of her inquiry, the one she had nearly forgotten in all her nostalgic musings.

She had never before seen the desk in full view. A twinge of guilt over her past infatuation with it prevented her from immediately beginning her search. For several minutes, she simply gazed at the piece, admiring the richness of the cherry, the delicacy of the legs, the detail of the woodworking. The harsh clanging sound of Elizabeth washing dishes soon reminded her, however, that this was not the past. Winifred had granted her permission to examine the desk and, by God, that's what she was going to do.

She pulled up on a small metal lever which released the drop front and revealed a narrow writing table with several drawers above it. The inside was much shallower than the broad exterior indicated, and relatively few items were stored there. In the smaller drawers were pencils, pens, ink, and stamps. One larger drawer held receipts and bills, and another paper and envelopes. She inspected each of these things and saw nothing of any significance, certainly nothing that would arouse suspicion. Not even one delinquent bill.

The rest of the drawers were empty, as were the spaces she searched in behind them. A careful examination of the outside of the desk was equally devoid of any clues. Elizabeth had found the spoon here somewhere, but there certainly was no trace of it now. The desk was immaculate; no watermark, no spilt sugar, no hint of anything out of the ordinary. She shook her head in dismay. Just a piece of furniture, an inanimate object that in her eagerness to find a solution she had imbued with special meaning. Perhaps Obee had meant the desk at work. Perhaps, as she initially thought, his wild reference had been completely meaningless.

Sarah looked the desk over once more before sliding her hand under the lid to pull it shut. But grappling for the lever on feeling alone, her hand missed it, and, instead, landed upon another smaller lever in back. Its out-of-the-way position rekindled an anxious hope that there might be something there yet, and so without hesitation, she gave it a forceful push.

At first, all she could do was ponder her curious finding. A secret compartment containing five large, leather-bound scrapbooks. Black leather of the finest quality. Two of them were empty save a picture of the judge glued to the front and back pages, two were filled to the brim, and one appeared to be a work in progress. Beside them were a pair of scissors, a jar of glue, several candles in various stages of melting, a box of matches and a tiny bottle of liquid that she instantly recognized as the dreaded laudanum. The compartment itself was cavernous, thus explaining why the exterior of the desk was so massive. The contents left room to spare and were simple for her to extract. Returning them as she had found them might prove more difficult, however, as they appeared to be arranged with forethought; with some aesthetic or perhaps ritualistic purpose in mind. Like a still life, each item had rested upon the other in a seemingly deliberate order. Like the wafer and the wine, they seemed designed for holy use. When she later got the courage to examine them in detail, she realized that this was not far from the truth. For those books indeed proved to be a kind of sacred document; only the story they told was of a man rather than a god, an all-too-human man who required a drug-induced numbing of the senses to confront the paradoxes of his life.

It seemed as if fate had something in store for Sarah, and so she decided to return the next day when she would be rested enough to face it head on. A cursory glance told her that the books were a kind of autobiography, and that the other items, including the laudanum, must have served one way or another in the creation of it. To make any judgement beyond that would require careful study, which she was simply too exhausted to begin.

What did she tell Winifred before she left? That she merely wanted to review some of Obee's books, that they were too cumbersome to take home. She put everything back as best she could, determined to return early the next morning with as much emotional detachment as possible. If there was something relevant in those books, she would be better equipped to deal with it if she didn't let her already overly tested feelings get in the way.

8

Easier said than done. It would be difficult for anyone, let alone someone who cared so deeply about a person, not to be affected by the pages of those documents. A kind of monument to the self, Sarah thought, wiping away tears after only a half hour of reading. A noble but flawed monument, that is, with visible dirt and cracks.

Regarding the books collectively at first, she figured that about ten percent of them were comprised of miscellaneous items: menus from events Obee had attended, speeches he had given, programs, postcards, awards, invitations. The rest were newspaper clippings. From *The Blade, The Bee,* from papers outside Toledo and even beyond Ohio. Obee had evidently cut out nearly every article ever written about him, important and trivial, positive, negative, and everything in-between. All of it was in chronological order, meticulously placed, with dates marked clearly on each. He had even penciled in future dates on the blank pages, doubtless in anticipation of articles yet to come. Each of the books began and ended with the same picture, too; a young, unsmiling O'Brien O'Donnell, with slick black hair and arched eyebrows. The haughty, serious expression belied the cheerful disposition usually attributed to him.

I am not what you supposed, but far different.

The line came back again as she recreated in her mind the ritual in which, to have amassed so much material, he must have regularly engaged: lighting a candle, a drop of laudanum on his tongue, scanning for articles, clipping, pasting, dating. The image was both heroic and tragic; a man who had truly made a difference seeking to quietly preserve the things he had done. But too quietly, too private. Sarah envisioned him there, alone for years, cutting his life, piecing the strands of it together for some anonymous posterity, and then finally for Winifred and the baby. A life in print, a representation for future generations, a form of confession, perhaps.

Seated at the desk's cane-back chair, Sarah looked out the bay window and admired the oak tree heavy with summer foliage. She took a sip of tea that Elizabeth had been kind, or perhaps curious, enough to bring her, and prepared herself for a long day. She would go over these books from here on out with a fine-tooth comb. If they contained something that could help Obee get out of this mess, she would find it. Settling back into a relaxed but very unladylike position, she opened the first book, annoyed that she had forgotten her reading glasses but pleased that she had decided to wear her trousers rather than her uncomfortably feminine frock.

The book was dated 1910-1914, and in examining it Sarah was reminded why she had been so honored to have been chosen to work for O'Brien O'Donnell. These were the early years in the judge's career, and yet already he had done a great deal to improve the quality of life in Toledo. For one, during this period he introduced the concept of the Big Brothers to the city, an act she believed that by itself should guarantee him a place in Toledo, if not Ohio history.

She heaved a deep sigh. So much time had elapsed since his speech on the topic was printed in *The Blade*! The date was February 24, 1913. She had been a probate officer in his court for five years by then, had heard him speak many times, but she remembered still being impressed by his eloquence:

"We are members of one great body. We cannot exist without mutual help. Circumstances may prevent us from conferring worldly gifts from the hand to the needy, but the heart possesses an inexhaustible supply of gifts more valuable. Kind words, and a helping hand, a touch of sympathy, are precious gifts which silver or gold cannot buy and, when applied frequently, are bound to make a little circle in which we move better and happier. Such influences stimulate and develop humanity. Every youth born into this life with the world against him should find one kind, sympathetic big brother, imbued with the spirit of brotherhood implies; you be that brother."

The clippings in this volume also recorded his emerging position on what—despite his missteps in the area of mental health—would become a life-long commitment to women's rights. On one page was an article about his support for female suffrage, on another his favoring of women in the fire department and the police force, and on another his central role in the creation of the very controversial Mother's Pension Act. There were articles here as well about his work with the Thalians, a group committed to curing tuberculosis, and others about his fairness in the courtroom to people of all races and creeds. And scores of miscellaneous entries filled the pages. Among them a cartoon teasing him about his sock collection; a ticket to the Newsies annual banquet; and two postcards, one, a gushing thank-you note from a satisfied client and another from a friend philosophically describing the grandeur of Niagara Falls.

Though feeling a bit voyeuristic reading these latter items, Sarah was determined to leave no stone unturned. She even scanned the advertisements attached to the news articles for clues, although all she really discovered in doing so was how much prices had risen in eleven years; how in 1913 one could get a skirt for a dollar and thirty-nine cents, while today, even though the shorter lengths required less material, it cost at least twice that.

Sarah took brief note of a few other entries: an editorial accusing some Toledoans of not voting for Obee because he was Catholic, one that praised his support of the Poles, and one that warned of the growing influence of the Ku Klux Klan.

She read the next two sets of articles more carefully. The first focused on none other than John O'Dwyer, and involved the court case that started all the trouble between him and Obee. Sarah hadn't remembered that it was Charley Northrup, of all people, who had defended O'Dwyer in that peculiar incident involving soliciting of votes for Walter F. Brown. Was that one of the reasons Obee had ultimately dismissed the case? The July 29th article, the last of the series that traced the case from beginning to end, seemed to suggest as much:

"A demurrer, filed by Attorney C. S. Northrup in probate court to the information of Prosecuting Attorney Milroy, alleging that the charges preferred against O'Dwyer of unlawful soliciting of votes for Brown within one hundred feet of a voting place in November 1911 did not constitute a violation of the law, was sustained Tuesday by Judge O'Donnell. Judge O'Donnell held that the information did not set forth a cause of action, inasmuch as it failed to say in what way O'Dwyer had committed a violation of the law."

In other words, Obee dismissed the case on a technicality, something he was usually loathe to do. He was convinced O'Dwyer was guilty and let him know it at the time. Thus, it was possible he didn't push things in court because of Charley, who, after all, was his former law partner and close friend. Although not exactly ethical, the exchanging of legal favors of this sort was common practice. Had the charge been a felony rather than a misdemeanor, however, Sarah was certain Obee would have had no part of it. His professional courtesy only went so far.

Yet, what did all this really matter anyway? An hour had already passed and she'd barely skimmed the surface of the material. Charley couldn't have written the note, and despite her general distrust of O'Dwyer, she didn't think that even he would stoop as low as blackmail of this sort. Especially since he had more than lived up to his promise to support Obee, campaigning for him vigorously since that day she saw him and Kenneth at the courthouse. But then again, perhaps she shouldn't rule him out altogether. The man was, if nothing else, an enigma, and if anyone could get hold of incriminating information, it was John O'Dwyer. No, although it was improbable that he was involved, she would not exclude him entirely from what she realized with a bit of a thrill was the beginning of her list of suspects.

The second group of articles, about forty in all, proved even more compelling, for ironically, they chronicled piece by piece Obee's tireless, or perhaps more precisely, obsessive efforts to regulate the sale of narcotics. Yes, narcotics and other addictive substances, collectively referred to as "dope." These were the years when cocaine and the opium derivatives morphine, heroin, and laudanum were casually prescribed by physicians and often sold over the counter by pharmacists. Obee was on the front lines in the fight to criminalize such activity. Of course, at the time no one, including Sarah, knew that already personal experience was helping to motivate that fight.

Hours later the sun shone directly overhead, and though unable to penetrate the density of the oak's leaves, lent to the tree a brilliance particular to a cloudless summer afternoon. But, it could just as easily have been the dead of winter. Reading with that fine-toothed comb was working, working so well that absent-mindedly sipping on her third cup of tea, Sarah had lost all track of time. Not only did the hours slip past, but so did the days, weeks, and years, until she felt herself as she was at twenty-eight back in the courtroom on that memorable afternoon in 1912 when Lester Swank, the first druggist prosecuted by county and state officials on a dope charge, was sentenced by none other than the Honorable O'Brien O'Donnell.

9

Lucas County Courthouse, 1912

"In passing sentence I cannot refrain from expressing regret that the persons equally guilty with you are not amenable to the law.

"The wonderful achievements accomplished by the medical

profession in behalf of mankind are fully appreciated by the civilized world and it is indeed too bad that human vultures, hiding under the cloak of this noble profession, can escape prosecution for trafficking in a substance the evil consequences of which are more destructive to mankind than the most obnoxious disease and results in filling the community with human derelicts.

"That this grand profession may become worthy of its growing influence and widening scope, it must protect the members thereof by seeing to it that technical knowledge alone is not sufficient to permit a person to become and continue as a member thereof, but in addition thereto the person must possess character, high ideals and a thorough appreciation of the duty owed to humanity by members of the profession. All barnacles who, instead of interpreting and assisting nature, are destroying it, should be removed. Under existing law, court machinery is practically powerless to reach persons who are now prostituting their profession by prescribing at one time enough cocaine to serve the average drug store for some time, but the State Medical Board has the power and it is its duty to remove all such members.

"Will it act? Time alone will tell."

Judge O'Donnell's powerful voice resonated throughout the courtroom packed with doctors and druggists who sensed—some with resignation, some with anger—that this was a man on a mission. O'Donnell made eye contact with every one of them but none more penetratingly than the ever-defiant Lester Swank.

"Mr. Swank, I order you to pay a fine of five hundred dollars and the costs of prosecution. That, unfortunately, is the maximum penalty under the current law, which," he added with a menacing scowl, "I intend to do everything in my power to change. You and Dr. Neal, by selling Billy Donaldson twenty grains of cocaine, started him on the path to what he has now become: a 'dope fiend.' No amount of money can repair the damage you've done. Mr. Swank, Billy is only fifteen years old. Do you have anything to say for yourself?"

"I've done nothing wrong Judge, nothing that all of the other druggists in this town haven't done," Swank responded blandly.

"Well, if that's true, Mr. Swank," O'Brien bellowed, glancing accusingly around the room, "I've got my work cut out for me, don't I? Court dismissed!"

O'Brien slammed his gavel with the finality of a guillotine and headed immediately for his chambers, leaving the stunned crowd to digest his bitter remarks on its own. For a few moments, no one, even the reporters, moved. The import of the judge's decision left everyone reeling, especially the physicians in attendance who bristled at having their authority questioned so publicly. Who was this man to decide what kind of prescriptions they could or could not write? What the hell did he know about the correct dosage? And, most importantly, what was that ominous reference to changing the law?

Oddly enough, it was Sarah to whom O'Brien first explained the meaning of that remark. Odd, because at the time, the two were little more than distant associates, he a judge of stature, she just one of several junior officers he had appointed. No real conversation had occurred between them, let alone the sharing of such a serious confidence. Therefore, upon finding him waiting in her office that evening, Sarah concluded he had come to announce his disappointment with her work. Why else would he want to see her so late in the day, when everyone else had gone home? Not that he'd ever found cause to criticize her before, but she'd heard stories from others. The judge had a reputation for being fair but demanding, and if one of his staff was not performing up to his high standards, he had no problem letting them know.

"Miss Kaufman! Here you are!"

It was only one of a handful of times in five years he had personally ventured into her office. On each of the previous occasions, his compact physique (which in those days was leaner if not taller) seemed to round out the square space with something more intangible. An enlarged intelligence or spirit. Not seen, but experienced. Today, as she anxiously entered the room, that same quality made her feel as if she couldn't breathe.

"Yes, Judge. How can I help you?" she said, steadying herself against her desk.

"Miss Kaufman . . . Miss Kaufman," O'Brien repeated, clearing his throat. "I, er, uh . . . well now, I can't believe it, now that you're here I'm positively tongue-tied."

The judge stammering? It must be something terrible indeed. He was never at a loss for words. "Is there something I've done to displease you, sir?" she asked.

"What? Oh, no . . . no . . . no, my dear. To the contrary! You've the wrong idea entirely."

The comment didn't register. She continued to wait for some sort of reprimand.

"Miss Kaufman," O'Brien said, recovering his speech, "this may sound presumptuous . . . perhaps even a bit crazy. But I was wondering . . . I mean I'd be honored if you would be so good as to accompany me to my quarters. There's an issue I need to discuss with someone, and I've come to believe you're just the person."

Sarah said nothing but heat fanned out over her cheeks and neck.

"I'd rather talk in my apartment because this is a very delicate matter, and, to tell you the truth," he confessed with an tired sigh, "it's been a long day and I could really use a drink . . . now, what d'ya say?"

Sarah remained silent. He added reassuringly, "I think you know you can trust me, Miss Kaufman."

O'Brien had misinterpreted her. Of course Sarah could trust him. She was baffled, flustered, taken off guard, but certainly not suspicious of his motives. Her contact with the judge thus far had been limited and strictly professional, so it was reasonable that she would respond with some surprise and even embarrassment to his request. And this, in essence, was how she explained her reaction when she finally composed herself enough to tell him that she would be happy to talk with him at his home, or wherever he felt most comfortable. Even if she had been disposed to decline, it would have been foolish to do so. Say no to the Honorable O'Brien O'Donnell? Unthinkable. No telling what might happen. Moreover, when they reached the stairs, she had to admit that she was a bit flattered and not just a little curious about why he had selected her of all people to discuss whatever topic it was he had in mind.

She would find out soon. The Monticello Hotel was on the corner of Michigan and Jefferson, an easy walk from the courthouse, especially on a balmy spring day. Automobiles had already begun to clog downtown's wooden block paved streets; the Model T had made its commercial appearance in 1908 and was now as common as the horse and buggy was before it. Still, many preferred to walk, and O'Brien, like Sarah herself, was an ardent supporter of such an antiquated method of transport.

Fruit vendors had taken advantage of the weather, and they slowed their pace to admire their seasonal harvest. A painterly display of overlapping colors and shapes. Unable to decide between a hard, thick-skinned orange and an even harder, green pear, they purchased a large bunch of slightly undersized but perfectly ripened purple grapes. As they strolled past the ivy covered, brick library on Madison, inhaling the sweet air tinged ever-so-slightly with the metallic fumes rising from the Libbey glass factory, O'Brien spoke continuously on a variety of subjects: the new Theodore Dreiser book, the national debates about corporate regulation, the election of Wilson, the Toledo Mud Hens. On each of these topics he offered a terse opinion—"Dreiser has captured the spirit of the age;" "regulation is necessary for the social good;" "it is refreshing to have a scholarly presence in the White House;" "this will be their year"—after which he took a grape and, with the finesse of a major leaguer, caught it like a pop fly into his perfectly positioned mouth.

A broad, contagious smile that Sarah had never noticed before accompanied his talk, and there was a robustness about him, a physicality that seemed to come alive in the open air. When he came to the topic of the Leo Frank trial, however, which he did just as they approached Jefferson, he stiffened. A story that had made national headlines, O'Brien argued that the Georgia case had made a "mockery of the legal system," that it "exposed the double standard of Southern justice: one for whites and one for minorities like Frank," who was Jewish. Frank was accused of a murder that he most certainly didn't commit and hung by a lynch mob after his death sentence was commuted. O'Brien was appalled at the action and expressed his fear to Sarah that the racist sentiments the trial had ignited would result in the growth of the Ku Klux Klan and other such groups. Time would of course prove him right, and that was one of the main reasons that both he and Sarah became involved with the NAACP, a new national organization designed to protect the rights of Negroes. O'Brien's impassioned speech to her on this topic was also how Sarah first came to know that in her daily struggle against antisemitism, she had perhaps found a potent ally.

O'Brien relaxed again when they arrived at the hotel. The namesake of Jefferson's Virginia home was a six-story concrete structure with gothic arches, bay windows and wide inviting balconies. A popular rendevous for actors, entertainers and traveling salesmen, the Monticello was also a permanent dwelling to a select group of prominent Toledo citizens. An ornate chandelier served as the focal point of the darkly elegant Victorian lobby, and its tear-drop prisms reflected the light like gleaming, polished gems off the revolving glass door through which, in separate chambers, Sarah and O'Brien entered the intimate room. Everyone present—a bored-looking bellmen, a young, bookish Oriental woman, a group of dapper businessmen and even an overweight hound lounging next to his blind master—examined the new arrivals curiously, making Sarah feel rather conspicuous as she waited for the judge to check his mail. Fortunately, he returned with his small bundle promptly and guided her past the prisms and the stares to the elevator. As they waited for the gilded cage to make its noisy descent, a uniformed, black gentleman seated behind a nearby desk waved to O'Brien and winked.

"That's Jimmy, the hotel clerk," O'Brien said. "Good man. Worth his weight in gold."

What O'Brien meant was that over the two years that he had lived there, Jimmy had developed an instinct for distinguishing legitimate callers from the hoards of disgruntled citizens who sought to take advantage of the judge's policy of "listening to the people." If not for Jimmy, he would have never made it to work. He couldn't have known it at the time, of course, but if it also weren't for Jimmy's unexpected retirement in 1917, he might not have gotten into the mess he would find himself in eight years later.

O'Brien extended his right arm and held the sliding door open with the other. "After you, my dear."

As they stood silently waiting in the elevator for what seemed like an interminably long period to reach the fourth floor, Sarah swallowed hard. She could feel perspiration gathering on her upper lip. What was she doing here? Why had this much esteemed person chosen her to confide in? What purpose could she possibly serve? The amusing sight that welcomed them as O'Brien opened his apartment door, however—a costumed man with the startled expression of a boy caught with his hand in the cookie jar—made her breathe a bit more easily.

"Ken!" O'Brien said, clearly startled himself, "I didn't know you were coming home so early. I thought you had a meeting."

"I did," the grinning man answered mischievously, "but seeing that the weather was so lovely and there were so many unnecessary people there anyway, I didn't think anyone would notice if I just slipped out quietly . . . and went to the golf course instead."

"Yes, so I can see," O'Brien said, critically eyeing the man up and down. Ken wore tan knickers and bright tartan knee socks, and though this was typical sporting attire, it looked so ridiculous Sarah nearly laughed out loud.

"Well, Obee, I can see what *you're* dressed for, too, with that staid, nobly suit: nothing fun, I assure you. My God, that collar looks like it's cutting off your circulation. Now you, Miss, are another matter. That's called a shirtwaist, isn't it? Usually those are very plain, but on you, especially that maroon color . . . very enticing, my dear."

"Miss Kaufman, this is my roommate, Kenneth Ballard. Believe it or not, he's an engineer."

Ken was enormously attractive then, energetic and charming, even in his knickers. Tall, wiry, with thick, straight, sandy hair and angular features, he exuded youth and vitality, looking more like an actor or an athlete than the plain, studious type one associates with his profession.

He offered Sarah his hand and smiled. "It's about time Obee brought home a lady," he said approvingly. "And such a lovely one, too. Kaufman, that's a Jewish name, isn't it?"

"Yes, yes it is."

"Well, you're lovely just the same." Kenneth looked at Sarah blankly and then laughed. "Forgive me Miss Kaufman. I was just kidding. I love to get Obee's ire up."

"Ignore him, Miss Kaufman," O'Brien said. "He has a detestable sense of humor."

Sarah smiled uncomfortably, thanked Kenneth for the half compliment, and started to ask him about his golf game. But O'Brien abruptly cut her off.

"Ken, we'd love to sit and chat, but it's getting late and I do have something important to discuss with Miss Kaufman, a matter that is strictly business."

"Oh, I'm sorry to hear that."

"I'm sure you are, considering how *seriously* you obviously take your own job," O'Brien said. "But that being the case, do you think you might give us a bit of privacy?"

Kenneth sighed in annoyance. "Oh, all right. But you work too much. He works too much, Miss Kaufman. I'll have to talk to you about it sometime."

Sarah joined in the fun, and told him that she would look forward to the conversation. "If, that is, you think a Jewess can be trusted with such information."

"Ha, that's good, that's very good!" Kenneth exclaimed. "I like her, Obee."

"So glad you approve, Kenneth . . . now shoo!" and O'Brien didn't take his eyes off the man until the bedroom door creaked shut.

"I'm sorry about Ken, Miss Kaufman. He's really a good chap, just a bit of a prankster. And, I'll wager he'll never tease you again. You stood up to him, and for that he'll respect you for life. Now, would you be so kind as to join me in a glass of sherry?"

Sarah wasn't much of a drinker, but this spirited exchange had made her feel rather adventurous. "Yes, I think I will. Thank you, Judge ... oh, and, Judge," she boldly added, "please call me Sarah."

While O'Brien was retrieving the sherry, Sarah had a brief opportunity to examine the apartment, which she quickly determined was at once comfortable and elegant. The spacious drawing room in which she was now seated on an embroidered burgundy satin couch was softened by a fireplace whose dark patina bore the cozy signs of frequent use. A formal dining room, a small kitchen and what appeared to be two bedrooms on opposite sides of a photograph-lined hall filled out the apartment. The bay window, that stretched nearly the entire length of the drawing room, let in abundant light, and on the connecting balcony were a pair of round chairs that faced Jefferson like two watchful eyes.

"Here we are!" O'Brien offered Sarah the amber liquid in an exquisite bit of cut crystal, ushering in what seemed to be an auspicious occasion. The judge had apparently as refined a taste in household items as he did in his clothes. So unusual for a man. They drank a toast, to what she did not yet know.

"Well, let me get right to the point," O'Brien said, resting his empty glass on a worn coaster that appeared to occupy a permanent place on his very chic, marble coffee table. "It's really not so mysterious after all; I actually have nothing to say that Ken couldn't hear. The truth is," O'Brien said with a sigh, "my roommate wouldn't be very interested. Kenneth's mind is too compartmentalized. Though, as you've witnessed, he does possess a bit of a wild streak, which, I'm pleased to report, his lady friend, Kate, does a pretty good job of taming. Still, Ken's an engineer, and a good one at that. He's a wonderful guy, a real friend, too. But when it comes to the betterment of society, well, if he doesn't have a statistical chart before him, he's rather lost. And, what I want to talk to you about, Miss Kaufman . . . I mean Sarah . . . is nothing less than the betterment of society. Do you mind if I smoke?" O'Brien asked, already lighting a pipe.

"No, no of course not. I rather enjoy the aroma, in fact."

"Really? Now, that *is* unusual. Reason enough to ask you here more often! Well," he said, ignoring Sarah's blush, "you know what happened today in court. You were there. You saw the response, the anger in the eyes of those predators who call themselves medical men."

"Well, I—"

"I'm sure you also saw the cover story in *The Blade* and that sketch of Toledo's dopers, you know, the one where they appear, to put it mildly, like descendants of Lucifer?"

"Yes, but—"

"Now, some have called that image an exaggeration, but I tell you, it's not far from the truth. Not far at all," O'Brien said, his widening eyes blinking rapidly. "Sarah, I know you've counseled some of these people."

"Yes, I—"

"I'm sure you've seen how destructive this vile stuff is," he continued. "Well, I intend to fix this problem, Sarah, the most permanent way I know how—by changing the law!"

"Yes, I heard you mention—"

"Wait a minute." O'Brien hurried out of the room and returned with a thick, hand-penned document. "See this? This is a bill I am going to propose, along with Warren Duffey. You know the assemblyman?"

This time Sarah just nodded.

"We're going to introduce a measure which would make illegal the possession of all of it: morphine, cocaine, heroin, and the sources of these drugs, too. See, right here." O'Brien pointed to a passage, but pulled it away, waving the entire document frantically in the air before Sarah had time to read it. "This will make the conviction of dealers, and by that I especially mean the druggists and doctors, much more possible. And, most importantly, Sarah, it will allow for their imprisonment. This is the key. Up until now, the only penalty for this terrible offense has been a fine. Prison should be a much more effective deterrent. This is the only solution, Sarah. Drug addiction is an epidemic. Dope is killing people!"

O'Brien uttered these last statements in an almost hypnotic fashion. His expression darkened, and he seemed to be staring at something outside or, something deep inside himself. For a moment, he seemed to nearly forget she was even there.

"Judge O'Donnell, are you all right?"

"Oh, yes, yes," O'Brien said, squaring his shoulders. "Well, my dear, what do you think?"

At last he seemed to desire a response. As she didn't know when she'd get another opportunity, Sarah chose her words carefully.

"I think it's a fine idea, Judge; truly a noble and important cause. And, yes, I have seen these victims. Anything, legal or otherwise, that can be done for them should be." She took a sip of sherry. "But, I must say, I'm a bit perplexed. I've enjoyed this visit immensely, of course, but I wonder why you invited me? You certainly don't need me to confirm an idea to which you are already so clearly committed."

Sarah waited for an answer while O'Brien puffed on his pipe and poured himself another drink.

"Well, my dear, you're right. I don't need any convincing about this matter. But, I didn't ask you here for that." O'Brien leaned toward her. In this light his eyes looked like freshly minted quarters. "Sarah, I've got a confession to make. I've been keeping track of you. Yes, in a manner of speaking, you could say I've been following you. I know about your volunteer work for the Jewish Women's Settlement House, for the Banner Club, the Traveler's Aid Society, the Girl Scouts, and I know you've been trying to organize a Toledo Chapter of the NAACP, which, by the way, I would be happy to help you with. I'm certainly also well aware of your successes in court: last year out of those five hundred couples seeking marital advice, it was only forty-five of them, wasn't it, that went through with a divorce after speaking with you? Well, these acts individually are noteworthy indeed. But more importantly, together they prove to me your social conscience, your dedication to humanity. You are bright, very bright, but you're also compassionate. An admirably unique combination."

Sarah smiled and glanced down at her folded hands. She had never received this kind of praise from anyone, let alone from someone of such esteem.

"If I may be so bold, I think your religion is partly responsible. You as a Jew, as do I as an Irish Catholic, know what it's like to be persecuted. I'm sure you're aware that there are many who can't abide the idea of a Catholic in office, who still believe that 'no Irish need apply.' Well, such a sentiment causes some to hide their origins, others to lash out at those they perceive as weaker than themselves. But, without sounding too arrogant, I hope, such attitudes have made me more empathetic, more caring, not just for people like myself, but for all victims of oppression. And, if I'm not mistaken, I believe such experiences have had a similar effect on you."

Now it was Sarah who poured herself another drink.

He stared at her, unblinking. "Sarah, I brought you here because I need more than your opinion. I need your help. I'm going to be taking on the medical establishment, and I need someone I can count on, someone who believes in the importance of fighting this battle." O'Brien got that far-off look again, and his words began to take on an evangelical quality. "This is only the beginning, Sarah, only the beginning! It will be a long haul, my dear, a very long haul. With tempers running so high, it could even be dangerous. But I have a vision! A vision of a drug-free city, where children will have no fear of becoming dopers. I will propose the building of a hospital, too; for while the perpetrators need punishment, the victims need rehabilitation. This problem needs to be attacked on multiple fronts. I know this is really not your territory, Sarah, but I'm asking for your assistance. I need support, but I don't just want a secretary. I'm asking you to lend your knowledge, expertise, and your heart. Of course, you will still retain your regular job, for unfortunately, this is extra work for which the city will be unable to remunerate you."

O'Brien sat back and puffed on his pipe. "Well, that's about it. I don't expect an immediate answer. You'll probably want to go home and do some thinking."

Sarah was silent, but not because she needed the extra time. She would accept his offer. The judge was right about her. She, too, had an affinity for the marginal, the downtrodden, for the victims of persecution, whatever its source, whomever its target. No, she only hesitated because of a vague sense of foreboding. O'Brien's passion was contagious, but something about it was also disquieting; exceeding the needs of the cause. That intermittent look was troubling as well. Captain Ahab came to mind. Was the judge, too, on some kind of monomaniacal quest, motivated by personal revenge? Surely, not all doctors were villains. Surely some of them had the welfare of the patient in mind when they prescribed these drugs. But, Sarah didn't linger on this idea for long. He had presented her with a once-in-a-lifetime opportunity; to work with one of the greatest thinkers of her city and, perhaps, help him change the course of history. She was susceptible to overreaction. No doubt her apprehension was due to the fact that she had simply never been in contact before with someone who cared so deeply about people.

"Judge, I don't need to think about anything. Of course, I would be honored to assist you."

"Wonderful!" he said, raising his glass in another toast. "I knew I was right about you."

The sun had long set by the time O'Brien finally escorted Sarah back through the lobby where they had walked in earlier as working acquaintances. From here on out, they would be friends. And if there was any doubt of that, O'Brien cast it away forever with a remark he reserved only for such individuals: he asked Sarah to call him Obee.

10

Despite many jumps and starts, the Duffey Bill was passed unanimously by the Ohio State Legislature on April 17, 1913. Sarah read the brief description quoted in *The Bee*:

"Prohibits the sale, peddling or giving away of dope of any kind, except on original prescription of a physician, dentist or veterinarian, and then only when such prescription is for the patient's necessary purposes; Finding of dope in possession of a person is prima-facie evidence of a violation; No prescription containing dope can be refilled. All dope prescriptions must be original; Dope users can be committed by the courts to an institution for treatment; For the first offense a penalty is provided of twenty-five to five hundred dollar fines or imprisonment in the county jail for from thirty days to six months, or both. For subsequent offenses the penalty is from one to five years in the penitentiary."

My God, who would have guessed the irony of Obee's response when he heard news of the bill's passage: "Nothing more satisfying than to see one's idea take shape and come to fruition," he had said. "These murderers will finally get their due."

That was indeed true for most of them, but as she would later discover, there was one who escaped such a fate by agreeing to provide Obee with the very substance for which the others were permanently marked with a criminal record.

Perhaps Obee didn't understand the psychological mechanism that allowed him to rationalize the double-standard he had come to live by. But then again, Sigmund Freud himself might even have had trouble. Because Obee knew the terrible consequences of addiction first-hand, he no doubt genuinely wanted to prevent its spread. One of its victims—and perhaps unconsciously even longed to be discovered—yet consciously he was somehow able to justify his use. He didn't have the profile of an addict. All dope did, whether tincture of laudanum, morphine sulphate, or those little white heroin pills, was make it easier for him to meet his demanding schedule, to tackle the endless needs of society. Others had wives and children to sustain them. He had only his commitment to protect the people. Who then would fault him for turning a blind eye to those who, however perniciously, protected him? Wasn't this just a case of sacrificing the individual for the good of the whole? A necessary evil in the service of a higher cause?

Sarah swallowed a remaining drop of cold tea. She contemplated asking Elizabeth for more but three cups were enough. Although she was tired and hungry, a walk around the room and a stale mint found lodged in a forgotten pocket of her handbag would have to suffice for now. She couldn't afford to waste time, and a clock chimed two bells somewhere in the house. Hopefully Tillie was making something tasty for dinner.

On the page before her was one the most volatile headlines involving Obee *The Blade* had ever run: *Stay Away or be Blown to Hell.* The day before the Lester Swank verdict was read, Swank's attorney, Paul J. Ragan, had directed this remark specifically toward the special agents of the State Board of Pharmacy who visited Swank's drug store and caused the druggist's arrest on the basis of an alleged improper prescription. "Tell these men that if they don't stay away from Toledo and cease defaming our city we will blow them to hell," were his exact words. But as Obee had arranged the agents' trip and was the presiding judge in Swank's trial, he, too, was likely at risk for whatever action that threat implied. The judge was undaunted, however, and fortunately, nothing serious ever materialized. Swank paid his fine and attorney Ragan moved quietly on to his next client.

During the year Sarah worked with him on the drug problem, Obee continued to receive his share of verbal abuse. But the bluster died down as people began to realize the inevitability of the Duffey Bill and all but disappeared after Dr. Alexander Lambert came to town. Theodore Roosevelt's personal physician and an authority on the treatment and cure of dopers, Lambert worked with Obee on the development of a rehabilitation hospital. Most citizens enthusiastically supported such an humanitarian effort, and the national attention Lambert's visit brought to Toledo shifted public attention away from the few remaining dissenting voices. In fact, despite the increase in addiction, a general optimism began to pervade the community. Positive action was being taken that would ultimately turn things around, people thought. With the judge at the helm, patients would get proper doses, children's futures would be safer, and the city would serve as a model. The fact that the drug trade would simply go underground and eventually thrive there was not of general concern. One thing at a time everyone said, a sentiment Obee construed to include himself.

If this period marked the beginning of Toledo's love affair with the Honorable O'Brien O'Donnell, it also saw the ripening of Sarah's friendship with him. Obee had meant what he said about not only wanting a secretary. Indeed, from the very first, he treated Sarah more like a trusted confidant, discussing with her all . . . well, nearly all . . . matters pertaining to what he termed his "war against dope." In daily conversations that often extended long into the evening, the nearly inseparable pair spoke about potential loopholes in the legislation, the newest methods of treatment, the architect who would design the hospital. They celebrated the Duffey Bill's passage together and bemoaned the unsuccessful but persistent attempts to derail it. And Obee listened to Sarah's opinions. It was Sarah, in fact, who counseled him to be lenient with both druggists and doctors on their first offenses. With some resistance and much rapid blinking, he followed that advice and quickly became known for his fairness on the issue, even by the most defiant of the medical establishment.

Yet, perhaps not every member of that illustrious crowd was so easily subdued. Sarah flipped through the next several pages of the scrapbook.

O'Donnell is Obdurate: Judge Refuses Plea of Friends to Suspend Sentence Imposed on druggist Thomas A. Huston; Dr. Lilly gets 6 Months for Ordering Dope; Dr. Lilly is Jailed as "Dopers"aid; Dr. Sickles to Fight Dope Law; Demands Jury.

Any of these individuals—Thomas Huston, Dr. Lilly, Dr. Sickles—could have theoretically harbored resentment toward Obee. His actions ruined their careers if not their lives. But, was it possible that they could also know all the intimacies exposed in that blackmail note? After all, Sarah, to whom Obee told almost everything, only just learned of the pregnancy and had yet to discover the significance of Frank Westfall. Tom Huston and even the obstinate Lester Swank never really knew the judge. Furthermore, both moved out of town years ago. Dr. Lilly and Dr. Sickles on the other hand still resided in Toledo. But both were infirmed and at least in their seventies, not really the profile of a blackmailer.

There were, however, two other doctors who Sarah knew to possess at least one critical piece of information: the obstetrician who delivered Winifred's baby and the charlatan who supplied O'Brien with drugs. The first was a long shot as a suspect because even though Sarah didn't know the man, he was surely unaware of O'Brien's addiction, and the possibility of him knowing of Frank Westfall was even more remote. Moreover, if, as she presumed, this doctor practiced out west, what reasonable motive could exist for him to demand O'Brien's withdrawal from a local political race in which he could surely have no interest?

The second was a different story. Sarah did know this one, a man who had lived in Toledo all his life, and was most probably still the judge's supplier. Samuel Evans was one of those slimy individuals whose thriving medical practice was due to the fact that he preyed on the fears of his patients. He was, unfortunately, very handsome, and most people mistook his pleasing appearance for a trustworthy character. A confidence man of highest order. Sarah herself would have put her health in his hands had she not by chance discovered the truth about his relationship with Obee; a terrible truth which she had reluctantly agreed to keep secret.

About six months after the Duffey Bill was passed, she noticed that Obee looked pale and tired, and that he was also becoming absent-minded. A person who prized and demanded punctuality, he started to forget appointments and was late to meetings. This was one of the main reasons she began her practice of calling him in the morning. By this time she was also well aware of Obee's extreme fastidiousness; she had come to believe, in fact, that such behavior was integral to his sense of self. Therefore, while others might not have noticed, she became concerned when he appeared ever-so-slightly disheveled at work, a collar not pressed quite enough, a tie slightly off-center. And, she became downright alarmed the day his uneven pant legs revealed two obviously mismatched socks.

Sure enough, not long after that event, Sarah was informed that Obee was in the hospital. When she went to visit him the evening after hearing the news, Dr. Evans, the attending physician, was at his bedside. Two weeks later, when Obee was released, Evans was understandably there again. But when Sarah continued to see the two men together outside the hospital, she began to wonder. Evans seemed to hover in the shadows of Obee's life, appearing out of nowhere, coming when she and everyone else was going. Even more suspiciously, Obee never explained the nature of their mysterious alliance. Indeed, whenever Sarah encountered them together, he acted as though the doctor were invisible. Until, that is, Sarah discovered the judge passed out in his chambers about a year after his hospitalization.

She had been coming to deliver some papers when she saw Evans skulking out of the room. Sensing trouble, she opened the door without her usual knock and saw Obee on the couch. He was out cold. After several minutes of shaking him and shouting his name, she succeeded in bringing him around. His pupils were constricted, and he was groggy, but in general seemed to be all right. At the very least, he was breathing. After assuring herself of this, Sarah decided she'd finally had enough.

"Obee, if you don't explain to me what's going on, I'll confront Evans myself."

This comment extinguished the residual signs of his stupor. "No, Sarah. Please, you can't do that!"

"Well then?"

In resignation, O'Brien told her what she wanted to know, but not before extracting a promise that she would keep every word of it confidential. The judge was subject to anxiety that had grown more severe in recent years. The source of it was unclear and the triggering mechanism random. But the symptoms were painfully real. Trembling, rapid heart beat, dyspepsia, and an amorphous sense of foreboding. The first time he had experienced them he thought he was going to die and admitted himself to the hospital. There he was treated by Dr. Evans with laudanum and recovered almost instantly. The calm this drug brought to him was a god-send, and he performed countless "Hail Marys" in thanks. Evans prescribed more for him to take at home, and for a while just knowing the "medication" was there proved comfort enough. For months he never touched it. But then he had another bad attack, either from the stress of an election or a trying case, he couldn't remember which. Before he knew it, he had come to increasingly rely on this substance. He would stop periodically, but would eventually start up again, and always Dr. Evans was there to keep him well-stocked.

"You see then, Sarah, why I need this man."

"What I see, Obee, is that you're a hypocrite! How can you . . . *you* of all people?"

"I know how it must seem, but—"

"I know how it *is*, Obee. You're an addict. And Evans is your supplier."

"It's not that simple. I'm not really what you would call addicted; I can do without it, if I absolutely have to. And Sam doesn't do this for anyone else. We have an arrangement that comes out of our . . . our . . . common humanity."

"Oh come on Obee, you're not seeing things clearly. Why are you any different than those dopers in the papers? Why is Dr. Evans any different than Dr. Lilly or Dr. Sickles? You called those men murderers. Remember?"

O'Brien reddened and blinked. "Look, Sarah. I understand how you feel."

"I don't think you do. I've come to greatly admire you, Obee." Her eyes burned, but she fought to keep the tears away. The depth of her affection surprised and embarrassed her. "I've trusted you, worked with you, been your friend. And now I come to find out that the whole thing has been a sham."

O'Brien swallowed hard. "Sarah, I hope you don't really believe that. I'm as committed to solving this problem as ever. Don't you see? My passion comes out of my own experience; out of my own pain. What does it matter if I'm a causality of the battle, as long as we win the war?"

"It matters to *me*. And it matters to this city. This isn't a melodrama, Obee. You've done great work here, and you were meant to do more."

"And I will do it. I promise you. But, Sarah you, too, must keep your promise!"

Sarah would have seen the fear in Obee's eyes even if his pupils were their normal size. There was already a paucity of honest leaders in the city. If Toledoans learned that their beloved favorite son was not among them, the eradication of dope and perhaps every other noble cause he had supported would be in jeopardy. No, Sarah could not let that happen. The judge was human after all, flawed like everyone else, and in a way, she felt closer to him for it. But the people still needed a hero. For them, he needed to remain on the pedestal they had carved out for him with their hopes and dreams. After all, his personal failures were not a gauge of his social conscience. His own weakness didn't mean that he couldn't, to use his own bellicose imagery, fight the battle. Nevertheless, something had do be done. If Obee kept this up, no matter how hard he tried, he would be useful to no one.

Sarah softened her expression and took his hand. "I will keep my promise, but only under one condition, Obee."

O'Brien returned her grasp but backed into himself a bit. "Go ahead."

"I want you to get help. Take the cure. Go away to do it, but do it . . . and soon."

After much squirming, sighing, and blinking, O'Brien agreed to her terms. A bit too willingly, she even thought at first. The judge was a master of oratory. He could convince anybody of just about anything. Even when he left town for three weeks she was skeptical. Although he told Sarah he was going directly to a clinic in New York, the papers covered the trip as a "long-needed rest to some unspecified location." Without the press keeping track of him, he could be in an opium den for all she knew. But, for many months after his return, he really did seem much better. He got to meetings on time. His collars were impeccable. His socks matched. Samuel Evans was nowhere to be found, either, although stories of his questionable medical ethics continued to circulate. Then, a year or two later, Obee wound up in the hospital again. This time there were no warning signs, despite the fact that he was sicker than ever. Sarah had heard that Evans was called in on the case, but she could never be certain because even she was barred from seeing the judge.

After his release, Obee left town, this time for two months. When he returned, he refused to answer any of Sarah's questions, and she eventually stopped asking. The judge was her friend, but she still worked for the man. She had been promoted to chief probation officer by then and had no intention of risking her job, even for the well-being of the court's most celebrated member. If he wanted to destroy himself, let him do it. But in 1920, when he came to work with no socks on at all, she couldn't maintain that hard line. In tears, she begged him to get help again, and in tears he again said he would. She was right, he admitted. He owed it to the city, to her, to himself. He would get clean and stay that way. And that's exactly what he did. Until a week ago when he ingested enough laudanum to take his own life.

Sarah sat back, massaged her temples, and considered the evidence. Samuel Evans was certainly around during Frank Westfall's time. He was about fifty now, near the age Frank would have been had he lived. He could have even been the commissioner's physician. In a moment of weakness, Obee may have let something slip about Westfall, the pregnancy, and who knows what else to Evans. A person in need of a fix will say anything. He might even mistake a doctor for a priest, especially when the medical remedy for a waning spirit makes the body of Christ seem bland by comparison. Yes, Sarah might be taking this detective stuff a bit too far, but Obee could very well have told Evans everything, more than she even knew. And as for motive, that wasn't hard. Although Evans was a professed Democrat, anyone who invented illnesses for profit certainly wouldn't be beyond working for another party if the price was right. Indeed, she would be surprised if this so-called doctor, who had already violated the Hippocratic oath ten times over, was not playing both sides of the political fence.

One scrapbook completed, three months to the election, the mystery of Frank Westfall yet to be discovered, and two names to investigate so far. Sarah sat in her kitchen munching on a piece of fresh challah Harry had picked up from Feldman's and absentmindedly watched Tillie cook. Her sister had already prepared cold chicken sandwiches and salad and was now making a spice cake from a recipe she had found in the "Our Cook Book" section of *The Blade*. To ensure absolute precision, it was her habit to read the directions aloud: "Stir one cup of butter, two cups of granulated sugar, and yolks of three eggs until very light." The efficient, maternal quality of Tillie's voice was comforting, but the specific measurements flew in one ear and out the other. "Add two teaspoons of cinnamon, one of allspice, one of cloves, one-half teaspoon of ginger, and one-half of nutmeg." *John O'Dwyer, Samuel Evans, Frank Westfall.* "Mix in one cup of buttermilk, one teaspoon of soda dissolved in one-third of a cup of hot water and three cups of flour." *Three months to the election.* "To this add the beaten whites of two eggs. Bake in three layers and use icing." *What in God's name have you've gotten me into, Obee?*

Sarah had become bleary-eyed scrutinizing the newspaper's fine print and, therefore, had asked for Winifred's permission to return the next day, this time with her reading glasses in tow. Fortunately, tomorrow was Sunday. She had contemplated taking a few days off, but decided against it. Not only would she further disable an already depleted staff, but she would risk arousing suspicion about the true nature of Obee's condition, especially from the press for whom she needed to be regularly available for damage control. Fortunately, detective work was not limited to daylight. Indeed, the great Holmes himself forwent sleep often, although, she added cynically to herself, not always unassisted. Perhaps Conan Doyle had his own friend after whom he modeled his brilliant but similarly tormented protagonist.

At any rate, time enough for sleep would be found later. Sarah surrendered to an exhausted yawn and immediately reconsidered that idea. It had been a very trying few days, and the aroma of the cake

11

Mitchell stared into his icebox, hoping in vain that something other than eggs and a moldy wedge of cheddar cheese would magically appear. His cramped apartment was sweltering even with all the windows open, and he was loathe to make it hotter by frying his usual omelette for dinner. But the truth was, with the way things were going in every other part of his life, he should have been grateful to find anything in there at all.

The affirmed bachelor had fallen hard for one Pamela Edwards at a fourth of July party. Petite, blue-eyed, and blond, the widowed thirty-five year old possessed his favorite combination of physical traits. Better still was the fact that she was not terribly bright. Mitchell decided long ago that a woman with too much intelligence was incapable of sustaining a loving relationship. Raised solely by his mother—a teacher, poet, and close friend of the brilliant Pauline Steinem, the first woman elected to Toledo's school board—he had come to resent the time she devoted to her many intellectual pursuits. Eleanor Dobrinski had actually given her son more attention than many of his friends' mothers did them, but he nonetheless felt—or chose to feel—neglected by her. He was twenty when she died. One week after the funeral, he vowed to never get involved with a woman with an IQ above 100. Thus when the simple Miss Edwards, a cashier at the Lion Department Store, whose only ambition was to find another husband to dote over, glanced admiringly his way as he threw a game-winning ringer, he begged off another round of horseshoes and asked her to join him in a bit of refreshment.

From that moment until Tuesday of last week, the two spent nearly every evening together. Pamela didn't really share Mitchell's interests—the theater, concerts, and especially long strolls around Riverside Park—but she agreed to go with him just the same. At this time of year, the hard-hitting newspaper man loved taking walks along the sandy river's edge, especially with his shoes off. Ice-skating here in the winter was also pleasurable, enhanced by the festive holiday atmosphere. But then one had to bundle up so. It felt liberating to go barefoot, and it was satisfying to offer nature, who gave so much to its inhabitants, this rare bit of homage.

Nothing so lofty occurred to Pamela as she and Mitchell made their way arm and arm amongst the other clinging lovers and picnicking families. Neither did she notice, as Mitchell did, the equalizing influence of this lovely place, how it temporarily suspended the divisions between generations, races, and classes. Pamela, in fact, had little curiosity beyond what kind of husband a man might make. She responded to his comments regarding such topics with an appreciative nod and an occasional "how interesting" or "that's wonderful." But he could tell that she really had no clue and couldn't care less.

Pamela was exactly what Mitchell had always envisioned for himself, and if he now had any doubts about his ideal woman coming to life, he didn't allow them to consciously surface. He was in that period in a relationship where all of those little internal warnings were silenced by the thrill of novelty. Pamela's lack of interest in worldly affairs was a relief, her vacuous expression engaging. What did it matter that she held few opinions of her own when she thought all of his were right? Why be troubled by her limited vocabulary when she called him "Mitch" in the sweetest of tones, when she prompted him to indulge for the first time in his life in the fantasy that maybe he, too, would finally have images of loved ones watching over him on his desk?

The physical side of the relationship had not advanced beyond a peck on the cheek, but this he also found appealing. Pamela was saving herself for a second marriage, a noble trait in these promiscuous times. All the more so if Mitchell were so lucky as to become husband number two. Yes, if that were the case, he could certainly be patient. The promise of what was yet to come would sustain him. It might even encourage him to take better care of himself. After all, he wasn't a bad looking man. More than one woman over the years had even said he was handsome, in a slightly imbalanced way that is.

All of Mitchell's features were, in fact, a little off, as if his Polish and English sides had been vying for dominance and had not quite settled the battle. His hair was still thick and curly, but the once black ringlets, which were now various shades of grey, were irregular in size and texture. Clean-shaven, he possessed an air of refinement, but a creeping blue shadow that threatened almost as soon as he laid down his razor usually lent him an earthier appearance. His jaw was just square enough to be masculine, the cleft in his chin just deep enough not to look like an accident of birth. His eyes were an unremarkable green, but with sufficient rest, flecks of gold appeared, giving them a curious sparkle. And though deep, craggy lines gathered around his eyes when he smiled, a smooth, wide mouth counterbalanced the signs of age. The only trait that could be said to be wholly unambiguous was his weight. At six feet, two inches, he was very thin at one hundred and sixty pounds. When he was younger he was called wiry, but without the muscle of youth, skinny came closer to describing his frame. Yet even this defect, with a little exercise and many more trips to the grocery store, could be improved upon. He had really become a bachelor out of neglect rather than desire, even though he had always claimed the opposite. And now that he saw the possibility of a different destiny within his grasp, he was ready to seize it.

Until last Tuesday. Without a word, the woman upon whom he was ready to stake his future left town to marry her high school sweetheart. Rumors that the man, whom she'd rejected three times before, had recently come into a family fortune apparently had nothing to do with her decision. The innocent little lady simply realized that she had loved him all along.

Shock quickly gave way to dejection, dejection to anger, and ultimately to swearing off the fairer sex for good. Too wounded to see that fate had perhaps intervened on his behalf, he made for the local speakeasy and got drunk for the first time in years to a gravelly rendition of "It Had to Be You." He smoked until his vocal cords were raw and then he smoked some more. And when he finally came up for air, he concluded that intelligence had nothing to do with it. It was inherent in the breed. Eve had doomed them all, every last one of them, to be rotten to the core.

Perhaps art would save him. As a response to his own pictorial void, Mitchell had developed a passion for photography in recent years. As a journalist he was of course aware of the growing documentary value of the medium. One of his most prized possessions was in fact a first edition of Jacob Riis' *How the Other Half Lives*. But his primary interest was aesthetic.

Even in Riis' wrenching shots of tenement squalor, it was the technique that attracted him, the tight framing, the conscious use of light and shadow. As a lover of books, he had read with great interest *The Art of Fiction* by Henry James and had come to believe that its central tenant could be also applied to photography. If there were to be social commentary, it should be as an outgrowth of the art, not the other way around.

Following the advice of Peter Henry Emerson, a physician and ardent amateur photographer, Mitchell also believed that photographers "should respect the photographic process, and limit their controls to those that were inherent." He therefore detested the "snapshot" and the accompanying principle—a consequence of Eastman's Kodak's "You Press the Button, We Do the Rest," system—that it could make an artist out of anyone. He would never purchase one of those "instant cameras." He preferred to do all the work himself, including the developing, which he did in a tiny dark room he devised in the closet of his apartment.

If Mitchell's vision was fundamentally aesthetic, his subjects were nevertheless in keeping with those of "Realists" such as Riis: actual people, actual scenes, very carefully studied, but once captured, never retouched. To this end, he would stand, sometimes for hours, staring purposefully out his third-story window onto Michigan Street, awaiting the moment in which everything was in balance; that is, until his eye was satisfied. Only when the light, action, and subject came as close to perfection as humanly possible, as close, he liked to think, as the striving figures in John Keats' "Ode to a Grecian Urn," would he release his gaze and press the button of his hand-held Ermanox.

This heightened attention to the "real," however, did not receive much praise from the world he was so patient to represent. Although he had initially picked up a camera for pleasure, he'd begun to think he might be able to make something more of it. A sideline, a supplement to his meager journalist's wages, perhaps even a second career as an artist. Thus, after much agonizing, he selected what he thought was his best work, a wide-angle shot of a fashionable elderly gentleman, shielding his poodle with an umbrella while failing to take any notice of a rain-sodden beggar directly in his path. Certainly the picture had a message, something about the disparity between rich and poor, about the absurd injustices to which wealth gives rise. But it was the delicate tonal rendering that he thought might convince a magazine of its value. And if he could get it published, no telling what might happen next. Exhibitions. Books. The sky might very well be the limit.

He had submitted the piece to *Camera Notes and Proceedings*, the handsome periodical founded by Albert Steiglitz, which included works by only the most talented European and American photographers. But, for someone who held the "real" in such esteem, he had been as unrealistic as Icarus about his chances. And he, too, got burned because of it:

"There is evidence of skill here, Mr. Dobrinski," the editor said with condescension, "but you seem to have not found the right subject . . . or perhaps it is that you have not mastered the platinotype paper. The image is moving enough, but it shows an immature eye. It is missing something . . . something ineffable. To be frank, sir, you don't seem to have caught the essence of the thing. Please feel at liberty to submit to us again when you've had more experience."

Mitchell was mortified. Another subject? Not mastered the paper? He didn't have the time for more experience; he had devoted too many hours to this blasted hobby as it was. And he stubbornly refused to consider a lesser publication. As with romance, it was all or nothing. For Christ's sake, what did they want? Having fumed about the letter for a week, he now stood before his icebox, whose door had been open so long the kitchen was beginning to feel chilly. Perhaps a slice of moldy cheese would be the "right subject." Or no, maybe just the mold, yes that's it, the mold by "itself" should be more to their liking! For a minute, he took this thought seriously, but then slammed the door without removing anything. He was too miserable to eat. Better to spend the remainder of the evening wallowing in a bit of old-fashioned self-pity. At least with that he was certain to have great success.

What made matters worse was that he could not use work as a refuge from such disappointments, because in that area, too, things had not gone particularly well. In fact, his hope that the inferences he had drawn from the O'Donnell articles would ripen into a story had instead as of late completely dried up. For days after his trip to the archives, Mitchell had felt paralyzed, unable to act on any of it: the marriage, the pregnancy, the seemingly hands-off collusion between the people and the press. Never before had he felt so caught between the proverbial rock and a hard place. If he printed a story without all the facts, he could be accused of libel. If he acquired the evidence and used it in an article, provided he could even get it past an editor, throngs of O'Donnell supporters would write to *The Blade*, accusing him of a personal vendetta, or worse, *Bee*-like sensationalism. If he did nothing, he'd be a fool. Finally, he decided that the safest and most ethical way to proceed was to approach O'Donnell directly and privately. Over lunch would be a nice touch. But on the very day he came to this conclusion, he was told the unbelievable news: the judge was once again in the hospital, prostrate with nervous exhaustion.

Of course, by itself, this should have been a tantalizing development. So, too, should have the widespread closing of ranks that followed its dissemination. Instead, it resulted in him being stymied in his pursuit. The official word was that this time the illness was a result of excessive campaigning. O'Donnell would recover shortly, but needed absolute bed rest. No one would be permitted to visit him in the hospital or know the name of his attending physician. All questions would be directed to Miss Sarah Kaufman, O'Donnell's trusted colleague and director of the Women's Probate Court.

"Miss Kaufman, are you sure the judge will recover in time for the election?"

"Absolutely, the doctor has the utmost confidence."

"Why are we not able to interview the doctor?"

"The doctor is a busy man. I've been selected to pass on any crucial information. No doubt the judge will be happy to talk about his stay after he's released."

"Why can we not at least know the hospital he's in, Miss Kaufman? He has many well-wishers, you know."

"The doctor has advised withholding his exact location. The judge needs peace and quiet."

"Miss Kaufman, do you know how Mrs. O'Donnell is faring? And the baby?"

"As far as I know, they are both fine."

"How will the court be able to manage without the judge?"

"Dick Clemens is filling in while he's away."

"Miss Kaufman, have you seen the judge?"

"No. But I've heard he's looking better already. Now, good day, gentlemen. I'll be happy to speak to you again when I have something further to report."

Sarah Kaufman, with whom Mitchell had limited contact over the years, met with the press regularly and always spoke to them in the same firm, laconic, and courteously evasive manner. She was adept at keeping the interaction superficial and brief. As any journalist worth his salt would do, Mitchell attempted to circumvent this worthy adversary by contacting his usual sources on the street and at every hospital in the Toledo vicinity and beyond. But his efforts proved fruitless. Either they really didn't know anything, or someone had gotten to them all. Even Chief of Police Dodd, who, ever since the Cavender case, had distanced himself from the judge, seemed unwilling to make waves.

During a meeting that Mitchell arranged with *The Blade*'s managing editor, however, his progress on this story was nearly brought to a halt.

"Jesus Christ, Steve, we're a *newspaper*," Mitchell said. "Shouldn't we probe this a bit more?"

"What's to probe? You know O'Donnell periodically has these episodes."

"Yeah, but so close to the election? Shouldn't we find out if he's really fit for duty?"

"They'll let us know if he's not."

"They? Since when do we let 'they' dictate to us!"

"Mitch, Mitch, my boy, calm down. I've never seen you so tense." The man sat back in his chair. "Hmm. Now, let me think." He twirled his thumbs and stared at some invisible spot on the wall. "Perhaps what you need, Mitch, is a change of venue. Covering politics can wear anyone out." He paused and stared at the wall thoughtfully again. "You know, we could use someone with experience to cover the

'Society Bandits.' Those girls are suspected in another robbery. It could be interesting."

Steven Marks was a large, vigorous man, who attempted to use his striking physical resemblance to Teddy Roosevelt to his advantage. Whenever he needed to convey something distasteful to one of his employees, he would intensify the resemblance by donning his wired spectacles and offering them his toothy-grin. When Mitchell was the recipient of this strategy, he would usually humor the man and acquiesce. He simply didn't have the heart to tell him that he was so transparent. This time, however, even with Steven's spectacles gleaming at him authoritatively, he was not about to go down without a fight.

"Oh, come on Steve. That's ridiculous. You know I don't write about that kind of trash."

"What do you mean, trash? When two sixteen-year old debutantes stick up a garage, that's news. And when they do it again, well that's something! I thought you liked it when the rich fell."

"You know what I'm talking about. This is not my—"

"Mitch, actually, I'm not giving you a choice," Steven said. "Until further notice, you're off the O'Donnell campaign."

Mitchell would have laughed at this incredible remark had he not understood from the "President's" refusal to discuss the issue further that the man was dead serious. No two ways about it, he was being officially reassigned.

"There's a press conference tomorrow about the girls' latest heist. I'll expect a story in the Sunday paper," were Steve's parting words as he abruptly escorted Mitchell to the door.

As Mitchell dumbfoundedly walked toward his desk, it eventually dawned on him that this was no spontaneous gesture. Steven must have been waiting for just the right moment to break the news. And no doubt he was delighted to have found one so made to order. Indeed, what could be better than having Mitchell arrange the meeting himself? This way the crafty roughrider could pretend that the idea wasn't premeditated, that he had simply responded on the spot to an employee in need.

But Mitchell knew better. This whole situation had too familiar a ring, and it convinced him that he had been on to something where O'Donnell was concerned. *The Blade's* management was clearly hiding something . . . that, or the judge really had cast a spell over the entire city. Either way, Mitchell felt more than ever that he was entitled to this story. At one point he would have been relieved to be given another assignment, now he was disappointed; disappointed and angry to be dismissed for such a flimsy, trumped-up cause.

Official or not, this story belonged to him. And in the midst of mourning his other losses, he decided that one way or another it would stay that way. He might never hold another woman in his arms, and his photographs might forever be worthless. But in his sticky apartment, with nothing but those eggs and moldy cheese to keep him company, he promised himself that this was one thing he was not going to surrender. The Society Bandits be damned! This was the story he needed, and somehow, someway, he would get it . . . with or without the permission of *The Blade.*

12

While most of Toledo was dressing for church, Sarah was already on the streetcar, halfway to the O'Donnell's, and nearly as far through her second newspaper. At times she envied her Christian neighbors, participating in their common weekly ritual. It wasn't always easy being out of step with the rest of the town, not to mention the country as a whole. Now and then it would be a relief to be on the inside looking out instead of the other way around.

This feeling usually didn't last very long, however. Although she didn't count herself among the most devout of Jews, she would have never really considered exchanging the occasional isolation she experienced for the untested pleasure of belonging to the majority. Furthermore, not celebrating the Sabbath on Sunday afforded her some extra sleep before the work week began, something for which Jews and Christians alike might be tempted to sell their very souls.

This particular Sunday, however, Sarah awoke early to the sound of her own restless thoughts. The night before, just as she was about to retire, Dr. Miller phoned to say that several newsmen had been nosing around again. With no small amount of effort, the hospital staff had managed to get rid of all of them. "All but one, that is," Miller said, "who refused to leave until he was allowed to speak to a doctor. Just a few words, Sarah, that's all he said he wanted."

Dr. Miller decided that it might look less suspicious if he agreed to meet with the man. "You know," he clarified, "satisfy the guy's curiosity while revealing nothing of any substance." When he realized it was Mitchell Dobrinski, that pesky writer from *The Blade* who had made the request, he wasn't so sure this strategy would work. "Of course, I denied having any knowledge of the O'Donnell case, and I eventually got the guy to leave. But I'm certain he'll be back. And," he added, "I fear it's only a matter of time before Dobrinski discovers the truth."

As both Dr. Miller and Sarah knew, Mitchell Dobrinski had a reputation for being both persistent and extremely resourceful. Dr. Miller would do everything in his power, but he was only one person. He trusted his staff, but then again, one could never tell.

This was why, as the sun was only just beginning to graze the eastern bank of the Maumee, Sarah was seated on the empty streetcar, scanning the morning headlines for the latest O'Donnell reports. Newspapers, once just daily sources of information on which she had always looked with a jaundiced eye, were now powerful forces to be reckoned with. While others were reading the Bible, she would be reading, in the lines of *The Blade* and even *The Bee*, judgements that might prove to be no less final. The articles of the past might hold the key to Obee's salvation. Those of the present could lead to his doom. In either, danger could be lurking on the very next page. Sticks, stones, and that tiny bottle of liquid might break his bones, but words could be far worse, blackening his reputation, as her hands were now blackened by the paper's ink. Indeed, time could only tell if the papers of the future would record his glory or his undoing.

As Sarah approached her destination, she breathed a sigh of relief even though the air was exceedingly humid. At least for today, nothing of any consequence regarding the judge had made its way to print. No new speculations about his health. Not a hint that this latest episode was anything other than a minor setback. Moreover, for the first time, all the reporters appeared to have quoted her correctly, including the troublesome Mr. Dobrinski. That didn't mean that this man didn't bear careful watching, however. In fact, last night Dr. Miller had really only confirmed her growing suspicions about him. Mitchell Dobrinski had covered politics for years and had been following Obee in particular for quite a while. A permanent fixture at *The Blade*, Dobrinski was known for his intelligence, objectivity, and clarity of expression. Sarah herself had respected his writing, and that was saying a lot since there were so few reporters' work which she did.

Although she had never spoken more than a few words to him, she had encountered him often. At press conferences, city affairs, at an occasional banquet. She frequently saw him at Riverside Park, most recently sometime last month, walking with an attractive blond woman. In the past, rumors spread that he had a drinking problem, but even then, his journalistic integrity had never been in question. Most importantly, in his treatment of Obee, he had been as fair as anyone else. That is, as far as she could recall, he had played by the same laissez-faire rules.

But lately his approach had changed. At these recent meetings, he was always the first to arrive and the last to leave. Barraging her with questions that he knew ahead of time she would refuse to answer, he seemed determined to wear her down. Most disconcerting of all, the man had a menacing way of making eye contact that she found nearly impossible to elude. First, he would tilt his head to one side and stare directly into her eyes until by some seemingly uncanny force she would move her head in the same direction and return his gaze. Once she did, his own eyes, hazel she believed, would lock hers in place until he decided to release them. Sarah didn't know what exactly he was looking for or what he could see from that angle, but he was clearly up to no good. And it bothered her considerably that she couldn't prevent herself from succumbing to this undoubtedly practiced maneuver.

Sarah couldn't have been more grateful to find Winifred indisposed. Eager to get right to work, she didn't relish the thought of another strained encounter with the fair beauty just now. She even hoped that Elizabeth was telling the truth, that the baby was once again asleep. For the task that lay ahead, the quieter the surroundings the better.

"Mrs. O'Donnell says I am to provide you with anything you need, ma'am. Just ring this bell."

Elizabeth had shown Sarah into the study where some tea and freshly baked scones already awaited her. She seemed to be in exceptionally good spirits. Very different from the day before.

"Thank you, Elizabeth. But I don't think I'll be needing anything else. This looks wonderful."

"Well, here's the bell just the same. You never know." And with that the woman smiled, turned, and closed the doors gently behind her.

What caused Elizabeth's change in attitude? Perhaps Winifred had something to do with it, or perhaps she just hoped to acquire some juicy gossip if she was friendly enough. Whichever, for the time being it was good to have the woman on her side.

Sarah's stomach growled at the smell of the scones, which were lightly toasted and plump with raisins. Since she had not had breakfast, they looked particularly inviting. If things were different, it would be delightful to sit back and enjoy them in view of the oak tree, whose shade kept the room remarkably cool. But there was no time to waste. Any eating would have to be done medicinally as she worked.

She reached in the desk, released the latch, and pulled out the next journal, dated 1915-1920. A tumultuous time in Toledo as in the rest of the country. On the positive side, reformers continued to see the fruits of their labors: improvements in many of the city's poor tenements, safer conditions for factory workers and, of course, women finally got the vote, an achievement Sarah held as the movement's crowning glory. But the period was not without its low points. The emergence of a new and more vicious KKK, the Volstead Act, which, while well-intended—indeed Sarah had been a supporter of it herself— initiated the dramatic increase in crime that had not yet been curbed, and, of course, there was the War. The Great War, as it came to be called, the first time in human history that all of civilization was threatened. A war that marked the beginning of America's rise to power. As soon as President Wilson ordered the country to organize for defense after the sinking of the Lusitania, she knew that soon she would be mourning some of her city's own. It took two years, but she was eventually proven right. Compared to Europe, of course, American casualties were light. But Toledoans, including two young men with whom she had worked, died in that fight.

It was a different kind of war that was chronicled in the initial pages of the journal, however, the one Obee continued to wage against drugs. Though the Duffey Bill had passed, it was eventually designated unconstitutional on a technicality of law. But the judge would not be defeated. Due in large part to his efforts, the bill was resurrected first as the Platt and finally the Lynch "Dope Bill." Several articles noted its resounding passage by the Ohio State Legislature and paid homage to the man behind it:

Lucas County Judge wins in Dope Fight; Toledo Starts Crusade; Toledo Judge Wins Big Victory: "Judge O'Brien O'Donnell, former Port Huron attorney, and now judge of the Lucas County Probate Court at Toledo, is making a reputation for himself in the state of Ohio." The articles spanned several days, from May 5 to May 11, 1915.

Sarah took a bite of a scone, marveled once again at the irony of such an achievement and turned the page. This journal was even thicker than the first, and as she continued to read, she realized that this was not only because of Obee's ever-growing reform efforts and accomplishments. Naturally, a number of reports surfaced along these lines. His call for a maternity hospital and a levy for orphans, his ongoing support of the Newsies and other boys' organizations were all there. Several pieces took particular note of his help in finding the proper treatment for "The Spider," a man with a "Jekyll and Hyde" personality who had terrorized Toledo for months. But by this time, the public had also started to develop their insatiable appetite for what she liked to refer to as "Obeeisms." Having bestowed on the judge their utmost respect, the good citizens of Toledo now felt entitled to have a few laughs at his expense . . . all in good fun of course. There was enough of this kind of stuff here to have kept them amused for quite awhile:

What Do You Do with Your Hand when Phoning? Psychologists Say Little Nothings You Draw Give Insight Into Character, the headline read. "Probate Judge O'Brien O'Donnell is fond of capital B's, with inside decorations. He also likes to make boxes with slats across the top."

Since there was no accompanying analysis, Sarah conducted a bit of it herself. The slats looked a bit like bars. Indicating what? Feelings of imprisonment, perhaps? Trapped in a box of conventions? And the B, for O'Brien no doubt—what might those marks represent? Arrows? Algebraic signs? Pointing to something? A way out? But she was wasting time, getting caught up herself in this drivel.

She turned to a short piece by *Blade* reporter Ezra Windfall:

"I see Probate Judge O'Donnell signing his name. It's a good thing I see the judge signs his name. For I would never know the hieroglyphics engrossed are those of the distinguished jurist. Of course, Horace Greeley and Theodore Roosevelt both had a terrible hand."

The next several articles were in the same vein.

"Judge O'Donnell of the probate court doesn't believe in wearing a vest. He says he always buys one when he orders a suit and has quite a collection adorning the walls of a clothes closet;" "Judge O'Donnell is an untiring collector of fancy socks;" "Judge O'Donnell gazed out at the greening courthouse lawn on Thursday and murmured something about steamboats and summer resorts;" "In this, a leap year, Judge O'Brien O'Donnell has been voted one of Toledo's most eligible bachelors;" "Bailiff Douglass, in Probate Judge O'Donnell's office was approached by a stranger Wednesday morning. 'Are you Judge O'Donnell?' he was asked, and was informed that he was not. 'Well, you'll do just as well; I suppose that you are Judge O'Brien?' which was also denied. The stranger departed still bearing the impression that Lucas County has two probate judges."

"For God's sake," Sarah said, "doesn't this crap ever end!"

This rather tame display of profanity would have sounded strange to anyone who knew her. She instinctively looked around to make sure she was alone. Not that she had any moral objection to employing a few choice words now and then, she had just never acquired the habit.

"And from the mighty *Blade*, no less," she added. "Oh, and here we have another vital message from *The Bee*:"

"Something to watch for on Easter Sunday–Judge O'Brien O'Donnell's button hole bouquet."

Sarah was just about to take her new expressiveness to a higher level when, out of the corner of her eye, she spotted the name she had been searching for, the one Obee had so fearfully moaned in his hospital room. A wave of adrenalin shot through her body. Frank Westfall. The unequivocal, black print underscored the man's historical reality. Frank Westfall, County Commissioner, a victim of a tragic accident. Until this moment, just a vague image of a dedicated public official who had met an untimely death. Now, a mysterious grouping of letters that filled her with dread.

She removed her glasses and pushed herself up from the chair. Her whole body was already aching. When she was a young girl at the piano, she found that she could release the tension of sitting in one place by twisting her spine from side to side until she felt it ease into a kind of balance. Over time, the remedy had become a custom, one that she employed now with great relish.

Sarah then eyed the nourishment before her and gave a passing thought to her waistline. She would need her strength. So, with what some may have viewed as a wild abandoning of conventionally female restraint, she devoured a second scone, took a large gulp of tea, and prepared to bring Frank Westfall to life.

The papers, however, ended up raising more questions about the man than they answered. This was partly because the only articles included in the journals were those that involved Obee specifically. She had hoped that there would be some record of the commissioner's work as well as the original accounts of his death. Her memory desperately needed refreshing. But, as with other events outside Obee's immediate experience, such references in the journals, if they appeared at all, did so only when they chanced to fall in a neighboring column. Though in reality the judge was a product of history, here that history was clipped to the dimensions of his own unique personality.

That meant that the articles on Westfall chronicled only the aftermath of his death, when Obee and two other designated officials were called upon to elect a replacement. What then had actually happened to the commissioner? Sarah could only recall the broadest of details. Late one night, in a heavy rainstorm, he had accidently driven his car with two passengers aboard through the draw of the Ash-Counsul Bridge into the Maumee. One of the passengers had survived. Westfall and the other had drowned. It had taken weeks to discover the bodies.

She had trouble remembering much more than this because she barely knew the commissioner, let alone the men who had been traveling with him. Once an officer in Obee's court, Westfall had left long before she had begun to work there, and his later duties had fallen far outside the scope of hers. Like everyone else in Toledo, she was of course shocked and saddened by the death, but she would have reacted similarly toward any of her fellow citizens.

Very soon after the accident, however, Obee had succumbed to another nervous attack, the very one which had forced him into a two-month leave of absence. The articles reminded her of how closely aligned the timing of these episodes were. In fact, as one report in *The*

Blade noted, he was hospitalized on the very day of Westfall's funeral, after serving as a pallbearer. A sick feeling stirred in the pit of her stomach. The timing. As she continued to sift through the numerous accounts that Obee had included on this topic, she wondered how she could have not questioned it before. For never had two events seemed more inextricably linked.

The papers presented the facts as these: immediately following the accident, the debate began over who would fill the commissioner's vacancy. Judge O'Donnell, County Auditor Charles J. Sanzenbacher, and County Recorder Landon W. Kumler were to make the official decision, but this clearly was not going to be easy. Indeed, forces were at work that would turn the appointment into one of the most contentious and controversial in Lucas County. What were those forces? In general, they appeared to be the usual competing political interests. County commissioners possessed a broad spectrum of duties, including everything from oversight of structural improvements to ensuring the rights of the indigent. Their power was not necessarily deep, but their influence was wide, making the competition for a vacancy predictably fierce.

But, the specifics of this contest were more difficult to unravel. After all, these articles and her own vague memories were at present Sarah's only source. A mosaic of preselected news. Fragments of condensed information. A special kind of map was what she needed, one that provided a larger context to lend meaning to the individual reports. Instead, for the time being, the name of O'Brien O'Donnell would have to suffice. Appearing in each of the articles, it alone would help chart the path, like a signpost unwittingly pointing the way to some as of yet unknown destination.

As far as she could determine, three main groups lobbied Obee and the other two members of the triumvirate: the Polish community, the Democrats, and the Buckeye and Huebner-Toledo breweries. The

Poles because Frank Westfall was Polish, the Democrats because he was a Democrat, and the breweries because they each wanted a candidate who would serve as an ally in their fight against the growing threat to the liquor industry. Initially, it seemed as though the Polish nominee, Republican attorney, Nicolas J. Walinski, was a shoo-in: auditor Sanzenbacher was willing to vote for him and, because the Poles were among O'Brien's most loyal constituency, it was assumed that he would be as well. But the Democrats, to whom O'Brien also was indebted, had someone else in mind, and they could be very persuasive when they needed to be.

It was when the breweries staked their claim, however, that things really started to heat up. Not surprisingly, both companies nominated a Republican. Former police chief John C. Newton was the choice of the Buckeye Brewery and John F. Kumler, an attorney and brother of County Recorder Langdon Kumler, was Toledo-Heubner's. Tempers ran high in the city when news of the nominations spread. Newton was bad enough. He had a reputation for strong-arm tactics and had been accused, though not convicted, of graft. But John F. Kumler crossed the line. How, people asked, could they even think of supporting a candidate whose brother was on the selection committee? Had they no shame at all?

Charges of nepotism, greed, bigotry, and other injustices were rampant, and it soon became clear that if put to a larger vote, neither man would win. But that was not the procedure, and these were powerful companies determined to see that things went their way. Moreover, they each had a formidable name behind them . . . formidable and very familiar: Walter F. Brown and John O'Dwyer. Brown was for Newton, which was understandable since he himself was the most infamous Republican in the city. O'Dwyer's support of Kumler, however, was something else again. Even given her general distrust of the man, this shift in alliances was difficult for Sarah to comprehend . . . almost as difficult as his recent change in attitude toward Obee. It was odd enough when this leading Democrat was caught stuffing ballots for Brown. But by all accounts, Kumler was even more conservative than Newton! Well, she said to herself, whoever came up with that phrase about politics making strange bedfellows must have known O'Dwyer. He seemed to have shared a pillow with at least as many enemies as friends.

Another strand in this increasingly complicated story involved the police investigation of the accident. It took several weeks for them to locate Westfall's body, and the mayor determined that no appointment would be made until that event occurred. Although the police were certain that the drowning was accidental, they needed verification before any official business could proceed. This allowed the various factions to continue lobbying. And the longer the vote was delayed, the more they intensified their efforts. So much so that by the time the body was found, the Democrats had withdrawn their candidate, and the Poles were celebrating, confident that O'Brien and Sachzenbacher would support Walinski. This made it all the more shocking when the final tally was announced: Kumler had won. Sachenzbacher had voted for Newton, Kumler for Kumler. And Judge O'Donnell? O'Donnell, the swing vote, had gone with Kumler.

It was, however, even longer than everyone expected before that vote was cast. After the body was discovered in early June, the mayor once again decided that the funeral should precede the appointment. They had waited this long already. For the family's sake, another day or two wouldn't matter. No one could have predicated that Judge O'Donnell would be hospitalized the afternoon of the funeral, leave for a Michigan sanitarium a week later, and not return until the end of July. But that's precisely what happened. Desperate requests to hold the meeting at his hospital bedside were denied. Press reports were halted. And, nobody knew of the judge's exact whereabouts until July 26th, when, as *The Blade* recorded, he "surprised his friends by appearing on Madison Avenue."

After that things moved quickly. On the 27th, the election was held in his office. A "Star Chamber" session, with "the doors of the probate court room locked and the shades drawn." Immediately after the vote, O'Donnell left the frustrated press and gasping town again for another two weeks. In private, people wondered and some even gossiped. But when he returned, everyone, including Sarah, acted as if nothing out of the ordinary had happened.

Sarah pondered her own collusion in what, where Obee was concerned, had become the regular Toledo practice of equating silence with innocence. Why had she, his closet friend, the one person who knew his innermost secret, not suspected something? How could she have been so unaware? Why hadn't she involved herself more? She glanced at the oak tree and tried to remember. Had she just been too busy? During those weeks the installment of the Mother's Pension Fund had caused that huge surge in clients. Everyone had to work overtime to finish processing the volume of new applications, but she had to work weekends as well to ensure that they had been processed correctly. That summer the department had also been preparing to move to another set of offices, an event which Sarah was additionally in charge of overseeing. Add to that her speaking engagement at the suffrage conference in Nashville and the funeral of a cousin she had to attend in Akron. To be sure, she had been spread very thin.

But as she continued to gaze at the tree, Sarah knew that these were just excuses. The unflinching oak mirrored the truth back to her: her disengagement from Obee had been much more deliberate. Helping him through his prior episode had cost her so much emotionally that she had been reluctant to put herself through it again. If Obee had made any attempt to contact her at all she would have relented. But when, like everyone else, she was forbidden to see him, she decided to immerse herself in other things and let time pass. The closeness between them eventually returned, but not before she succeeded in blocking out almost entirely the events of those days.

Now that her defenses were down, however, they came rushing in. Poor Obee. He must have been under extraordinary pressure. To betray his principles and especially the people who had such faith in him, no wonder he got "sick" again. What could have possibly persuaded him to vote for Kumler? Someone who stood for everything he was against. The answer chilled her. No doubt it lay behind a series of locked doors: the Star Chamber's, the sanitarium's, and Obee's many hospital rooms. Doors of the past to which someone besides Obee presently possessed the key. Dr. Evans perhaps? John O'Dwyer? If she were going to help him, she needed to find out who. Something had happened, something treacherous enough to induce a blackmailer to boldly show his hand ten years later. Something about Frank Westfall.

It was clear that she needed to learn more about this man, more about his death. What were the circumstances surrounding the body? Who were the other people in the car? What did they have to do with Obee? Certainly other questions would arise. She scanned the remaining pages of the journal. Funny, one would hardly know that a war, other than Obee's "war" on drugs, had occurred in these years. There were only a few oblique references.

What did make it into the journal in some depth—evidently because of its proximity to a large spread about renovations being made to the courthouse—was the July 4, 1919 World Heavyweight Championship fight between Jess Willard and Jack Dempsey. Toledo was chosen as the site of this internationally publicized event because it was one of the largest rail centers in the country, and plus, few other cities offered to host it. *Blade* staff writer, Ralph E. Phelps, called it "Toledo's Most Exciting Day." Sarah didn't know about that but she did remember that it was filled with controversy. The much bulkier

Willard had already killed one boxer, and most feared that Dempsey was simply not a match for him. So when Dempsey won, foul play was on everyone's mind. Though never proven, the rumor was that his manager had loaded his gloves with cement.

Some sort of foul play had also been at the bottom of all the strange occurrences in the summer of 1915. Precisely what sort she wasn't certain. She would need more than these few articles. The Willard-Dempsey fight remained a rumor because the contents of those gloves were never definitively established. To avoid the same fate, Sarah needed to find material as unambiguous as cement.

She closed the second scrapbook. Although she hadn't followed the Westfall story closely at the time, she knew that the papers had covered it in detail for weeks. What if she could see some of those papers now? Not just clippings, but entire copies. At the very least, they could help fill in the gaps in her memory. At best . . . well, at best, it remained to be seen. But time was short. The library was out of the question. She doubted whether the meager facility even had editions going back that far. No, she must have quick and complete access. And, to get that, she needed assistance. An expert, an insider who could bypass any cumbersome formalities. She poured herself another cup of tea and considered the possibilities. Adriane, Sheila, Helen, perhaps Anthony, she went through her list of potential candidates, crossing each of them off for one reason or another. Then, suddenly, a name appeared to her as if in a vision. She shook her head, attempting to jar it loose, to will it away, but the words forced themselves into her consciousness and settled there intractably. Of course, it would be risky. If she told Dr. Miller, he would think that the pressure had finally gotten to her, too. But try as she might to deny it, she really had no other choice. She would have to take a chance. And the sooner the better.

13

"Mr. Dobrinski," Sarah said extending her hand, "thank you for seeing me on such short notice. I'm sorry to intrude at work, but I have a rather urgent matter to discuss with you."

Mitchell stood before his desk erect and stiff, as if dressed in protective armor. "Please, sit down, Miss Kaufman."

The clock read 10 a.m., peak work hour at *The Blade*. People running every which way, typewriters clicking frantically, phones ringing non-stop.

Sarah looked around the room disconcertedly. "Mr. Dobrinski, is there a place we might speak privately? What I have to talk over with you, well . . . it's somewhat sensitive."

Mitchell stared at her unblinking. What the devil was he looking at, anyway? With difficulty, she maintained eye-contact.

"Of course. Follow me," he said.

Mitchell led her down a hall to a small conference room. Along the way, he gestured to a young woman who regarded them inquisitively. When the woman asked if they wanted a cup of coffee, Sarah presumed it was his secretary. Mitchell directed one raised eyebrow toward Sarah.

"Miss Kaufman?"

"Yes, thank you. Coffee would be nice."

"How do you take it?" Mitchell asked.

"Black, please."

"Really? Most women prefer cream and sugar."

"I didn't know that." She had seen that self-satisfied look before, that came over men who thought of independent women as little more than disobedient children. Some other time she would be happy to take his prejudices on full force. But not now. Not when she required his services. Instead, she blinked innocently and added, "Well I do like cream and sugar in my tea."

"Two black coffees, and Sally, please bring me an ashtray."

"But, Mitch, I thought you were trying to stop smo—"

Mitchell glared at the woman. "Sally, bring me an ashtray."

"As you wish, sir."

Mitchell lit a cigarette and inhaled so deeply that a long, snake-like ash began to recoil upon itself before he was through. "Okay, Miss Kaufman, what can I do for you?"

"Well, Mr. Dobrinski, I'm really here because of what I hope we can do for each other."

Mitchell exhaled three perfectly shaped smoke rings. He blinked and leaned back in his chair. "Go on," he said.

"Now, Mr. Dobrinski, I know how important it is for you to get what you call "the facts" on Judge O'Donnell. I can't say that I always approve of your tactics, but I understand that you're just doing your job."

"Glad to hear you feel that way, ma'am."

"Well, then. Let me get right to the point. I've come to propose a deal, or more precisely, an exchange. Information about the judge for access to your archives. Unofficial, private access that is. I would prefer that no one knows beside yourself.

"I'm still listening, Miss Kaufman." Mitchell's eyes widened slightly. "May I ask what kind of information we're talking about?"

"Yes, of course. But before I divulge anything, I have one condition that I must insist upon. One absolute requirement." She drained her cup and looked at him just as he unsuccessfully attempted to blow another ring. "You must agree to postpone printing anything until the judge is completely well. Upon this point there can be no negotiation."

"But what if the judge doesn't get well, Miss Kaufman?"

"Well, now, that's the chance you'll have to take. He always has before. And with all due respect, I think my risk is far greater."

Mitchell nodded slowly. "Hmm, yes, I guess I see your point. It would, of course, be relatively easy on my end. But I do wonder if you'll be able to find what you need on your own. Were you planning on telling me, well, what you'd be looking for? Perhaps I could be of some help."

"In fact, sir, I'm counting on it. I don't have the skill or the time to tackle this problem alone. But let me be frank. I make this proposition with great trepidation. I don't really know you at all. If you agree, I have only your reputation as a man of your word."

Mitchell used his thumb to smash the remaining embers of his cigarette. He stood up and walked around the tiny room, running his fingers through his thick hair, mumbling under his breath. After several moments, he sat back down and looked at her with a half smile.

"All right, Miss Kaufman. I will enter into this, this . . . shall we call it a covenant?"

"I would be honored if you took it that seriously."

"So then, where do I sign?"

"I take your promise as your signature, Mr. Dobrinski . . . your signature in blood, that is."

Sarah's assessment of Mitchell had been right. The potential for an exclusive story on Obee was irresistible, even if he were forced to ultimately table it. A Holmesian move if there ever was one. So, she would tell him about the blackmail note. With all the seriousness such a confidence warranted, she would explain that this was the source of Obee's illness. However—and this was critical to her plan—she would reveal only the part about Westfall. Nothing else. She would take from Mr. Dobrinski what she needed and hopefully provide him with just enough of "the facts" to keep him interested.

It was a calculated risk. Obee's recovery might depend on her ability to figure out the hold the Westfall episode had over him. At the very least, the totality of the threat could not be fully understood without solving this crucial part of the puzzle. Nor could the identity of the blackmailer ever be discovered without it. If she were unsuccessful or, God forbid, she found evidence that incriminated Obee in some way, well then he would most likely continue to be plagued with one form of illness or another. His bid for office would be over in any case, even if the noble reporter adhered to his end of the bargain. If she were luckier, however, Obee would finally be able to put his past and, maybe, his addiction behind him. And, as for Mr. Dobrinski, he would get his story. A sufficiently juicy story, too, no doubt, but one that in the end would assure its readers that their faith in the judge had not been misplaced. A fantasy perhaps. But it was where Sarah set her sights. Therefore, before returning to the courthouse, she conveyed her version of events to Mitchell, who afterwards gazed at the ceiling as if thanking whatever forces had decided to shine on him with favor.

TOLEDO DAILY BLADE

OMMISSIONER

IS CHOSEN

BOARD MADE POWERLESS BY T
RIVER TRAGEDY IS COMPLETED

SELECTION OF WESTFALL'S SUCCE
SOR ORDERED—FIGHT BETWEEN
BREWERIES HELPS IN DELAY

The vacancy that was caused in the county c
missioners has been filled by the appointment
John F. Kumler.

DECLARE BRIDGES
POORLY GUARDED

Grand Jury Probes Cause of
Auto Plunge Into Maumee
River.

SAYS ROPE BARRIERS
ON DRAW INSUFFICIENT

Service Director Asked to
Act to Prevent Further
Fatal Accidents.

O'DONNELL BACK;
CONTEST REVIVED

Officials to Meet Tuesday to
Fill Vacancy on the Com-
missioners' Board.

Judge O'Brien O'Donnell returned to
the city Sunday night. He has been
at a sanitarium resort in Michigan for
several weeks, recuperating from a
severe attack of nervous prostration.
The return of the judge immediately
revived interest in the question of appointment of a county commissioner to
succeed Frank W. Westfall, who was
drowned in the Maumee river last May.
An effort will be made to decide upon
a successor to Westfall at a meeting
to be held at Judge O'Donnell's office
Tuesday morning at 9. The meeting
was arranged Monday by the three
county officials who constitute the appointing power — Judge O'Donnell,
County Auditor Charles J. Sanzenbacher and County Recorder Langdon W.
Kumler.
Politicians renewed their activity
Monday in connection with the va-

BURY WESTFALL,
THEN FILL PLACE

Appointment of Successor to
Commissioner Deferred
Till After Funeral.

BODY IS RECOVERED
FROM MAUMEE RIVER

Officials Decide There is No
Reason for Acting
Hastily.

Appointment of a successor to the
late County Commissioner Frank W.
Westfall was deferred Thursday.
County Auditor Sanzenbacher insisted that there is no official business

14

Five o'clock. At last, the city clock bells sounded the end of the work day. Even if Mr. Dobrinski's eagerness was selfishly motivated, Sarah was grateful he had made the offer to meet her that evening. Now that the plan was in place, waiting would have been intolerable.

On the way over, she would pick up some sandwiches to show her appreciation.

Mitchell was pacing outside when she arrived. "You're late," he said.

"Yes, I know," she said breathing heavily, "I'm sorry."

Mitchell ignored her apology. "What's that?" he asked, pointing to her bag.

"Sandwiches. I thought we might get hungry. I didn't think Betty's would be so busy."

"Oh," Mitchell said and grunted. "Thanks."

"Not at all. I hope you like turkey."

He reached his arm behind her and checked the lock on the entrance doors. "It's one of my favorites. Now, please Miss Kaufman, follow me."

Silently wending their way through the dark, Sarah felt as if she were being watched. Goose bumps crept down one side of her body and then the other. Maybe because she was in a place where people made it their business to monitor the actions of others. They say that a building often takes on the character of its inhabitants. Perhaps her recent efforts to raise the dead awakened the spirits of some long-gone reporters, too. Or perhaps it had something to do with Mr. Dobrinski, whose gaze was so piercing he might very well have been staring at her through eyes in the back of his head. Whichever, when they reached their destination and he turned on the light, she could finally breathe again.

Mitchell told her to relax while he searched for the papers in question, those dating from the day of the drowning until Obee's return to work in September. Approximately four months worth. She half-heartedly leaned back in a chair as file drawers creaked and slammed. But relaxation would only really come when Obee was back on the bench. Instead, she took the opportunity to observe the man that only yesterday she would have done anything to avoid. In appearance, he was everything Obee was not. Tall, gangly, somewhat unkempt. Thick hair, narrow face, fair complexion—currently darkened with a five, or now indeed, six o'clock shadow—and long, tapered fingers. Those she had noticed earlier. His hands were the exact opposite of Obee's, whose stockiness and square shape emphasized function over form. Hands had always been a physical feature to which Sarah was strangely drawn. A sign of a person's disposition and talents, they had a personality all their own. Obee's fit the image of a judge perfectly. Strong, mature, and evenly—deceptively evenly—balanced, they seemed designed for a gavel. In contrast, Mr. Dobrinski's were graceful and expressive, indicative more of an artist than a reporter.

Artist or not, however, his hands were certainly resourceful. The stack of papers resulting from his search was enormous. Fortunately, in recent days she had become adept at sorting the wheat from chaff. Together she was confident they would make short shrift of this material. And, in fact, in less than an hour they had culled out all the articles on Frank Westfall, O'Brien O'Donnell, and the contest for county commissioner. Next would come the more onerous task of reading, cross-checking, and interpreting.

"How 'bout those sandwiches before we begin?" Mitchell asked. "I'll make some coffee to go with them. Black coffee," he added with a grin.

"Certainly." Sarah started to reach for the bag, but Mitchell stopped her in mid-grasp.

"Wait a minute, I have a better idea. Why don't we move everything into the conference room where we met earlier. There's more space there. We'll be much more comfortable."

"Whatever you wish." It seemed like a waste of time, but she wasn't about to argue. She picked up the bag and as many of the papers as she could carry, and, for the third time today, followed Mr. Dobrinski as he led the way.

"This really hits the spot," Mitchell said swallowing audibly.

"Good. I hope wheat bread is all right with you. They say it's better for the digestion than white. Personally, I just like the taste."

Mitchell looked thoughtfully at the remaining half of his sandwich. "I hadn't noticed but now that you mention it, it does add something to the flavor." He took another bite and then regarded Sarah inquisitively. "You know, Miss Kaufman, since we've now shared a meal, not to mention taken an oath—in blood no less—don't you think we should start calling each other by our first names? If nothing else, it would help us conserve our energy. This Miss and Mr. stuff is getting exhausting."

Sarah had been thinking the same thing, but having recalled a similar conversation with Obee years ago, had decided not to act too impulsively. Considering what that seemingly simple step led to, it was perhaps wise to maintain the formal address. But now that he raised the issue, it seemed ridiculous to put up a fight.

"All right. You can call me Sarah, if you'd like. And would you prefer Mitchell or Mitch? I heard your secretary say—"

"Mitchell. Definitely Mitchell," he said. He lit a cigarette. "So Sarah, you enjoy your job, don't you?"

Hearing him speak her name caused a wince. The familiarity sounded terribly artificial. "Very much so . . . Mitchell."

"How did you choose this line of work?"

"Well," she said clearing her throat, "there aren't many choices for a woman, you know. I've always been interested in the law, but up until a few years ago, I wasn't even permitted to vote, let alone think about law school. Besides, I had to earn a living. So I tried to find a job that would combine my interests and needs. I was lucky to be hired by Judge O'Donnell."

Mitchell inhaled. Not that she would have accepted, but why had he not offered her a cigarette? Maybe he wasn't aware that women were now permitted to smoke.

"You're Jewish," he said matter-of-factly. "Education is highly valued by your people, is it not?"

"By some, I suppose, although I don't put much stalk in such generalities. You, for instance. I believe you're Polish, and you're obviously educated."

"Well, that's true. I didn't mean any offense, Sarah. I have the utmost respect for both the Jews and the Poles. But actually, it was my mother, an Englishwoman, who was the educated one. Acquiring knowledge was of great importance to her. In fact, that was all she really cared about."

He glanced away and pursed his lips. For a moment, the grown man looked like a little boy who had been put to bed without any supper.

"I'm sure she cared about you, too. It's possible for a woman to do both, you know."

"Oh, she fed and clothed me if that's what you mean."

Sarah believed him. He had nothing against the Jews. It was women he resented, and she was beginning to understand why.

"Well, that does—"

"Never mind. It's all in the past. Besides, we were talking about you." He leaned toward her. "Tell me Sarah, have you ever been married?"

"No. No, I haven't."

"Never found the right person, I suppose."

Sarah was silent. She'd found the right person all right. He just hadn't found her. That question always had a sting to it though, not just because of Obee, but because it reminded her that while society tolerated, even admired the bachelor, an unmarried woman of her age was simply to be pitied. This was especially true in her case, as she had crossed the threshold of the "old maid" years ago. *I'm sure he wouldn't have spoken so freely had I remained "Miss Kaufman." I should have trusted my instincts.*

"Not that it's really any of your business, but as you may know, it's a rare breed of man who isn't threatened by a woman with a career."

"I can see that I have offended you. I'm sorry."

"I'm not offended." Sarah should have let it drop, but now that the topic had been broached, she couldn't resist turning the tables. "And you, have you ever been married?" She thought of that woman she saw him with in the park. *Quite a romantic scene, as she recalled.*

"No."

"Never found the right woman, I suppose?"

"That's not it at all." Mitchell bristled. "I just enjoy being single."

"Now it is I who have apparently offended you," Sarah said.

"No, I'm not offended either, Sarah. But perhaps we would be better to stick to the subject at hand. Shall we get back to work?"

"Gladly. After all, that's why we're here, isn't it?"

When they finally picked up their heads, it was midnight, long past both of their usual bedtimes. Had circumstances been different, they would have surely postponed examining their findings until the next day. As it was, however, they decided to proceed, each spurred on by their own motivations and more black coffee.

What did more to revive them than anything else were the articles themselves. The papers had covered every twist and turn of the Westfall episode. After comparing notes and discarding the duplicates, they singled out several for further scrutiny. To prevent any careless oversights, Mitchell read them aloud as Sarah took notes.

Mustn't Call on O'Donnell. Visitors Told Judge is in Hospital for Absolute Rest. Appointment of a county commissioner probably will be deferred for several days:

"Dr. T. J. Cunningham Wednesday said that Probate Judge O'Donnell will be unable to leave St. Vincent's hospital for several days. In the meantime visitors have been excluded from his room. Overwork, he said, has affected his nervous system and upset his digestion."

Mitchell took a swig of coffee as Sarah wrote. When she laid down her pencil, he went on to the next article.

O'Donnell Prolongs Trip:

"No hope of appointing a successor until at least July 4. Judge O'Donnell has gone up into Michigan, and friends here have received information that he will not be able to return to work until the last of this weekend and probably not then. He was in Toledo Saturday, at the Union Station, between trains.

"Judge O'Brien O'Donnell returned to the city Sunday night. He has been at a sanitarium resort in Michigan for several weeks, recuperating from a severe attack of nervous prostration.

"Charles Northrup, who accompanied O'Donnell, said that the judge has recovered to the point that he can walk short distances, but that his convalescence is slow."

Sarah leaned forward. "Mitchell, could you read that last sentence again, please?"

"Charles Northrup, who accompanied O'Donnell—"

"Okay, that's enough." She made a note. Charley was with Obee. Hmm. Interesting. Perhaps she should talk to him. "All right. Go on."

"Here's that editorial I found," Mitchell said.

The Commissionership Fight:

"Judge O'Brien O'Donnell holds too high a place in the respect and esteem of the people of Toledo to be made the sacrifice of an unhallowed political machine. All good citizens will earnestly hope that the vicious effort to hang the O'Dwyer-Pilliod tag on a citizen who holds promise of so great usefulness in future public service, will meet with the failure it deserves."

Mitchell could have carved a hole into her with his gaze. "I remember thinking at the time that the pressure on O'Donnell must have been very great, a man with such a sense of duty. I imagine he's just prone to taking things a bit too hard."

"Yes, he is." Sarah glanced to the side as she answered, then hoped Mitchell didn't notice.

"Please Mitchell, continue."

Poles ask recognition in County appointment: Demand that Walinski Pole, Succeed Westfall:

"Our entire Polish population has united its energy in securing the appointment of Nicholas J. Walinski, a very prominent Pole and well known lawyer, and call upon you to heed to the Polish voice and make this appointment. We feel certain that our appeal will not be disregarded.

"Shall I continue?"

Sarah nodded.

"Two other men, Councilman Tafelski and Peter Matis, liquor salesman, were passengers in Westfall's car. Tafelski survived. Matis's body was recovered on Friday morning, the day after the drowning. While dragging the river with grappling hooks Monday afternoon,

Patrolmen Sheeder and Koke brought to the surface one of the cushion seats of Westfall's automobile, but not Westfall."

"That's right," Sarah said. "It was the councilman who survived ... and a ... a ... liquor salesman who drowned." She didn't know the salesman at all, and she only knew of Tafelski by name. He wasn't in politics anymore as far as she could recall.

"Listen to this one, Sarah!" Mitchell said, tightening his grasp on the paper:

Bodies Missing; Auto Found on River Bed:

"Councilman Tafelski said that the automobile plunged through the open draw without warning. He said he saw no guard rope or red signal light on the bridge. Soon after he arrived at the hospital, Tafelski told the following story of the tragedy:

'Matis was my countryman and I had known him a long time. He called to see me early in the evening and, after visiting a little while, he asked me to go with him to the East Side. He said he had some business in Ironville and Birmingham and wanted me to introduce him to several Hungarian saloon keepers who are friends of mine. I agreed to go and I got Frank Westfall to drive us in his automobile.

'We left my place about eight and drove to John Strick's saloon on Front street. We stayed there nearly an hour and after visiting several other places started for home about ten. Westfall was driving and Matis and I occupied the back seat. When we started across the Ash Street Bridge I looked ahead. No other vehicle or any obstacle was in sight. We were driving about fifteen miles an hour, I think.'

'I was talking to Matis when, without warning, I felt the automobile suddenly pitch forward and fall into space. I leaned out the side of the machine and the next thing I knew I was in the water.

'I think I fell out of the auto before striking the river. I guess I sank nearly to the bottom of the river and then I rose to the surface. I had on a heavy overcoat and although I am a good swimmer, I had to work hard to keep afloat. The wind was blowing hard and the water was very rough.'

'Soon I spied some piling near the pier of the draw, about thirty feet away. I managed to swim to one of the piles and clung to it with both arms and legs until I was rescued.'

"Now this is a man who knows how to tell a story," Mitchell said, nodding and smiling.

Sarah shuddered. "It's a gruesome story."

"Precisely."

"It sounds as if they may have had a bit too much to drink," she said.

"Believe me, they had more than a bit too much."

Sarah remembered the rumors about Mitchell. Undoubtedly he knew what he was talking about. "What's next?" she asked.

"Maybe the most important piece yet: *Body of Westfall Found.*"

Sarah stiffened as Mitchell recited the facts.

"The body of Frank Westfall was discovered by Walter LaBeau, 22, of 1787 Summit Street and Carl Murphy 21, and Westfall's son, John Westfall, 22. The body was discovered at 10:45, Thursday, June 3, floating near the middle of the channel 300 feet north of the Ash Street Bridge. A few minutes before, a freighter, a passenger steamship and a tug, all outbound, had passed through the draw of the bridge a short distance apart. It is believed that the churning of the water by the propellers caused the body to rise to the surface. The body was so badly decomposed that the features were not recognizable. His son identified the body by a diamond ring on the little finger of the left hand, the clothing, and a gold watch and several business papers in the pockets."

Mitchell shook his head. "This would be laughable if it wasn't true. Sounds like something from *The Bee.* Glad I didn't have to write it."

"Yet it *must* have been true, Mitchell." Sarah recalled that the body had been missing for days. But she didn't remember that it had decomposed to the point that even his son could not identify him. The mental image she conjured up made her blood run cold.

"Maybe it wasn't Westfall at all," Mitchell said half-jokingly. "Maybe his ring, watch, even the papers were planted on the body."

"Talk about *The Bee*! Don't be ridiculous. What could possibly be the motive?"

"I'm surprised you ask. You've read about the battles that ensued after the death. No doubt the acrimony started long before. Maybe the answer was in those business papers."

Sarah had considered this, too, but refused to admit it. They were both overwrought, letting their imaginations run away with them.

"You're talking crazy. I'm sure that once an autopsy was done, his identity was confirmed. And if those papers were suspicious, the police surely would have noticed."

"You're probably right, although there doesn't appear to be any news of it here. I think it's worth looking into at any rate."

"Perhaps," Sarah said. "How many more articles do we have left?"

"Just a couple."

"Let's finish up then."

"All right. Let's see here."

Declare Bridges Poorly Guarded: Prompted by the drowning of Frank Westfall and Peter Matis, the Grand Jury Probes Cause of Auto Plunge Into Maumee River; Says Rope Barriers on Draw Insufficient:

"The grand jury is unanimously of the opinion that the use of ropes as a guard to pedestrians or vehicles is wholly insufficient by reason of the fact that ropes are not easily discernable in the dark and would not stand a heavy blow that is liable to occur at any time on these approaches." Mitchell shifted in his chair.

"Here's another one on the same topic. *Mayor Certain Bridge Tenders Did Full Duty:*

"Mayor Keller said Thursday that he is satisfied the Ash-Consul bridge tenders took proper precautions against accident. He investigated the circumstances. 'I am certain the city is blameless,' he said. 'The guard rope was in place and the red lantern was displayed in its proper place.'

"Officials were interested in the marks of the automobile wheels on the bridge surface. There were marks indicating that Westfall may have seen his danger and applied the brakes fifty feet from the edge of the draw. The wheels had, apparently, scraped only at intervals, suggesting that the brakes of the automobile may not have worked properly."

"Seems to contradict the councilman, doesn't it?" Mitchell said. "Just like a politician to deny any responsibility."

Sarah nodded absentmindedly. She might have challenged that remark, told him that all politicians are not created equal. But her thoughts were frozen on the last sentence of the article: *the brakes of the automobile may not have been working properly.* My God. Perhaps Mitchell had not been far off. Mitchell looked at her and appeared to read her mind. His deep voice rose an octave.

"Sarah, are you thinking what I'm thinking?"

"I don't know what you mean."

"What I mean is that perhaps there was a different kind of foul play at work here than I initially thought. Maybe Westfall *was* recovered from the river after all. But maybe, just maybe his drowning was deliberate. The papers call it an accident. I'm not so sure. I don't think you are either. And, Sarah, if it was deliberate, it's possible that Judge O'Donnell knew—"

"Stop! Please, Mitchell, don't say any more."

"Don't say any more! Why not? Isn't that what we're here for? To discover why the judge is being blackmailed? You aren't going to shrink from this now, now that we finally may be on to something?"

"No, no of course not. It's just that . . . that . . . Look, we've made a great start. But this is an extremely grave point you're about to make, so grave that I would prefer to discuss it when I'm fresh. That coffee is wearing off, and I simply can't stomach anymore at this hour." Her throat tightened. A lump was forming that at any moment could dissolve into tears.

"Forgive me. Perhaps you're right. How about we meet at the park tomorrow at noon. Do you know the benches by the gazebo?"

"I know them quite well. All right," Sarah said as she stood up. "I'll meet you there. Good night, then."

"Wait a minute," Mitchell said, grabbing her arm with more force than was necessary. "Sorry, but just how do you plan to get home? There are no trains or cabs at this hour."

"I'll walk. I'm used to it."

"By yourself? Oh, no you don't. I'll accompany you. Let me put these papers away and then—"

"No, please Mitchell, I'll be fine."

"Listen Sarah, I know you're an independent sort, but it's not safe this late at night. I'd walk you home even if you were a man."

Ordinarily, Sarah would have continued to protest. She longed to be alone. But clearly Mitchell wouldn't go down with out a fight, and she was simply too drained to take on that kind of resolve.

"All right, as you wish. But you must promise me not to speak of the judge. I want no more of that talk tonight."

"Fair enough."

Sarah thought Mitchell's chivalry quaint, but unnecessary. She was convinced that if a woman were aware of her environment, she could avoid trouble. It was those taken off guard, oblivious to their surroundings, who were most vulnerable to attack.

"You see, there's no danger. Even the mob's in bed at this hour," she said, as they walked without incident down the dark, empty streets.

DOPE MERCHANT MURDERER,
D

Sędzia O'Brien O'Donnell

Kandydat na Sędziego do

Probacyjnego Sądu

"Przyjaciel i obrońca kobiet i dzieci, który prawdo-podobnie najwięcej zrobił dla ludzkości w Toledo niż kto kolwiek inny." (z The Ohio Woman's Magazine)

O'Brien O'Donnell jest uczciwym bezpartyjnym, ciężko pracującym probacyjnym sędzią i jego administracya tego urzędu była taka, że niżej podpisani członkowie stowarzyszenia prawników chętnie informują publiczność, że pozostawienie jego na dalszy termin na zajmowanem stanowisku jest wysoce pożądane.

To polityczne ogłoszenie jest wolnem przyczynieniem się; bez wiedzy sędziego O'Donnell'a od wielu zwolenników jego zasad o sprawiedliwości i humanitarności.

RING JUVENILE
HERE INFORMED
Gathering Containers and An-

BY MURDER AND
BECOME COUNT
Two Boys Arraigned for Alleged
Bootlegger—Another Admits

15

A light breeze blew over the Maumee as Sarah approached
Riverside Park. With the sun finally unhindered by the typical summer
haze, the effect was magical, changing what for weeks had been a mud-

colored flow into a mass of shimmering opals. This was the kind of day that could make even the most dedicated atheist wonder. Flat and faded just hours before, the landscape suddenly emerged in all its contrasting shapes and forms, each bush and flower sharpened to the finest edge. A few of the tallest oaks were showing burnt orange at the tips of their leaves, flickering like a thousand flames against the clear, blue sky.

But for Sarah, these signs of the approach of autumn meant only one thing: the election was drawing near. For the first time in her life, she felt nature mocking her with its splendor.

But, of course, Sarah was not quite herself. Her very skin felt raw. As if sensitized by fever, she recoiled at even this, the world's most benevolent touch. Such a strange night. When she thought of it, how she'd gone to Mitchell—for Mitchell now it was—how she'd been there alone with him reading those papers, well, the whole thing seemed like a dream. She might have still been wondering if that were the case had she not had a real dream with which to compare it. A seemingly endless, tortuous nightmare that, at a time she needed rest more than anything else, had interrupted much of her sleep. There was only one saving grace. At least now she didn't feel guilty that she had asked Tillie to call her work and tell them she was sick. Anyone who saw her would have been certain she was telling the truth.

Was she now fully awake? Would she turn a corner and find herself still participating in the horrifying tale of her own mind's creation? She could see it all so clearly. The house made of yellowing newspapers. The walk down the hall she was repeatedly compelled to make. The eight doors she was forced to open, each embossed with the name of someone involved in this incredible matter. No doubt Conan Doyle would see all of it as some kind of message from the beyond. But what did she think? Each time she would begin the short journey, she was nearly paralyzed with fear. Vaguely aware of dreaming, she was nevertheless terrified of what phantom of her imagination awaited behind the doors.

At first she was relieved, encountering upon each twist of the nob nothing more than a news photograph of the person whose name the door announced. In order were the inanimate faces of John O'Dwyer, Dr. Evans, Winifred, Councilman Tafelski, Charles Northrup, Obee, Frank Westfall, and Mitchell. So innocuous were these images and so predictable was their appearance in her dream that even as she slept Sarah wondered at the simplicity of her unconscious. Freud, she thought, would have been extremely bored.

Soon, however, that thought was replaced with the old adage "be careful what you wish for." For suddenly the darker recesses of her mind took flight, revealing a faceless presence that hovered over each of the images, bringing them to life and changing them into something uniquely sinister. First to alter was John O'Dwyer. Having grown to monstrous proportions, he was greedily counting money with one hand while tending barrels of fermenting grain with the other. Then came Dr. Evans. When Sarah opened his door, he was directly on the other side, holding a giant syringe with a gleaming, metallic needle. He laughed hideously when Sarah shrieked. Next was Councilman Taflelski, sitting on Obee's bench and wearing his robe. With a self-satisfied look, he repeatedly recited one of the most absurd bits of doggerel Sarah had ever heard: "Quid pro quo, quid pro quo, every thug in town is free to go!" In reality the verse was ridiculous, in her dream it was a frighteningly vicious proclamation.

After that a ghostly Winifred appeared, threatening a screaming, disfigured child, and she was followed by Charley Northrup, who was furiously burying a key to Obee's hospital door. And Obee's room? Obee was in there all right, blinking wildly, as he aimed a loaded gun at his head.

Sensing the worst was yet to come, Sarah tried to resist the impulse to open the next door. But it was no use. The door exploded open on its own, revealing a bloated and purple Frank Westfall, still alive and gasping for air in the water that was rapidly filling the room. She thought she would be sick, but didn't have the time. The torrent of water immediately enveloped her, trapping her in its turbulent current. Westfall's bulging eyes were pleading for help, but she could do nothing. She, too, was in a fight for her life. And in the midst of it all, bearing down on her with oppressive force, was that same, faceless, ominous presence. Amorphous but visceral, concealed behind an invisible veil, this was an evil Sarah knew was bent on her destruction.

There was only one chance left. With all her remaining strength, she managed to push open the last door. There, in unadulterated form, sat Mitchell, immersed in a copy of *The Blade*. She tried to speak, to scream out his name, but was made mute by her submergence in what now seemed like a flood of biblical proportions. Desperate to get his attention, all she could do as the life drained from her was stare at him as determinedly as he had so often at her. And for a moment she thought she was saved. Instantly, like steel to a magnet, his gaze pulled upward and he was alerted to her dire condition. Yes, he was running to help her, yes, but a rush of water was preventing him from getting through his door. He reached out his hands. "Swim toward me Sarah, swim!" he shouted. But by this time her body had gone limp, and she was unable to return his grasp. His eyes had witnessed her struggle, but his hands, so long and elegant, were still outstretched when she heard the distant sound of Tillie's voice.

"Sarah dear, Sarah wake up. It's nearly ten. Sarah! Why, Sarah, you look awful! You really *are* ill."

"No, no Tillie, I'm not. I just didn't sleep very well . . . but, please dear, no questions right now, okay?"

"Whatever you say, Your Highness. Shall I get you some breakfast?"

Sarah was in no mood for Tillie's special brand of sarcasm. This time she was not going to let it make her feel guilty. If her sister was offended, so be it. Better that than have her worrying to distraction, which is exactly what she would do if she knew the real source of Sarah's distress.

"Just some toast, please. I'm having an early lunch."

Tillie shook her head disapprovingly as she started for the kitchen.

"By the way, Sarah," she said over her shoulder, you might be interested in the morning paper."

"Oh?"

"Yes, there's an article on the new synagogue. Looks as if it'll be open for the holidays. They're not far off you know, just a couple of weeks away."

"Uh, huh . . . that's nice," Sarah mumbled.

"Well, if that doesn't interest you," Tillie said with annoyance, "there's another article that might. It's about Dr. Evans, that doctor who treated Obee years ago. He's dead. Now then, I'll get your toast."

"There you are. I was beginning to think . . . hey, Miss, you don't look so good."

"So I've been told."

"Have a seat," Mitchell said, as he brushed off a small pile of dry leaves that had accumulated on the bench.

Sarah silently obeyed. This was her favorite spot in the park, and for a few moments she gazed at the familiar vista. The bench was situated exactly at the bend of the Maumee where Swan Creek made its delicate contribution. From here the view was like a perfectly balanced painting, with the vast expanse of the river in the distance and the white, wooden gazebo, where chamber groups played in the summer, centered in the foreground. She loved this respectful coupling of nature and culture. The contrast enhanced the beauty of both.

Two of Toledo's five bridges framed the scene, one the Cherry Street and the other, the infamous Ash-Counsell. Since the time of the drowning, all the bridges had been modernized, thanks to the Progressive march led by none other than O'Brien O'Donnell. Was Obee's involvement in this issue personal, too? Perhaps, just as it had been in his fight against drugs. But there was no doubt in her mind that even if he'd had no connection to Westfall whatsoever, he would have argued for such improvements. As early as 1906, he spoke on behalf of Ohio Electric, the company that eventually built the largest reinforced concrete bridge in the world across the Maumee. Private demons aside, he was still more committed to the public welfare than any person she knew. If he recovered, even this very location would one day be the beneficiary of his efforts. Developers had long been encroaching on this bit of pristine land, and Obee promised to do everything in his power to thwart them. "More parks and fewer buildings," he had said in a recent speech, "open space for future generations."

"Will you tell me what's troubling you, Sarah?" The sound of Mitchell's voice reminded her of the hurdles she would have to surmount in order to ensure that Obee would be healthy enough to carry out his noble goals. "You mean other than finding a blackmailer, solving an unspeakable crime, saving the judge from ruin? Oh, nothing really."

Turning from the river, Sarah saw by Mitchell's bemused expression that he was just as surprised at her remark as she was. Where did she get such a sharp tongue? The two stood there for a moment exchanging a bewildered glance before simultaneously bursting into laughter.

"I don't think I've ever seen you laugh," Mitchell said. "It becomes you."

She could feel herself blush. Not only because she was taken off guard by the compliment, but because once again she had been thinking the same thing about him. What was with this fellow, anyway? It was as though he had read her mind in reverse. She wondered at the extent of his powers.

She tried to adopt a more serious expression, but when she glanced at the corner of the bench her mouth spontaneously curved back into a grateful smile. There, neatly displayed on a red checkered napkin, was what appeared to be lunch. It was nothing, Mitchell said as he handed her one of his home-made sandwiches, only a return for the previous night's favor. But the last time Sarah could remember someone of the opposite sex cooking for her was when her next door neighbor, little Dave Bernstein, made her mud cakes for her eighth birthday. Now it was cheese and lettuce on white (for which he apologized), but her delight was the same.

After wiping some crumbs off her skirt, she cleared her throat and made an announcement. "Okay, now I am ready."

"You are?"

"Yes." She looked at Mitchell almost as intently as she had in her dream. "Last night you were about to say that Frank Westfall was murdered and that Obee must have somehow been involved. Am I right?"

Mitchell jolted upright. "Why, yes, that pretty much covers it. I didn't realize just how ready you were."

"It seems absolutely incredible, of course," she said, "yet I have no choice but to accept your theory as a possibility. Besides, if I'm ever

180

to get any sleep again, I need to find out what, if any, part of the equation is true."

"Ah, so that's it. Bad night, huh?"

"*That* is an understatement."

With very little prompting, she told Mitchell about her dream, excluding the part about Winifred and, of course, Dr. Evans, who she now had removed from her list of suspects. As soon as Tillie had nonchalantly dropped that bomb on her about the man, she had raced to the paper. The timing was phenomenal, but there it was. The obituary said that Dr. Samuel Evans, noted Toledo physician, had died of cancer of the lung. He had been sick for some time and hospitalized for the past month. "Hospitalized with cancer." She reread the line, something she was becoming accustomed to doing these days. Her mother had died of that dreaded disease. The word conjured up her horrible end, the wasting away of the body, the surrender of the spirit. She wouldn't wish such a thing even on this scoundrel, but then again if anyone deserved it... At any rate, Dr. Evans was too sick to have even put pen to paper, let alone carry out such a diabolical plan. Obee must have a different supplier now, perhaps more than one. Evans had done enough evil for one lifetime. If he appeared in her dreams now, she would just have to lock his door and throw away the key.

It wasn't like Sarah to speak so freely about such a private experience. Two days ago she would have perished the thought. But that was then. Life was no longer predictable, and she was learning to accommodate her behavior accordingly. Because she had brought Mitchell into her "investigation," it seemed natural that she should tell him—however selectively—about a dream so obviously related to it.

"And then my sister woke me up," she said, heaving a sigh of relief. "You know, I've never had a dream linger so. Thank you for listening, Dr. Freud. I think I'm cured." Describing the dream had in fact greatly diminished its power, and Sarah was now wondering how she could have let nothing more than a bunch of overactive grey matter bother her so much. She felt silly. Even that ominous presence struck her as something she had unconsciously devised simply to scare herself.

"May the doctor offer his opinion?"

Sarah hesitated. "As long as it doesn't involve my childhood."

"I'll save that for another time. For now, I think what we need to do, Sarah, is explore those rooms, so to speak. Find out everything we can in each of them. And if we are met with resistance, use whatever means we have to force our way in."

"I know it's my dream, but could you translate?"

"What I mean is that we focus on the tangibles, questioning—discreetly, of course—each of the individuals you envisioned in those rooms. I could begin by nosing around the Lagrange Street area."

"You mean Little Poland?"

"I've never heard it called that, but it might as well be. When I lived there as a kid, it was twenty percent Polish, now it's about forty. As far as I know, Charles Tafelski still lives there. I could talk to him, see how he acts, what he remembers. I could tell him I'm considering writing an article about his years as a councilman. The ego of a politician never fails. And while I'm there, I could pay a visit to Westfall's widow. She lives somewhere around there, too. It would be very interesting to find out what her thoughts are on her husband's death."

"And I?"

"You? I think the first person you should see is John O'Dwyer. You know him pretty well, don't you?"

"Not exactly well, but yes, I know him." Sarah shuddered at the thought of O'Dwyer's unctuous smile. "And just how am I to get information without making the man suspicious? He's involved with Obee's reelection campaign for God's sake. As you can imagine, he's already quite curious."

"I'll leave that to you, Sarah, although you might consider the guy's reputation with the ladies."

"I don't think I'm his type."

"Well, maybe that's because you haven't tried to make him like you."

"Just what are you suggesting, Mr. Dobrinski?"

"Nothing dangerous . . . some harmless flirting, perhaps. You're a dick now, you know. You have to be willing to use whatever talents are at your disposal."

Sarah smiled mischievously. "You mean, I should play the part of a dumb Dora. Bat my eyelashes. Use my feminine wiles and all that. Aren't I a bit . . . mature for such tricks?"

"You're a fascinating woman, Sarah. I wager you could get any man's attention if you put your mind to it."

Sarah felt the blood rush to her face. "Well, I think you may be overstating things just a bit," she said. "It might, however, be interesting to try out your theory." A disguise of sorts, following in the footsteps of her beloved Sherlock, who, regrettably, she hadn't read in weeks. "I can't say as I relish the thought of playing up to O'Dwyer, but it does give me an excuse to go to the beauty parlor."

Simultaneously they rose and talked over their plan as they walked to Water Street, where their paths diverged. Mitchell would head east toward *The Blade*, Sarah north toward the courthouse. Before they parted, they smiled and shook hands.

It had been productive. Like two countries, they had joined forces to achieve a goal. They were allies not friends, even if their parting was shaded by the exchange of a long, curious look from which neither seemed eager to retreat.

16

By two in the afternoon Sarah was saving another marriage. An annoying mother-in-law could be dealt with. Waiting in the lobby was a couple whose problems wouldn't be so easy to remedy, having already divided their property down to the last butter knife. Sarah glanced at the clock and frowned. Before going home, she wanted to visit Obee and speak to Dr. Miller about this confusing turn of events. She owed it to him to explain why she'd suddenly allowed Mitchell into their inner circle and yet still wanted him prohibited from learning the most basic facts about Obee's hospitalization. Dr. Miller would puff on his pipe and nod in understanding. He would accept her decision and abide by it. But he would also tell her what she had been already telling herself, that she should remember that phrase about the tangled webs we weave.

Sarah and Mitchell had left the park with a plan. She would make an appointment with O'Dwyer and pay a visit to Charley Northrup. Charley, she was certain, had nothing to do with the letter, but he might be able to shed some light on the situation. Especially, since according to the papers, he was with Obee during his breakdown after the drowning. There was no telling what he knew. As for Winifred, Sarah already had access to her "room," indeed to nearly her entire house. But, she was even less likely to be the culprit than Charley. Not only did the frail beauty presumably lack all the facts, she had no motive. While undoubtedly some women would go so far as to blackmail their husbands to keep them home, Winifred was not one of them. She would loathe for Obee to quit the bench. Her identity was wrapped up in being the wife of a judge.

It was Wednesday, the third of September. On Sunday, Sarah and Mitchell would meet at the same spot and compare notes. They each had their tasks. One way or another, all rooms would be accounted for, with the exception of Mitchell's, that is, whose significance in the dream was conspicuously absent from their conversation.

Even if she could have afforded it, Sarah wouldn't have adopted what had become for many women a ritual: the weekly trip to the beauty shop. She preferred to do her own hair. But this was a special occasion. The girls at work recommended Faye, a rising star at Aphrodite's. Faye apparently could work wonders, determining at a glance which style would flatter a woman most. "Anyone who's anyone goes to her," they all said, "including Mrs. O'Donnell." That clinched it. Sarah called and, fortunately, the much-sought-after operator had a cancellation on Saturday at ten, just a few hours before the meeting she had scheduled with John O'Dwyer.

Faye, an attractive, voluptuous woman in her mid-thirties, had every right to be proud of the ample cleavage she displayed. Her low-cut lemon yellow frock would have been garish on just about anyone else, but on her it seemed appropriate. A more subdued color would have dulled her rich Mediterranean complexion. No doubt that was why she was the only operator who didn't wear the shop's official light pink work jacket. Washing hair was one thing, looking washed-out quite another.

Seating Sarah in her swivel chair, Faye adjusted the height and eyed her from various angles. After a couple of minutes of intense scrutiny, the verdict was in. "Well, kiddo, you've got the face for a bob, but I don't figure you for the guillotine. Just some minor trimming, crimping, dips in the front and a bit of henna for brightening."

Sarah was impressed with the woman's efficiency and self-assurance. "All right. But, are you sure those dips won't emphasize my nose?"

"Baloney. Just the opposite. Besides, what's wrong with your nose? You wouldn't want one of those little turned up things, would you? That would make you just like any other Jane. So boring. Look at me," Faye said, proudly showing off her own strong, aquiline profile.

Sarah smiled. She liked this woman.

"You know, I've seen you in the paper before," she said as she whipped Sarah's hair into a meringue-like lather. With the judge. I'm a big fan of his you know. Heart of gold, that man. I don't believe the rumors, of course, but I wouldn't care if they were true."

"Rumors, what rumors?" Sarah asked nonchalantly.

"Oh, you know, that he knocked up his wife. They say that's why he's sick. Cause he had to marry someone he didn't love."

Sarah was glad she was lying down. "From whom do you hear such things, Faye?"

"Oh, from different people, here and there. But I mind my potatoes. Although I did always think it was a strange match, the missus being so young and all. You know I used to do her hair, permanent wave every six months. She was such a nervous little bunny."

"Used to?"

"Haven't seen her since the day before her wedding."

Faye rinsed out the shampoo, sat Sarah up and twisted a towel on her head into the shape of a turban. "I'm glad you don't go in for gossip," Sarah said, as she shakily followed Faye to her station.

"Not me. I get an earful in here. I'd never get any work done if I let it get to me. Now, honey, here we go." Faye was then all business. With authority, she rubbed Sarah's hair with tonics, and cut, curled, dried, and brushed it carefully, placing each strand in a preordained spot.

"There, you're quite a doll, Miss Kaufman." Faye spun Sarah around so she could see the full scope of her artistry in the mirror.

"It looks fine," Sarah said, although she was still unconvinced about the dips.

Faye took the brown felt hat Sarah had brought and positioned it at a stylish angle. "So, do we kiss now or later?"

"What?"

"Cash or check?"

"Oh. Cash."

Sarah paid her the required two dollars and gave her a good tip. She had gotten much more than she'd bargained for.

As she walked to O'Dywer's office, she admonished herself for being so naive. If the pregnancy had occurred to her, why not to others? And if this, what else? Just what were the good citizens of Toledo saying now?

"Excuse me . . . oh, Mr. O'Dwyer!"

Lost in the imagined whispers and innuendos of her high-minded townsmen, Sarah failed to see the person directly in her path outside the tall, brick building that housed Democratic headquarters.

"Miss Kaufman, it is Miss Kaufman, isn't it? You look like a woman on a mission."

Sarah patted her hair and checked the position of her hat. The collision had fortunately not disrupted the hard-won saucy look. "In fact, I was on my way to see you, Mr. O'Dwyer. I had an appointment."

"Oh, my dear, I'm so sorry. I don't usually work on Saturdays, and I'm heading to the ball game. Last game of the season, you know."

"But Mr. O'Dwyer, we had an appointment!" Sarah had to restrain herself from stomping her feet.

"My secretary should have known. Can it wait 'till Monday?"

"No! I mean, I may be going out of town tomorrow . . . and . . . and, I could be gone for several days."

"Is this about the judge? He's improving, isn't he?"

"Yes, he's doing fine. But, well, it does involve him . . . indirectly."

O'Dywer looked her up and down. The corners of his thin mouth twitched. "I'll tell you what, Miss Kaufman, why don't you come along?"

"Oh, no. Couldn't you just spare a few—"

"Why not? Come as my date. We can talk there. C'mon. It'll be fun."

O'Dwyer took Sarah's perplexed silence as a yes. Before she knew what was happening, he locked her arm and swept her into a cab. "Swayne Field," he commanded.

Despite the Mud Hens' mediocre eighty-two/eighty-three season, a sold-out crowd packed what was generally considered the best minor league ball park in America. Under other circumstances, Sarah would have been delighted to be there. And not just because of the hot dogs. Obee's passion for the game had been contagious. "People who insist baseball is boring don't have an appreciation for subtlety," he'd say. She wasn't a sports fan, but she couldn't resist the implied challenge in her friend's remark. It took a while, but she eventually realized he was right. Baseball was a game of strategy and nuance. Only an untrained, impatient eye would find it slow. She was hooked, and secretly proud that she knew a pick-off from a squeeze play. Most women went to the games to show off their finery. She went to observe the rise and fall of ERAs. Except for today, that is, when she was too preoccupied to even notice who was pitching.

The Mud Hens acquired their moniker from the bird that frequented the field where they used to play. Bay View Park was surrounded by marshland that was home to the American Coot, a disproportionate bird with short wings and long legs. The team now played at Swayne Field, located downtown at Detroit and Monroe. Named for noted attorney Noah H. Swayne, the urban park no longer had the birds to contend with, but the colorful moniker, known by more Americans than any minor league team, stuck.

Like most members of the Toledo elite, O'Dwyer had season tickets. His box was located directly behind home plate, close to Obee's, whose vacancy today stood out like a proverbial sore thumb. Before taking his seat, O'Dwyer winked at all his chums, who regarded Sarah curiously.

She was just about to sit down herself when she heard a familiar, deep voice bellow out her name. "Sarah, Sarah my love!" She turned around and saw Kenneth Ballard waving to her enthusiastically several rows up. Tanned and dapper as usual, Ken stood out from the group of styleless, grey-faced men with whom he was sharing a box. Now, *they* looked like engineers.

Sprinting athletically down the steps that separated them, Kenneth motioned to Sarah to join him in the aisle.

"I'll be right back," she told O'Dwyer, who was in the middle of making eyes at the young woman selling peanuts.

"How's it going, Sarah?" Kenneth asked, eyeing O'Dwyer suspiciously.

"Fine. And don't get any ideas, Ken. Mr. O'Dwyer had some extra tickets, that's all. You know how I feel about the game."

Kenneth rolled his eyes. "Obee all right, I hope? I'd like so much to see him."

"I know, Ken. But, it's better off this way. And, yes, he's doing well. He'll be back before you know it."

"Anything I can do in the meantime?"

"No, but thanks."

As she had predicted, Kenneth had failed to follow through on his promise to campaign for Obee. She didn't hold it against the man. He meant well. It was hard enough for someone of his voluble disposition to do the dry work of an engineer, whatever knack he may have for it. Something had to suffer.

"Well, if you need anything, my love, you know you can count on me."

"I know, Ken," she said, giving him a friendly hug.

"By the way," he said, as he started back up the stairs, "you look gorgeous. Far too good for that fellow you're with."

"But I told you, I'm not . . . oh, never mind." She shook her head in dismay and headed back to her seat. On the way, she spotted a number of regular attendees. Among them, as luck would have it, was Charley Northrup, who noticed her at the same time. This unplanned excursion might prove to be productive after all. Two birds, or should she say, two rooms with one stone.

"Charley, it's so good to see you. I should have known you'd be here."

"Can't say as I would've thought the same about you, Sarah. Who'd you come with anyway?"

"Well, Mr. O'Dwyer had some extra tickets and–"

"O'Dwyer! You're kidding of course."

"No, I'm not. It was only an opportunity to see the last game, Charley."

He narrowed his eyes and nudged her with his elbow. "I suppose you know to be careful with that one, Sarah. He's got a wife, but that doesn't stop him."

"I know. Don't worry about me. I can handle myself."

"I guess at least you'll be able to tell Obee about the game. I can imagine how disappointed he is that he's not here. Why didn't you just take his seats?"

"He didn't offer, Charley. But, yes, I'll relay every detail to him, although I'm interested, too, you know."

"So you are," he said nodding. He smiled apologetically. "I'd forgotten. How is Obee anyway? Just another one of his nervous attacks, I understand. *I've* been kept in the dark as much as everyone else."

191

"He's all right, but—"

"Howard Balllldwinnn. Paul Strrrannndd." The team was being announced over the loud speaker. Soon the game would begin, and that would make conversation nearly impossible.

"Charley, I've got to get back to my seat, but I'm actually glad I ran into you. This may sound strange, but I wonder if we could meet at some point later today. Do you have any time to spare?"

Charley cocked his head like a dog hearing a new sound. "I guess I could put off my quiet evening at home until tomorrow. Are you free for dinner, or are you eating with Boss Tweed?"

"Pfff. Yes, I'm free."

"The River's Edge, at seven?"

"Fine. And thanks, Charley."

Sarah waved at a couple of other acquaintances as she shuffled through the crowd to her seat.

"Where have you been, young lady?" O'Dwyer offered her some peanuts and slipped his arm around her chair.

"No, thanks," she said, as the noise level started to rise. Mr. O'Dwyer, I need to ask you something."

"Hey Sarah, Stengel's throwing the first pitch!"

"Mr. O'Dywer."

"Please, call me John," he said, motioning to the field.

The response to the great Casey Stengel was deafening. Sarah had met the man several times at Obee's; him, Bert Lents, Roger Bresnahan ("the Duke of Tralee") the whole lot of them. A great bunch of guys she had easily won over with her baseball knowledge. Unfortunately, O'Dwyer would require a different approach.

"John," she said touching his leg suggestively.

"Yes, Sarah. Why, yes, what is it my dear?"

"What do you remember of Frank Westfall's death?"

The first pitch by Ben Fray was a strike. The crowd applauded.

"What's that you say?"

Sarah repeated the question.

The second pitch was a strike, the applause more vigorous. "You'll have to speak up, Sarah," O'Dwyer said, pressing her hand on his leg encouragingly.

"What do you remember of Frank Westfall's death!"

Strike three.

The crowd went wild, but O'Dwyer was silent. He turned and glared at her. "What do you mean?"

Now she had his attention. "I was doing some research recently . . . on another matter, and came across his name. I'd forgotten how horrible the drowning was, John, not finding the body for so long and all. And, I didn't realize how difficult the appointment of a new commissioner was. It made me wonder. Your name was mentioned often, you know, in conjunction with John Kumler. Quite frankly, John, I'm puzzled why you, a Democrat, pushed so hard for Kumler, and even more, why Obee voted with you. He was so close to the Poles." Sarah smiled innocently and lightly massaged the man's thigh.

O'Dwyer's eyes grew moist. He licked his cracked lips. "You're a curious little thing, aren't you?"

She looked at him seductively and rubbed a little higher. "I suppose so. In fact, that got me wondering about something else, too, John, why Obee dismissed the case against you in nineteen twelve, you know, for stuffing ballots for Brown."

O'Dwyer removed her hand forcefully. "Listen, what are you up to anyway? You best mind your own business. All of that is in the past. You'd be wise to leave it there."

"No need to get upset, John. As you said, I'm just curious."

"It's Mr. O'Dwyer to you!" the reddening man barked as he turned toward the game. "If that's why you wanted to see me, consider the meeting over. I believe you can find your own way home."

Sarah could think of nothing she'd rather do. A femme fatale she was not, even if she had performed the role surprisingly well. Anyway, O'Dwyer's rejection of her hand didn't mean she would leave the ballpark completely empty-handed. Responding to a new round of cheers, she looked to the field just in time to witness the results of Moe Berg's expertise. The crafty shortstop could decode the other teams' signs with the skill of a spy, and, in this case, he had just thwarted an attempted steal by orchestrating a pitch-out. Like her kinsman and favorite player, Sarah, too, had conducted a bit of espionage. O'Dywer definitely had something to hide. Holmes would have been proud.

When she told Mitchell about the encounter the next afternoon, he concurred. "O'Dwyer's room does look pretty dirty," he said.

It all made sense. The guy's campaigning for O'Brien must have been a ruse, a clever way to mask the fact that he was actually working *against* his reelection. It was worthy of the brute. As for motivation, he could be blackmailing the judge for mere revenge or to get paid off by the other side. He was capable of either. Of course, there was still the matter of how he had acquired *all* the information. Westfall, Sarah understood. Undoubtedly O'Dwyer knew what really happened to the commissioner and what Obee's connection may have been. But, although he might have had his suspicions about the marriage, how could he have known for sure? And the drugs. That seemed nearly impossible. Of course, since Mitchell knew nothing of these matters, Sarah kept such concerns to herself. O'Dwyer still appeared to be the most likely suspect. Especially when compared to the others whose *rooms*, as Mitchell put it, now "appeared to be clean."

First there was Charley Northrop. After Sarah's dinner with him, she was convinced more than ever that he was innocent. Charley himself brought up the topic of O'Dwyer. Before slicing into his rare porterhouse steak, he informed Sarah that he was still disturbed at seeing her with him at the ball game.

"You should talk," she said, seizing the opportunity. You defended him when he was accused of ballot stuffing for Brown. Remember?"

"Unfortunately I do. But, that's my job. I'm not required to like my clients."

Sarah cut into her own well-done filet. Too well done. She twirled her fork around and contemplated the charred morsel. "You know, Charley, I've always wondered why Obee threw out that case. Do you know?"

"Because there wasn't enough evidence, Sarah. Obee would have preferred to throw the guy to the lions. For that matter, so would've I. But, there were no credible witnesses. Obee had no choice."

Charley's tone was even, his expression frank. No trace of deception surfaced. Nor did any when she asked him the more delicate question about his accompanying Obee to the sanitarium.

"What precisely was wrong with him, Charley?"

A frown joined his bushy, dark eyebrows. "What do you mean, what was wrong with him? He was exhausted. He had just cast that agonizing tie-breaking vote in the commissioner's race. He didn't want to do it, you know. He liked Walinski. But he was worried about all those workers."

"Workers?"

"You know, the employees who would lose their job if the breweries went under. Nick was a teetotaler and his wife, as you no doubt remember, was a leader of the temperance movement, president of the WCTM. Of course, Volstead ended up making the whole thing a moot point."

"So Obee was genuinely torn."

Charley jutted his neck forward and grimaced. "Torn? He was ripped in half. I'm surprised you don't know about all this."

Sarah shrugged. "We just weren't as close then."

"I actually didn't stay with him, you know," Charley added. "The Northern Michigan Asylum wasn't my idea of a place to holiday."

"Where did you stay then?"

"I was at a nearby lodge in Traverse City. I checked in on Obee every once and a while. But the doctors pretty much kept me at a distance. I have to admit, I didn't mind too much. The place was nightmarish." Charley closed his brown eyes and shook himself. "Creepy. You know, Sarah, they initially put Obee in the *most disturbed* ward. I couldn't figure that out."

Interesting. Charley was either still protecting Obee or didn't know anything about the drugs at all. From the transparency of his remarks, she'd have bet on the latter. Moreover, it seemed as though Obee might in fact have had a legitimate reason for voting for Kumler. But then again, he may have kept his real reasons hidden from Charley, too.

"I guess the Frank Westfall matter got to him more than even you realized, Charley."

"I suppose so. It was incredibly tragic," he said, sucking in his breath. "Remember the body, Sarah? Terrible for the family. The ring, papers, that's all that was left . . . hey, why all these questions, anyway? Writing a book?"

"Hardly. I just—"

"You know, come to think of it, those events do have the makings of a novel, a bad one I might add. *Murder in the Maumee*, you could call it."

Sarah gave him an ironic look that he misinterpreted as disgust.

"I'm sorry, that was uncalled for. The accident was bad enough as it was."

She saw her opening and proceeded cautiously. "Charley, did you ever actually wonder if the drowning could have been anything other than an accident?"

Charley smirked. "No, of course not."

She finally put down her fork. "But there were so many conflicting accounts of the episode. So many questions. Whether the draw was up or down. If the brakes on the car had malfunctioned. And then the intense battle afterward, and, as you said, the condition of the body . . ."

"Sarah . . . Sarah, you're serious, Charley said with a short laugh. Of course it was an accident. If it makes you feel any better, I was present at the autopsy. No sign of foul play there, if that's what you're thinking. And the breaks on the car were eventually found to have been in fine working order. I didn't realize you were so suggestible, my dear."

"I'm not, not really. I guess my nerves are a little frayed, you know with the election so near and Obee still not on his feet. Why don't we change the subject. I'd rather hear about your fishing trip anyway. The papers said you caught a whopper."

"Obee will be all right, Sarah," Charley said reassuringly. "I suspect these bouts are necessary. He'd never rest otherwise."

"I know. Now, tell me about the one that didn't get away."

Charley was more than happy to oblige. As Sarah pretended to finish her meal, he relayed to her the story of the twenty-pound rainbow trout. If his spontaneous reference to murder wasn't evidence enough of his innocence, this unexpectedly philosophical account clinched it. Was he proud of his catch? Of course. It was one of the largest ever recorded in Lake Michigan. But a person who grew misty as he described the "poor creature" laboring to breathe, who indeed was now rethinking his participation in the sport because of it, had too much of a conscience to be the blackmailer.

"It was the size of the thing" Charley said, as they were walking out of the restaurant. "My own lungs tightened as I saw it suffocating in the air. And its eyes. So pleading. For the first time I wondered if a fish had a soul."

No pun intended, she thought smiling to herself, but Charley was definitely off the hook. As he closed the door to her cab, she knowingly mixed metaphors and closed the door to his room.

"I've come to a similar conclusion about Charles Tafelski," Mitchell said. "Poor guy."

Ten years had passed since the drowning, but the man was still distraught over the death of his friends. He told Mitchell that a day hadn't gone by that the images of that night didn't come back to haunt him. The retired councilman didn't need the enticement of an article to talk about Frank Westfall. In fact, his only request was that Mitchell promise to do no such thing.

"I don't want you to write about me," he said, "my life isn't worth the paper."

At first he just summarized the facts as they had appeared in *The Blade*. He, Peter Matis, and Westfall had visited a few bars on the east side. About ten they started over the bridge, on which he could recall seeing no guard rope or red light. He later thought, however, that this could have been because he and Peter were talking in the back seat. At any rate, he suddenly felt the car "pitch into space." Before he knew it, he was in the water and managed to swim to some nearby piling. He hung onto it until he was rescued.

"It was ironic. Damn ironic," he said, shaking his now balding head regretfully. "During the evening, Frank had talked about his plans for improving the bridges. That was part of the commissioner's job you know. If only I hadn't asked him to drive," he said with the hypnotic gaze of someone who had repeated this to himself many times before.

"It's not your fault," Mitchell said. "These things happen." Mitchell really believed this, but he knew that to Tafleski his words must have sounded like empty platitudes.

"Frank was such a great guy, Mr. Dobrinski. Followed the straight and narrow all the way. Why is it that the good die young, and scum like, like, well like John O'Dwyer and his gang of thugs live long and multiply? You know, that same night Frank told us that earlier in the day O'Dwyer had come to see him about a contract for some highway improvement. Offered him a great deal of money to go with a particular construction company."

"And?" Mitchell asked, with practiced journalistic calmness.

"He refused, of course. That was Frank."

Sarah gasped. "O'Dwyer tried to bribe him the day of the drowning? That's unbelievable . . . O'Dwyer must be our man. But, why, may I ask, did you wait so long to spring this on me?"

"If you don't know by now, Sarah, I enjoy a bit of suspense."

"I'm up to here with suspense," she said, raising her hand far above her head. "Anything else you're keeping from me?"

Mitchell shook his head. "Only that Tafelski didn't seem resentful over the Kumler appointment. Disappointed, yes. No one in the Polish community had been happy about O'Donnell's choice, he said. Nick Walinksi would have made a terrific commissioner and was a great friend to the judge. But they understood politics. O'Donnell must have had his reasons. The Westfalls had a similar response. From what I could surmise, even Mrs. Westfall, with pictures of her husband filling every nook and cranny of her living room, had never questioned the cause of his death. And she certainly didn't hold any grudges. 'For whom are you going to vote for Probate Judge?' I asked her. 'O'Brien O'Donnell, of course,' she answered without hesitation. 'I pray for his recovery every day.'"

Mitchell then said that it looked like the nightmare, Sarah's as well as the judge's, might be just about over. As soon as he himself had a little talk with O'Dwyer, that is. The man would be on his guard now, and Mitchell had experience with this kind of thing. If the cause were noble enough, he wasn't beyond a bit of blackmail himself. The threat of a reporter itching for a scoop could be quite persuasive.

"I suppose so," Sarah said vaguely, as she fidgeted with a leaf that had drifted on her lap. More troubled than reassured by Mitchell's words, she stood and walked toward the lazy river. How could the source of so much pain be so peaceful? A smooth and glassy surface today. Rough and turbulent tomorrow. And beneath, who knew? *I am not what you supposed, but far different.*

When she returned to the bench where Mitchell sat watching her curiously, all that was left of the tortured leaf was a tiny, black stem. "I can't let you go to O'Dywer, Mitchell," she said, "I mean before I fill you in. It's only fair."

"Fill me in?" he repeated. "About what?"

"I didn't quite tell you everything that was in the letter. I had no intention of ever doing so. But since you're willing to take this risk with O'Dwyer, I must take another risk with you. Knowing that you'd be within your rights to ruin Obee for good."

When she was finished explaining about the drugs and the pregnancy, Sarah stared at the river in silence. Despite her own suspicions, as well as those, if one believed her hairdresser, of many others in the city, she still assumed Mitchell would be shocked. But all he said was, "I'm glad you told me, Sarah."

"You are?"

"Yes. It explains a great deal."

"Well, I couldn't let you take the Boss on unaware."

"You could, but you chose not to."

"Yes."

"I'm even more glad about that."

17

September 18th, Yom Kippur, the Day of Atonement. Last week on Rosh Hashanah, the book of life for the year 5684 was opened and this evening it would be sealed. In between, according to Jewish belief, God decided the fate of his children.

Who shall live and who shall die. The congregation was chanting those familiar lines as Sarah searched the pews for Tillie; she had promised she would join her after visiting Obee. Sarah usually went to high holiday services for the same reason she lit Sabbath candles: to honor her ancestors and participate in a cultural ritual. But after seeing how little Obee had improved, she considered some prayers might be in order as well.

The new synagogue was a modern structure of concrete and glass. Functional, but not inspiring. Shomer Imunim was a reformed congregation, meaning that it viewed Judaism as a dynamic, evolving faith. Here women and men sat together. Not so in the orthodox temples. There, amidst dark, weathered wood and unadorned walls, all practices were fixed. God's laws, according to this most hierarchal branch of the religion, were eternal, not some human invention that changed with the times. A trade-off, of sorts. The reformed temples had greater equality, but lacked the physical sense of the sacred that so many of the orthodox temples possessed. A place for the mind and body more than the spirit.

Sarah soon spied Tillie and hurried to the seat she had saved for her. "Better late than never," she whispered to her sister.

Tillie frowned. "More like just in time. You almost missed the shofar."

That would have in fact disappointed Sarah, but not for the same reasons as Tillie. To her sister, the annual blowing of the ram's horn was a literal communication with an attentive God. Failing to bear witness to this divine moment was not only disrespectful, it was dangerous. God was just, but He demanded adoration. To Sarah, the primitive sounds were more symbolic; representative of the eternal human longing to understand the mysteries of existence. Either way, the ritual was moving and an honor to the man—and, even here, it was always a man—selected to carry it out. Tonight was an especially emotional occasion because the performer was an amputee, an army commander who lost his right arm in the war. With the ram's horn poised in the crook of his left arm, he stood humbly before the waiting crowd as the rabbi chanted the introductory Hebrew plea. The tone that followed was rich and clear, the effect incantatory. Three lingering, ancient wails attempting to penetrate the heavens, with the final triumphant blow lasting so long that people found themselves gasping for air. When the sound finally ceased, not a dry eye could be found in the room. Tears of joy for the hopeful year the one-armed man had wrought.

Before breaking the day-long fast, the rabbi blessed the congregation and urged each member to fight hate with love. Antisemitism was a fact of life. Yes, the Ku Klux Klan was a growing threat. "But we as Jews cannot adopt the methods of our detractors. As always, we must serve as an example of peace and tolerance. *L'Shana Tovah*. Happy New Year."

Tillie took Sarah by the arm and headed for the buffet table laden with challah and grape juice. As they nudged their way through the crowd, several members tried to get Sarah's attention, probably due to their curiosity about Judge O'Donnell. No one, especially on this most holy of days, would dare show it overtly, however. The most they felt they could do without impunity was ask her to give him their best.

Sarah said she would be happy to pass on their well wishes for the judge, but she had no intention of addressing their unspoken questions. Today might be a holiday, but tomorrow there would be nothing to prevent their jaws from getting back to business. It was, after all, another year until the book was opened again. By then God might very well forget.

Hopefully, such questions would soon disappear altogether. Mitchell's meeting with O'Dywer was presumably over. If things went according to plan, she would soon be able to give her dear, sick friend the news, the only news, she now believed, that would aid in his recovery. At the hospital, Obee hadn't seemed nearly as agitated, but in a way that was more disturbing. She would rather he be agitated than as apathetic as he appeared, especially since Dr. Miller told her once again that in his current state the possibility of shock therapy loomed larger.

"Are you coming?" Tillie asked as she started for the exit. The crowd had begun to thin out, and Tillie needed to get home to attend to the holiday feast.

"I need to make a quick stop by the courthouse," Sarah said. "You go on home, and I'll be there before the meal is ready."

"But Sarah—"

"Now, dear, you know I'm a working woman. All I'm going to do is check tomorrow's schedule." And before her sister could protest further, Sarah kissed her on the cheek and was off.

In truth, work had nothing to do with her abrupt departure. She and Mitchell had planned for him to call her at her office at 7:30 and the time was now 7:15. They decided this would be a good place to communicate since it was close to the synagogue, and at this hour, the building would be empty. Had it not been for Tillie, they would have met in person. But Sarah dare not make other plans on the holiday. The world might be coming to an end, but if provoked, her sister could make life so miserable it wouldn't matter.

Sarah reached the courthouse in a matter of minutes. It was dark, but the building was well-lit, making it easy for her to find the pass key in her purse. The unlocking procedure required three steps. She inserted the key and quickly accomplished the first two. Midway though the third, however, something made her stop.

"What was that?" she said aloud. She looked around. Nothing. It wasn't really a noise. More like a sensation. She shook herself.

Ridiculous. She repeated the unlocking procedure and was just about done when once more she stopped. A thumping noise. Footsteps?

"What in the . . . ?" My God, yes, someone was there all right, but there was no way to see, no time to think. Was this another nightmare? Unfortunately, no. Instantly someone grabbed her. A cloth sealed her mouth and gloved hands forced her to the ground. What felt like the barrel of a gun was pushed into the small of her back. She was ordered to stand up and march into an area of thick brush hidden from the street.

She could hardly breathe. Pain seared through her knees from hitting a concrete step. Who was it? The force with which she was being restrained suggested a man . . . a large man. But when the person spoke, the tone was so muffled she couldn't be sure. The voice sounded strangely distant, too, as if transported through time as well as space. With tears welling up in her eyes, Sarah thought of the shofar. Was this her punishment for pondering the universe when God was waiting for her to beg forgiveness?

"Now, Miss Kaufman. We're going to have a little chat. Only I'm going to do all the talking. You understand?"

She nodded. If she'd had any doubt that this was not a random attack, the familiar address put it to rest.

"You're lucky, you know that, little lady? You know why? You know *why* I say!"

She shook her head.

"Because I'm giving you a warning this time. Your *only* warning."

She strained to hear something recognizable in the voice. Nothing. The masking device, whatever it was, worked. It would have disguised a voice as familiar as her own.

"Now, listen to me carefully. I want you to stay the hell out of this business with the judge. Do you hear? Forget it entirely. That is, if you want you and your perverted little family to live. You understand?"

Again she nodded.

"You Jews are always causing trouble. What you need is to be taught a lesson."

The person pressed closer. His hot breath swept the back of her neck. A vaguely familiar, heavy musky scent filled her nostrils.

"Perhaps if you had something between your legs now and then, you might not be so restless. I would take care of that myself . . . if you didn't have horns." He touched her hair lasciviously and then withdrew in an exaggerated gesture of disgust. "I must say, you do a good job of hiding them."

She pushed down the bitter taste that was rising in her mouth. At least her stomach was empty.

"Now, in a minute I'm going to leave. What I want you to do is count slowly to a hundred before turning around. You understand? And remember what I've said. Stay out of this business, or you'll regret it. Today your God has spared you. Next time your fate will be in my hands."

One . . . two . . . three . . . the heavy footsteps trailed off and by the time she reached one hundred were gone. For a few minutes she stood motionless, afraid to trust her own ears. When finally she had the courage to move, she instinctively started running, her purse somehow undisturbed dangling on her arm, the cloth still stuffed in her mouth.

Tillie screamed as she burst through the door.

Fortunately, she looked worse than she was. A lump on her forehead and a few minor cuts here and there. A small nick on her lip had made her injuries appear more serious. The bleeding from this area was profuse, staining the handkerchief that was now hanging limply around her neck a shockingly bright red.

Sarah put up no resistance as her sister cleaned her wounds and fed her some broth. She might have been a grown woman, but at this moment she was in desperate need of some mothering. In this detective business she was a child, a beginner, an amateur. How dangerous that could be. To herself as well as to those she loved. The vicarious experience of reading was one thing. As Holmes lay injured in the Scottish moors or a darkened alley, she could close the book and walk away. But now she was a real victim, and whoever had attacked her had threatened her family as well. If anything happened to them . . . she let out a moan.

"What's hurting you, dear?"

"Nothing, Til. I'm just so sorry about all this."

"Sorry? Certainly you're not to blame for what happened. You didn't ask to be robbed."

Knowing Tillie's capacity for worry, Sarah had told her that she was the victim of an attempted theft. The attacker only wanted money, she said, and when he found none, ran away. She never saw who it was.

"Shouldn't we call the police?" Tillie had asked.

No, that would be pointless. She doubted if the person was still in town. The main thing was that she was safe.

"Yes," Tillie said, "thank God."

Her story completed, Sarah hugged her brother, who had already resumed his meal, and told Tillie she was going to bed.

"Is there anything else I can do for you dear?"

"No. I just need some rest."

"Good night then, Sarah," Tillie said. "I love you."

Sarah smiled faintly. "I love you, too," she replied. And she meant it. She did love her sister and brother both. Tremendously. Yet, as she fell into bed, exhausted, in pain, and still in disbelief over the evening's horrific events, she was struck by the infrequency with which during the course of her life she had uttered those achingly simple words.

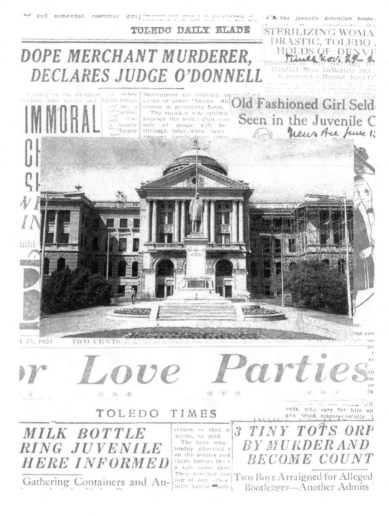

18

"Cause of Death: Accidental Drowning." Mitchell read that line once more before replacing Frank Westfall's death certificate in the court files. O'Dwyer said he had fifteen minutes this morning that he could "generously" spare. In an imperious tone, he had commanded

210

Mitchell to be at his office on time. Fifteen minutes to perform his mission. Quite a challenge considering he was not yet clear of his course. Better stop by county records. Before taking a path of potentially no return, he had to make absolutely certain of this one fact: "Cause of Death: Accidental Drowning."

He left the building with those words imprinted on his brain, and with a half an hour to spare, walked across the street to the courthouse. He was interested to see what Sarah would have to say for herself. Why hadn't she answered the phone last night? He thought this matter was important. Not that he'd really had anything to report. All he was going to tell her, in fact, was that O'Dwyer postponed their appointment until today. She had probably underestimated her holiday obligations. Still, it was inconsiderate.

But though it was already 9 a.m., Sarah had not yet arrived for work. Had she called in? No. When do you expect her? Soon.

"Shall I give her a message, Mr. Dobrinski?"

"No, thank you." Mitchell glanced at his timepiece. Surely the holiday celebrating had concluded by now. He would have to call her later. "Women!" he muttered to himself as he left. Just as he was about to put himself on the line again. Just when he was beginning to believe in the highly improbable chance that she was different.

"All right Mr. Dobrinski, the clock is ticking."

O'Dwyer was sitting at his desk, drumming his fingers impatiently. The man looked troubled. Dark circles deepened under his filmy, bloodshot eyes.

"Then I'll get right to the point, sir. I've been working on a story, about the contest for county commissioner in 1915."

O'Dwyer stopped drumming. "What about it?"

"As I say, I'm writing a story and have been reading some of the old news accounts. Your name comes up frequently, Mr. O'Dwyer. And not always in a, how should I put it, complimentary fashion. I was wondering if you might shed some light on the matter for me."

"Hey, what is this anyway?" O'Dwyer bolted up out of his chair. His red face blanched. "I see that conniving little woman has gotten you to do her bidding. Well, let me tell you something. I had nothing to say to her and I'll say nothing—"

"I have information," Mitchell lied. "About the supposedly accidental drowning. I intend to print it, too, if you don't retract your threat."

"Threat? What threat? What the devil are you talking about?"

"Come on, O'Dwyer. Does a letter to a certain colleague of yours ring a bell? Think about it. And think about this, too. I can destroy your already questionable reputation with a headline."

O'Dwyer laughed nervously. "You've either been spending too much time reading comic books or you're insane. Get out! Get out before—"

"All right. I'll go. But I mean what I say. I'll give you twenty-four hours to reply. You can reach me at *The Blade*.

Well, I'll never make it in the movies, Mitchell thought as he walked toward the courthouse. O'Dwyer had something there. I sounded like a character out of *Dick Tracy*. No, there would be no curtain calls, but he was nevertheless pleased with the results of his performance. O'Dwyer was clearly shaken. It wouldn't be long before the man would heed his warning.

To be seen at the courthouse again would be a bit risky, but Mitchell couldn't wait to tell Sarah the good news. Surely, she'd be in by now. But when he reached her office, the receptionist told him that Sarah had called in sick . . . again. "It's a good thing, too, the woman said. She needs a break."

"Will she be in tomorrow?" he asked.

"I'm not sure."

He started to ask what was wrong with her when the phone on the woman's desk rang. The call would apparently require her extended attention because she started thumbing frantically though some files and waved him off. He turned and walked dazed toward the exit. Sarah couldn't be sick. What the hell was she up to? He was halfway down the stairs pondering this question when the secretary called out his name. She was out of breath when she reached him.

"Mr. Dobrinski, I almost forgot. Sarah wanted me to give you a message. She said you'd understand."

The woman ran back up the stairs. With mounting excitement, he unfolded the small piece of paper. As he read the terse lines, however, his face dropped. "All bets are off," it said. "Thank you very much for your efforts."

Sarah was wrong. He did *not* understand. Not at all. But he'd be damned if he wasn't going to very soon.

19

"Tillie," Sarah said, "someone's at the door."

Tillie hurried in from the kitchen, wiping her hands on her flour-coated apron. She opened the tiny, peep hole. "Who is it?" she asked, gripping the door tightly.

"Miss Kaufman?"

"Yes?"

"I'm Mitchell Dobrinski. I'm a friend of Sarah's."

"Sarah's not well, sir. You'll have to call on her another time."

"Can you please open the door a little, ma'am? I'd like to talk to you."

"No. I have to go now."

"Please, Miss Kaufman. This is important."

"It's all right, Til," Sarah said, "you can let him in."

"Maybe he's the thief," Tillie whispered to Sarah.

"No, I don't think so. Go ahead, dear. Let him in."

Tillie reluctantly moved to one side and opened the door.

"Come in sir. Sarah is really in no position to receive visitors, as you can see for yourself. But I know better than to argue with her."

Tillie limped off into the kitchen. Sarah was lying on the sofa in a bathrobe, her hair loose around her shoulders. Not exactly dressed for company. Mitchell reddened.

"You shouldn't have come, Mitchell. Didn't you get my message?"

"Yeah, I got it. But I must say I was—"

The sun shone through the window straight onto Sarah.

"What in the hell! Sarah, what happened to you?"

Sarah attempted a calm response, but found it impossible to suppress her emotions. The question prompted a flood of tears.

Mitchell sat down, put his arms around her and asked the question again, "What happened, Sarah?"

With tears streaming down her face, she looked at him curiously but did not immediately pull away. Instead, she let herself feel the comfort of the embrace as she conveyed the events of the previous night. When Mitchell told her what had occurred between him and O'Dwyer, it wasn't hard for them to put two and two together.

"But why did you give me that message, Sarah? All bets are off? It doesn't make sense, when the identity of our blackmailer seems certain."

Tillie came in with some tea. She shifted her stunned gaze from one to the other, laid down the pot, and silently left the room.

"What I didn't tell you," Sarah continued, when she was certain Tillie was out of hearing range, "was that O'Dwyer, or I should say the man who attacked me, also threatened my family. And that, Mitchell, is where I draw the line. Blood is, as they say, thicker than water. My sister and brother come before even Obee."

Mitchell nodded. "Listen Sarah, I know I don't have the right to intrude on such a private decision, but before you give up entirely, would you let me have one more crack at it? I won't wait for O'Dwyer to contact me. I'll pay him another visit today. And, if that doesn't work, you may do as you wish."

"But, what will you say to him?"

"You leave that to me."

Sarah sighed deeply. Maybe it was his persistence, maybe it was because he had proven himself reliable. Or maybe, she hesitated to admit, she simply wanted to see him again. The idea annoyed her. How could she even have such thoughts with everything she knew about him? She was obviously not in her right mind.

"All right, one more crack."

Mitchell reached over to her again and gently touched the cut on her lip. He moved closer, but Sarah instinctively drew back. Right mind or not, she knew better than to encourage something for which she was clearly not ready.

"Please Mitchell. Let's keep this—"

"Sorry, I just thought—"

"I know. I'm sorry, too. I didn't mean to mislead you. I was just feeling a little vulnerable."

216

Mitchell shook his head. "All right, Sarah. From now on, we keep this strictly professional. That is what you were about to say, wasn't it?"

"Yes. I think it would be better."

Mitchell ran his hand through his tangled hair melodramatically and stood up. "Fine. I'll talk to you after I see O'Dwyer then. Goodbye."

"Mitchell," Sarah called out as he was opening the door, "you know I do appreciate all you're doing. I know it will pay off in a story."

"It better," Mitchell grumbled, and turned and walked out.

TOLEDO DAILY BLADE

STERILIZING WOMA
RASTIC, TOLEDO
OLDS OF DENVE

DOPE MERC
DECLARES

Wilson Paid
Toledo Visit
in July, 1916

ioned Girl Seld
the Juvenile C

IMMORAL
CHILDREN
SHOCKING
WHITE S
IN JUVE

Spoke for 15 Minutes at Union Station on His Only
Appearance Here.

Woodrow Wilson was in Toledo
only 15 minutes while he was chief
executive of the United States. He
stopped here for a short speech at
the Union station on Monday, July
10, 1916, at 4:25 o'clock.

Fifteen hundred Toledoans greeted the president. He had been to
Detroit to address the World's Sales-
manship Congress. Congressman
Sherwood, Frank B. Niles and
George Parrish, then postmaster, arranged for the surprise visit of President Wilson and met the presiden-
tial party in Detroit.

Mr. Wilson was advocating his
preparedness policy at the time of
his Toledo visit. Congressman Sherwood took exceptions to his policy
in introducing him. The president
came back with a rap at Sherwood
and received the applause of the
crowd.

John A. O'Dwyer was the only
citizen to get a personal interview
with Mr. Wilson while the special
train was in Toledo railroad yards.
He told the president that Toledo
was with him in his preparedness

hild Under Sixteen
History of Lit

MILK BO'
RING JUV
HERE INFORMED

Gathering Containers and An-

Y TOTS ORP
URDER AND
BECOME COUNT

Two Boys Arraigned for Alleged
Bootlegger——Another Admits

20

Everything, even his ashtray, was gone. No typewriter, no
phone, the drawers had been emptied, the desktop wiped clean.

"What in Christ's name is this about?" Mitchell demanded,
after storming into Steven Marks' office.

Steven didn't look up from his newspaper. "You're fired."

"I'm what?"

"You *heard* me," he said. "I warned you, Mitch." You can pick up your final check along with your belongings in Personnel."

"I think I'm due a bit more of an explanation, Mr. President."

Steven glowered at Mitchell. "Think what you like. You're fired. And now, if you'll excuse me, I've got work to do."

Mitchell would have grabbed the man by the throat mobster fashion if he thought it would have done any good. Instead, he asked the question to which he already knew the answer. "Does Mr. John O'Dwyer per chance have anything to do with this?"

"Who? O'Dwyer? I don't know what you're talking about, Mitch. Now, like I said, I'm busy. I heard *The Bee* is looking for writers. Why don't you try them?"

"If I do, you'll regret it."

Steven snickered. "I'll not worry too much, Mitch, considering *The Bee*'s audience. You know as well as I do that they don't care if what they're reading is fact or fiction."

"You know, Steve," Mitchell said contemptuously, "looking like a great man can only go so far. At some point, you have to show yourself worthy of the respect you think that random act of fate gave you the right to demand."

With every eye in the newsroom upon him, Mitchell marched determinedly toward Personnel, offered no goodbyes, and exited the building with one burning desire: to bring down the man responsible for creating all this havoc.

"O'Dwyer, you bastard!" he shouted, as he forced his way into the office he had been thrown out of only a few hours before.

"Mr. Dobrinski. Twice in one day. But I don't think we had an appointment."

"Get off it, O'Dwyer. You know why I'm here."

"I think I shall have to call the police," O'Dwyer said, his thick, freckled finger already on the receiver.

"Go ahead. We can talk to them together."

O'Dwyer had nothing to gain by taking Mitchell up on his challenge. But without concrete evidence, neither did Mitchell. Chief Dodd, after all, had participated in the unspoken "hands-off O'Donnell" policy. It was a stretch to assume that he would condone this level of evil, but the web of corruption undoubtedly ran deep; at the very least he would surely take O'Dwyer's word over his. Therefore, it would be to Mitchell's benefit at this point to keep the cops out of it. But he wasn't about to let O'Dwyer know that. He continued, aware of the fine line he walked.

"I'm sure the police would be interested to learn of your latest deed. You know, it was clever of you to disguise your voice, but that cloth you shoved in Sarah's, uh, I mean, Miss Kaufman's mouth. I don't know much about forensics, still I wonder if it might reveal something. Perhaps you forgot about it."

O'Dwyer screwed up his plethoric face into a look of confused disgust.

"Dobrinski, what in the hell are you talking about?"

"Let me refresh your memory. Last night? The courthouse? Miss Kaufman? Violence! Shall I go on?"

"You're talking in riddles. Speak your mind, man!"

"You attacked Miss Kaufman last night, did you not?"

"Attacked Miss . . . you really are crazy. Why would I?"

"Why? Okay, O'Dwyer, I'll humor you. Because she knows about Frank Westfall. Because she knows that you wrote a vicious letter to a man to whom you profess your allegiance. Because she knows what you're trying to do!"

"What letter are you talking about?"

"The blackmail letter, you creep."

"To whom?"

Mitchell shook his head in exasperation. O'Dwyer was toying with him. Or was he? Just as Mitchell was about to tell him that he was not one of the gullible masses, that he'd had it with his games, he caught something in the man's eyes. Not their beady shape or faded color, but confusion; sincere confusion. The sight of it made his stomach turn. Although he would now admit that his interpretive powers had occasionally let him down, he didn't think he was wrong this time. The look was genuine. To be absolutely sure, he took a more direct approach.

"Do you deny that you were involved in the murder of Frank Westfall and that you sent a blackmail note to one of the other, shall we say, conspirators?"

"Murder! Conspirators? Blackmail?" O'Dwyer looked at Mitchell in utter disbelief before bursting into guttural laughter. "Is that what you're getting at? Is that what you really think?"

Mitchell desperately needed a cigarette. Something to calm him down. A wave of heat shot through his body. Sweat was dripping down his back. He took in a few deep breaths and tried to carry on as if his career and perhaps his relationship with Sarah did not depend on what happened in the next few minutes.

"You didn't think it was so funny when Miss Kaufman mentioned Westfall's name at the ball game. Or when I did earlier today. Why were you trying to bribe Westfall the night of his death? Why did you cancel our meeting last night? If there wasn't some truth to any of this, why did you get so upset? Upset enough to have me fired!"

O'Dwyer's laughter gradually died down. He covered his lower lip with his crooked, greyish teeth and nodded.

"Look Dobrinski, I'm a reasonable man. When you string those questions together like that, I can perhaps see how you could have reached your balled-up conclusion. But I'll tell you honestly, I have explanations for each of them. Not that they would necessarily satisfy your high ethical standards, but I can assure you they do not equal the crimes you accuse me of. And, I'd be willing to tell you, too, for a—"

"For a price?"

"Well, yes, in manner of speaking. I was thinking of it more as a deal."

Great. Another deal.

Both men were standing up, eyeing each other cautiously. "Do you want to hear my offer then?"

Not waiting for a response, O'Dwyer moved closer to Mitchell and spoke in a low, confidential tone. "My explanation—and perhaps even my assistance with whatever you and Miss Kaufman have obviously gotten yourselves into—for your silence . . . and the return of your job."

Mitchell smiled cynically. "So you did call Steven."

"Oh yes, that's one accusation I cannot deny. Now, what do you say, Mr. Dobrinski?" O'Dwyer said, offering Mitchell a chair.

Mitchell remained standing for a few moments. He owed it to Sarah to at least hear the man out. If O'Dwyer was telling the truth, they would be back to square one, with the election drawing nearer every day. She would want to be absolutely certain that "closing his door" was justified, since doing so would likely mean closing as well the door on O'Donnell's future. Mitchell, moreover, had more than just a passing interest in the matter himself, seeing as though his job might very well hinge on his willingness to listen. Thus, with a mixture of apprehension and curiosity, he asked O'Dwyer for a cigarette and sat down.

His own anxiety somewhat abated, O'Dywer clasped his hands behind his head and adopted the wistful look of a storyteller. "It all started with my father," he began. "A terrible, terrible injustice." The narrative that followed was something Mitchell could have never predicted. Edward O'Dywer was a police captain, who, at the turn of the century, was stripped of his command for no other reason than his religion. The APA, or Apes as the viciously anti-Catholic movement was called, assumed power and elected a completely new county and city ticket. Edward was one of its victims. Up until this time, the O'Dwyers had been Republican. But because the APA was in control of that party, the family became Democrats . . . ardent, powerful, sometimes ruthless Democrats.

Although Edward was eventually reinstated, he was never the same. And neither was his son. John, a young teenager at the time and an impressionable youth, loved his father dearly. The ordeal affected him profoundly, shaping his own attitudes about right and wrong. It was, as he said, "why he was the way he was." It made him willing to accept graft, to gamble, and to even occasionally cheat on his wife. "One kind of deceit invariably leads to another," he said, when Mitchell raised an eyebrow. It made him lose his faith in the inherent goodness of people. If a decent man, who upheld the law, could be removed from office because of another's bigotry, what was the point of following the straight and narrow? Yes, he stuffed ballots for Brown, but that was because a former APA member was running for the Democratic seat. Yes, he was against Walinski filling Westfall's vacancy, but that was because someone in the Walinksi family had also been an Ape. Walinski himself was a Catholic, but as far as O'Dwyer was concerned, one person was sufficient to mark the whole lot of them. And, yes, he had tried to bribe Frank Westfall, but who in Toledo didn't use such tactics now and then?

"But, Mr. Dobrinski," O'Dwyer stated firmly, "just because I see the world in shades of grey, doesn't mean I can't distinguish black from white. I have my limits. Blackmail is black; murder blacker still. And, while I admit to still having a roving eye, I would never strike a woman. You must know that I love women. In fact," he confessed, "it was because of a member of that delightful sex that I was forced to cancel our appointment last night."

Mitchell was amazed, not only by the details of the account, but by O'Dywer's ability to describe them in such philosophical, almost poetic terms. His grasp on his own psychology was startling. Still, why had he reacted to him and Sarah with such hostility? Why was he so defensive about Walter Brown, Westfall, and the rest? To this O'Dwyer also had an answer. It involved President Wilson's 1916 visit to Toledo, when he came to rally support for the war. Although all of the city's dignitaries were in attendance, O'Dwyer was the only one invited for a personal meeting with the president.

"Look it up," O'Dwyer said, his beefy chest puffing out. "Your paper covered the event. During that meeting, the President encouraged me to seek higher office. He planted the seed, and I've been tending it ever since. Can you imagine, Mr. Dobrinski, Wilson even offered to campaign for me!"

With that tantalizing prospect, O'Dywer was determined to change his ways, to be a good citizen, to mend fences, as he had recently done with Judge O'Donnell. He couldn't have predicted that after the war Wilson would fall into such disfavor that he would have been a liability rather than an asset to anyone associated with him. As indeed he was for James Cox, who Wilson predicted would win the presidency in a landslide. Nevertheless, O'Dywer still held onto the dream Wilson had sparked, believing that had Cox not been such a wishy-washy

Progressive, their fellow Ohioan, Republican Warren Harding, wouldn't be president now. Cox's running mate, Franklin Roosevelt, would have certainly had more luck.

O'Dwyer wasn't so bold as to consider running for president, not just yet anyway. A senate seat was good for a start. After that, who knew? Perhaps one day an Ohio Democrat would sit in the White House. But, these grand ambitions required an equally grand character. Local politics was one thing. The national scene demanded more from its leaders.

O'Dwyer said he'd worked hard to meet the challenge. His taste for women was the only thing he'd failed to sufficiently reform, but men, at least, usually forgave such weakness. Therefore, when Sarah and then Mitchell brought up his past, he panicked, thinking they somehow might know of his aspirations and for some reason want to prevent him from reaching them. Stuffing ballots for a Republican. How would it look? He was especially worried about the Westfall incident because during that period he'd had a rather profitable interest in the Pilliod breweries. "To be a pro-business Democrat, especially in the liquor industry," he said. "Well, that would spell the end."

"What about *The Blade*?" Mitchell asked. "How do you come to have such power over the management there?"

"Oh, that. They just do what's expedient. You know, there's a kind of unspoken agreement. No official conspiracy, Mr. Dobrinski, if that's what you're thinking. The paper just knows who butters its bread is all. That's the way things work in this town. You'll have an uphill battle if you want to change it."

"But having me fired seems like the kind of behavior you supposedly renounced, O'Dwyer. Not very senatorial."

O'Dwyer smirked. "Self-survival is the strongest instinct, Mr. Dobrinski. In that case, I felt my entire future in Toledo, not to mention the country as a whole, was threatened."

"So you threatened mine instead."

"Natural selection, sir. According to Mr. Darwin, you would do the same if you could."

This was an unexpected allusion to which Mitchell could summon no quick response.

"But look Dobrinski, I've just told you more than I ever have anyone else. Turn about's fair play, and I now have a couple of questions for you. How did you and Miss Kaufman ever come to think Westfall was murdered? And who in the devil is being blackmailed?"

O'Dwyer had been surprisingly open, that was true. But it was not up to Mitchell to say anymore.

"I'm sorry, but I'm not at liberty to go into that."

"You may not believe it, sir, but I can be quite discreet when need be."

"It's not that."

"Come on, I'd really like to know—"

"Drop it, O'Dywer."

"All right, all right. Suit yourself. But, as I said, if you need me—"

"As a matter of fact, I do have one request," Mitchell said sternly. That you demonstrate you can do what you claim; be discreet, and keep all this to yourself."

"As long as you do the same, sir. However," he added, grinning like the Cheshire cat, "I don't suppose you'd mind me talking to Steven Marks again."

Mitchell gazed unseeingly at an oversized picture of President Wilson hanging on the wall. "Perhaps at some point," he finally said. "But not now. I'm not extinct yet. Who knows, in another environment, I may thrive."

As proud of this comeback as Mitchell was, he would have never imagined that it would have led to a handshake. Yet, that's exactly how he left O'Dwyer's office, with a handshake and the belief that this completely unscrupulous individual was in fact telling the truth. Including what he'd suggested about *The Blade*. Though depressing to admit, based on Mitchell's own experience it made sense. The hands-off treatment of O'Donnell, his removal from the story, and so many other inexplicable decisions he had witnessed over the years were not single acts that one could expose and be done with. Rather, they were like filaments in a barely visible web, one that could only be viewed in a dim, sickly light. In the scheme of things, he was nothing more than window dressing, his much-touted journalistic integrity a thin patina overlaying the paper's insidious, illusive system of favors. The best one could hope for was to work as honorably as possible within that system and wait for the public to grow weary of its complicity in it.

And that is precisely what he would try to do if and when he allowed O'Dwyer to work his magic on Steven Marks. For the moment, however, he had a more pressing task ahead of him. O'Dywer had committed many of the deadly sins and no doubt broken even more of the Commandments, but the mandate not to kill wasn't one of them. Of that he was certain. Now he would have to convince Sarah that they still needed to figure out who was behind the letter. Whether or not a murder had occurred, someone was bent on O'Donnell's destruction and would apparently not let anyone stand in their way. No one, including her family, was safe with such a person on the loose. As for the police, Sarah would surely agree that if even a flicker of hope remained for the judge, calling them in would extinguish it for good. So what he would tell her was this: that she was mistaken to believe her family would be protected by turning the other cheek, that the only way to ensure their safety was to discover the culprit's identity and settle for nothing else than an eye for an eye.

When it came down to contacting her, however, Mitchell almost lost his nerve. Their last encounter had been humiliating. And depressing. Because the truth was, his motives for involving himself in this matter had become personal. Otherwise, he would have certainly broken their covenant by now. He was all for rooting out evil, of course, but he had no particular allegiance to O'Donnell. It was irresponsible of him not to have taken this story to the public already. But fight it as he may, Sarah had gotten under his skin. Indeed, foremost on his mind was not what she would feel about continuing their investigation, but how she felt about him. Apparently, what had occurred between them was only a passing moment, the arbitrary consequence of a traumatic experience. Pain and fear could make people do things they might later regret. She might very well look on their embrace now with embarrassment, or even disgust. He had thought that perhaps she was becoming a little fond of him, but God knows, he'd been wrong before.

His hopes were nevertheless slightly raised again when Sarah quickly agreed to meet him at his apartment. When he had finally summoned the courage to call her, he had joked, with obvious double-meaning, that he thought it was about time for her to see *his* room. A calculated move. By referring to her dream in a light-hearted way he sought to put her at ease and redirect her attention to the subject of which the call was ostensibly about. But Sarah apparently didn't need any rhetorical coaxing. She had been, as she put it, "waiting on the edge of her seat," and despite her increasingly visible bruises, would come immediately.

When she arrived less than an hour later, however, she acted as if nothing had happened between them at all. She was friendly enough, indeed she made her own joke about her rather alarming appearance. But the barrier around her was palpable.

21

On her way to Mitchell's, Sarah had a talk with herself. Probably Mitchell thought her a tease. If he knew what *she* had been thinking, however, he might not judge her so harshly. The threats she had received had thrown her own life into sharp focus, allowing her to see how time had left its mark. She had known Obee for years and had grown old, or at least older, waiting for something to happen. She had known Mitchell for only a few weeks and, despite her present condition, felt younger in his presence.

True, he was a reporter—an occupation she had often loathed and always distrusted. But there was nevertheless a kindness in the man, a soft center within the hard shell that had started to affect her own firm exterior. Upon reflection, she could see that her reaction to his attempted kiss was in part defensive. If she didn't care at all, she would have taken it as a compliment and let it go at that. However, she was also convinced that this was no time to let her emotions take over. Far too much was at stake. The safety of her family. Obee's health. Reelection. These required her undivided attention. Besides, she still had her concerns about Mitchell. Despite his general open-mindedness, the man had a deeply rooted negative attitude toward women such as herself, and one didn't get over that kind of conditioning quickly. Moreover, the two of them had come together artificially, under extraordinary circumstances. In such a state, it was easy to mistake one kind of feeling for another. Better to wait until this matter was resolved, when day-to-day life resumed to see if there was really anything to their attraction.

Keeping these realizations to herself, she entered Mitchell's apartment with the single-minded purpose of learning what had happened with O'Dywer. Her resolve to stay on task broke down a bit, however, when she looked around his meager, unadorned little flat, especially because he seemed embarrassed about it.

"I know it's not much," he said, but at least I now begin to understand Thoreau."

"Henry David?"

"The very one. Despite the beauty of Walden Pond, I could never fathom how he found such peace in that shack he lived in. But,

230

now, I do see how one's response to a place can change. Yesterday this room felt empty and oppressive. Today, it, well, it feels lighter. It's nice to have company."

Sarah was flattered by such a lofty comparison, but she recalled reading somewhere that Thoreau had been devastated over being rejected by Louisa May Alcott. Perhaps the author's reverence for a solitary life in the woods had been partially a case of sour grapes. She felt no need to share this thought with Mitchell, however, who had doubtlessly intended the remark as a compliment.

"That's a nice thing to say, Mitchell. But you know, this isn't a bad apartment. A coat of paint, and," she added, observing only a threadbare couch to sit on, "a few chairs would do wonders." She noticed several photographs scattered about the room. "Did you do these?"

"Uh, huh."

"Why do you grunt like that? They're wonderful."

As she picked one up, a bitter look briefly crossed his face. "You're one of the few who thinks so."

"Who doesn't?"

"It doesn't matter."

"Well, there's no accounting for taste," she said. "I envy you for having such a creative hobby."

"I used to think it might be more than that." Mitchell turned his head from side to side and framed her face with his hands. "I might think so again . . . if I had the right subject."

Sarah frowned. "Oh, no you don't. I've been photographed enough for one lifetime. The papers . . . especially *your* paper . . . won't leave me alone."

"Those aren't photographs, Sarah, they're mug shots."

"You mean they're not doctored. All the more reason to believe them. You know, Mitchell, some very smart woman once said that she was happier than most of her friends because after forty she stopped

231

looking in mirrors. I don't have that luxury. Even if I covered every mirror in my house, the papers would be there to throw my image back in my face. To date, they've documented each and every grey hair."

"Oh, come now. I've seen much younger women who can't hold a candle to you."

Much to her dismay, Sarah felt herself blushing.

"Don't worry," Mitchell said, "I won't take your picture if you don't want me to."

They continued on in this manner for a while, but inevitably things turned to their predicament. "Well?" Sarah asked after an uncomfortable moment of silence. Mitchell responded by telling her the whole story, about how he got fired and why he wasn't especially worried about it, why he believed O'Dwyer was not their guy, why he felt they needed to continue their search.

Sarah sighed deeply. "So, we're back to square one, then?"

"I suppose there are, in reality, a number of groups that could be behind this. The KKK, the Nativists—those bigots that pass themselves off as Progressives–even the Housewives League. Or from whomever the judge got his latest batch of drugs. Yet, considering how much the blackmailer knows, I still think it must be somebody closer."

"It was so naive to rely on my silly dream," she said, shaking her head.

"Oh, I don't know. It was a reasonable place to begin."

Frustrated, Sarah agreed that they couldn't stop their investigation now, that she had realized herself even before Mitchell's call that she couldn't let Obee down like that, though she still worried about her family.

"You must be hungry," Mitchell said. "It's nearly dinner time."

"I am, a little."

"I'll make us an omelette. And don't worry. It's just a meal between partners . . . business partners."

"All right. Thanks. As long as it's no trouble."

"No trouble at all. It's my speciality. Here's something to tide you over." He tossed her an apple. "Nothing like the first apples of fall."

Fall. So it was. Good God. Sarah took a bite. The apple was delicious, crisp and sweet. As she listened to the familiar sounds of someone cooking for her, her eyes fell on the file cabinet that Mitchell was using for a table. On it were stacks of *The Blade*. She took another bite and looked over at Mitchell whisking the eggs. It was, she had to admit, an endearing sight.

She glanced back at the papers. Perhaps. Yes, it was definitely worth a try.

"Mitchell, may I use your telephone?"

"Of course. It's over there," he said, pointing to another file cabinet. He watched her pick up the receiver and then poured the mixture of eggs, green pepper, and onion into the heated skillet.

"Hello, hello Elizabeth, may I speak to Mrs. O'Donnell, please? This is Sarah Kaufman."

"Why, she's not here Miss Kaufman."

"No?"

"I guess you haven't heard."

"Heard? Heard what?"

"Seems as though someone started a rumor that the judge is pulling outa the race. Caught hold like wild fire, ma'am. Nobody could find you, so the missus got all gussied up and went downtown to assure everyone that it wasn't true. She even called a meeting with the press. All on her own. I suppose she can handle things if she has to. Why don't you try her later?"

"Yes, yes I will," Sarah replied in a shaky voice. "Thank you, Elizabeth." She steadied herself against the wall.

"What is it, Sarah?"

Receiving no response, Mitchell turned down the gas on the stove, walked over to her and, encountering no resistance, put his hands on her shoulders. "Sarah, what is it?"

She remained silent.

"Sarah?"

"The serpent has struck again, Mitchell," she finally said. "He's struck again." Mitchell asked Sarah to explain, and when she was done, he nodded in agreement, took the remaining bit of apple from her trembling hand, and finished it himself.

22

Sarah immediately surmised that the person who started the rumor, who sent Obee the blackmail note, and who attacked her were one and the same. Mitchell agreed. He also agreed to her proposal: that they reexamine the scrapbooks. Sarah remembered she hadn't bothered to read one of them very carefully. At the time, she didn't think it necessary. But now that O'Dwyer was no longer a suspect, and the whole Westfall matter up in the air, it might be a worthwhile pursuit. If nothing else, to know she had exhausted this avenue of investigation would give her some measure of satisfaction.

Fortunately Winifred was amenable. Even though she still seemed uninterested in the details of Sarah's visit, she apparently was convinced of her good intentions. So much so, that she didn't even ask her to explain why she wanted to bring Mitchell along. "Of course," she said, upon receiving Sarah's call later that evening, "I trust you. Bring whomever you wish. I'll be at the hospital tomorrow, but Elizabeth will be here to let you in. Good luck Sarah, and thank you. I know you're doing everything you can."

If one positive thing had come out of this latest development, it was that it had given Winifred a purpose. Considering the upheaval in her own life, Sarah was happy to let the woman assume the role of the spokesman. It was, after all, right that she should finally do so. Whether from the love of her husband or the love of position, she had risen to the occasion, showing that she could ascend to the throne with formidable strength. Her comments to the press were the talk of the town and, more importantly, were, either willfully or in truth, believed.

"Who would know better than his beautiful wife?" *The Blade* asked somewhat obsequiously. "Wife says, O'Donnell still in!" *The Bee* exclaimed, no doubt relieved that they had not yet printed an article announcing the judge's certain withdrawal. Yes, Winifred apparently had a talent for subduing the press, and, having broken the ice with them, she would perhaps be better prepared to answer their inevitable questions about Margaret. If they believed her comments about Obee, they would be more inclined to do the same when she would tell them that although their daughter was advanced for her age, she was a sensitive child and needed a bit more time at home before making her public debut.

Winifred had, as Obee might have said, stepped up to the plate. But, like any rookie, in order to stay in the game, she would have to get a hit. She would have to deliver on her promise. Even if she had sworn on a Bible that her husband was the picture of health, the rumors would surface again if he didn't soon appear in the flesh. Sarah knew this better than anyone and therefore decided to put her idea into action immediately. With permission granted from a voice striking in its new self-assured tone, she found herself the next morning once again in Obee's study, this time with Mitchell by her side.

The scrapbook in question was the thinnest of the volumes. It was also the only one that appeared haphazard in its organization. When Sarah had scanned it before, it struck her as a catch-all for items Obee found insignificant or unworthy of permanent display. Randomly dated, some perhaps were duplicates or articles so close in content that they would have disrupted the narrative-like flow of the books. Some he may have been considering discarding. Several had frayed edges, a few were even ripped, many not yet glued in, such as a Western Union telegram announcing Margaret's birth. As Mitchell sifted through the volumes she had previously read, Sarah now scrutinized these piece by piece. "Okay," she commanded as if to a crystal ball, "speak to me."

Judge O'Donnell has a 'new nationalism,' long before Colonel Roosevelt appointed himself defender of the decalogue.

Even though Sarah knew this article was irrelevant, she couldn't help quickly reading the first few lines: "Judge O'Donnell has done pioneer work along many lines of civic reform. . . . Toledo is one of the first cities in the country to open day nurseries, where children of mothers compelled to go out of their homes to work could be given proper care. The first to ask for women inspectors of workshops and factories."

Irrelevant to Sarah's current pursuit, but true, and despite the urgency of moving on, she wondered again if history would record this as well as all of Obee's other great achievements. Would he ever get the recognition he deserved? Lesser men had received at least a footnote. But who made those decisions and the criteria they employed had always puzzled Sarah. Making war would guarantee a chapter in a school textbook, but beyond that she didn't have a clue.

Paperclipped to the article was a cartoon with the headline *Father Must Do Housework*. It depicted a man performing domestic chores with comical incompetence. Below was a description of what inspired the creation: "Men whose wives go out to work to support the family must attend to the household duties or go to jail. Judge O'Donnell said this would be the rule in juvenile court hereafter when men are brought before him charged with neglect. 'If you want your wife to work I'll fit you out with an apron and you can pitch in and do the housework, Judge O'Donnell told a defendant on Saturday.'"

A cartoon, but to Obee this was no laughing matter. And for that, too, he should be commended. Today people might take his idea for a joke, but perhaps in the future. Sarah looked over at Mitchell and tried to imagine him in an apron. It would suit him well.

Sarah read the next couple of headlines:

O'Donnell will speak at Suffrage Banquet; Tell Troubles to O'Donnell, new slogan. She then perused a bit of the next article. "How does it feel to be the only survivor of your party when all others go down in a landslide to the opposition? To have come through with a plurality that keeps pace with the big figures by which your political co-workers went down to defeat? Probate Judge O'Brien O'Donnell says it is 'very, very gratifying.' And, the judge added, 'It makes one feel a deep sense of duty to the community made up of those voters.'"

"Find anything, Sarah?"

"No. Not yet. How 'bout you?"

"Nothing you hadn't already mentioned. Why don't we take a break? The aroma of that stuff is making me weak."

"I thought you'd never ask," Sarah said. This was a friendly exchange; she could keep Mitchell at arm's length, and still be congenial. If nothing else, working together this way was much easier. "Elizabeth has outdone herself today," she continued. "Muffins and scones. Tea and coffee. Which do you prefer?"

"Hmm, I think I'll have tea for a change," Mitchell replied, already sampling the baked goods.

How odd, Sarah thought, as she poured the tea with what an onlooker might have misinterpreted as wifely expertise, to be here in Obee's study with this relative stranger. Very odd, but she was nevertheless feeling something of what Mitchell had described yesterday. A kind of spacial transformation. For him, it had been the cramped quarters of his apartment. For her, it was a room that only days before had been alive with painful memories. The familiar objects were of course still there, in the same configuration. But the longing for what they had represented was fading. It was, as he had said, nice to have company. Whether Mitchell's company in particular was producing this effect, however, she wasn't prepared to say.

The first item she saw when she returned to the journal was a news photo of Obee's eyes. A caption underneath asked, "Whose eyes? Usually he wears glasses and these eyes blink repeatedly. Can you identify him?"

Of course. Sarah knew them as well as her own. Or at least she used to think she did. Those eyes were so many things, intelligent, generous and open, and yet, as she now knew, at times she had misread them, times when Obee had intentionally obscured their meaning. The article she turned to next reminded her that there were also things from which Obee believed the eyes should be shielded.

Essentially, the piece was a rant against the nickel picture shows. Although Sarah didn't agree with him, she knew the argument well. "It would open your eyes," Obee said to a group of parents who apparently had also been using their organ of sight improperly, "if you would but realize the condition that exists right here in our own city. The theaters are the ruination of many boys and girls of Toledo, and if I can find where one of these places is guilty to contributing to the delinquency of a child, I'll get them."

Next was a speech Obee had given on drama.

"Every performance is a lesson. Purify and elevate the drama. Don't degrade the morals and tastes of humanity. After the good lesson in drama, you depart breathing sweetness, loveliness and purity. After the lesson in which morality is assailed, and lewdness parading hand in hand with immoral suggestions to the coarse music, the lesson has injured you. There is a bad taste, and you depart, sorely in need of a strong disinfectant."

"Very Platonic," Sarah remembered telling Obee. "And inconsistent, too. For you advocate reading just about anything. How is drama different?" To which Obee responded, "Books improve mental skills and use the imagination! Drama is spoon-fed, my dear."

That didn't really answer her question, but Sarah had let it drop. Just as she had done when he'd made comments like the one she now read.

"In order to make their education more worthwhile, it is necessary for the Modern American Boy to get back to a simpler form of existence, to resist the encroachments that the unnatural amusements are making upon his time and attention."

Unnatural amusements. What did Obee mean by that exactly? The term invoked a disquieting echo, a memory of her past suspicions, which she tried to suppress by turning to the next page. Here was a cartoon depicting an event for the Newsies held at Toledo Beach. The attached article stated that "Judge O'Brien O'Donnell offered two dollars for the boy who had the courage to say no when tempted to do a dishonorable act. But the prize ended up going to O'Donnell himself for saying no when being urged to take a dip in the water." Sarah remembered this because she was one of the many who did the urging. "He said no so many times that he was awarded the prize," she was quoted as saying.

Why was swimming dishonorable? The echo grew louder. Why did Obee resist it so?

Perhaps if she read on. No, probably not. This next piece was part of a regular, banal little column entitled *Blithesome Sketches About People You Know*.

"In the beginning of things, every male person in Gael was a monarch. By the time Gael became Ireland—about the time St. Patrick was driving out the snakes—the doctrine of the survival of the fittest working thru the medium of the shillalah, had reduced the royal houses to two: the O'Donnells and the O'Briens. Being equally fit, they both insisted on surviving."

The suggestion? That Obee, being of royal lineage through and through, was destined by nature to be a great leader. The author in fact went on to say as much, noting in particular the judge's ability to lead the juvenile court without the benefit of having children himself, "being a bachelor—tho Lord only knows why."

Sarah was just about to ask Mitchell if he thought the writer could really have been serious about this shillalah business when she noticed that wedged in-between this article and the next was a letter that appeared to offer an opinion on that very topic. Typewritten on pale blue letterhead from The Toledo Machine and Tool Company, the single-paged little epistle, dated Nov. 14, 1910, was addressed to "My dear friend" and signed by a Henry J. Hinde. Initially it struck Sarah as a joke, as tongue in cheek as the article seemed itself. But as she reread it, she began to think otherwise. It wasn't so much what this fellow Hinde said, but how he said it.

"My own father was a direct descendent of one of the first and foremost so-called Irish Kings from the Galway Section in the county of the same name Ireland. It would not be possible to excel the way my father handled this weapon. The memory is one that will remain long with us. I expect and presume that you will on receipt of this immediately recognize that there was at least one other kingly family in Ireland besides the O'Briens and O'Donnells."

Sarah shook her head in disbelief. Amazing. No, not even a trace of humor here. This man was really offended.

"Mitchell you've got to see—"

"What?"

"Wait, wait just a minute," she said, raising her hand like a cop in traffic.

"What is it Sarah?"

"Shhh!"

This time Mitchell obeyed.

"I agree with the historian in one part and that is the absolute mystery of the facts as to why you remain a bachelor. Our mutual friend, Danny Nolan, however, may throw some light on this subject."

To what did that refer? Obviously, to the part in the sketch that referred to Obee's bachelorhood: "tho Lord only knows why." According to Mr. Hinde, the author of that line was wrong; at least one other human being also possessed that knowledge.

Our mutual friend, Danny Nolan, may throw some light on this subject.

242

A specific name, but enigmatic words. Alarming in their vagueness. Sarah sensed that in these terse lines was in fact embedded the real purpose of the letter. Henry Hinde. Who was he anyway? Sarah had never heard of him. Had he harbored some sort of grudge? The tone suggested as much. Subtly threatening.

Our mutual friend, Danny Nolan, may throw some light on this subject.

What kind of light? Soft or harsh? A ray of truth or a blinding beam? However the symbol was intended, it sparked in her a familiar uneasiness, a feeling that reminded her somehow of her dream, of the echo, of something illusive around which she could still only partially form her thoughts. She shivered, and not because of the wind that had picked up outside.

"Mitchell, do you know a Henry Hinde or Danny Nolan?"

"Hinde, Hinde. No, don't think I do. But Danny Nolan. I can't place him exactly, but the name sounds familiar. Why? What do you have there, Sarah?"

Sarah answered Mitchell more cryptically than she intended. She valued precision in language, yet here it seemed that the words to describe her suspicions were just out of reach. She told herself that it was because the meaning of the letter itself was so murky. She was looking for something denotative to describe something that was connotative at best.

"Well then," Mitchell said, "we need to pay them a visit. I'm pretty sure Toledo Machine and Tool went out of business a few years ago. But we can find out . . . Nolan, Nolan. I know!" Mitchell said sitting upright. "I know! I know where I've heard of Danny Nolan. He was part of that human rights group. I covered their convention for the paper just a few months ago."

"Human rights? What kind of human rights?" Sarah asked slowly.

"Well, you know, for men who don't care for women. Inverts. Homosexuals. Remember? They had a meeting in Chicago."

She widened her eyes and blanched. She could barely hear for the echo.

"Sarah, what's wrong? You looked shocked. Like you've seen the proverbial ghost." Mitchell smiled mischievously. "It couldn't be prejudice? Some moral objection?"

"Prejudice! Of course not. No. No, it's not that."

What it was, though, she wasn't sure. She did remember reading about that convention. But this was one cause in which she had never involved herself. She wished these people well, but it was not her battle. Or so she'd come to believe. Now she felt confused, as though suddenly immersed in a fog that she thought had already lifted. Just when she assumed the sky had cleared, she turned a corner and encountered an even thicker pocket. Hadn't these questions had been put to rest with Obee's marriage?

"I just don't understand how this could pertain to Obee, Mitchell. I mean, I used to think perhaps . . . but he did finally marry. And he fathered a child."

Mitchell listened and tried to decipher her code. "You mean, you thought the judge was homosexual? Why didn't you tell me?"

"I don't know what I think. Only this letter touches on something I've sensed before; something I suppose I've chosen not to confront. But now perhaps I must. If I'm not mistaken, this letter is a threat. And, if someone threatened Obee before, they might be inclined to do so again. So whatever it is, I'm in it now. It may very well be that this matter has its roots even further back than I imagined."

Mitchell lit a cigarette. Between puffs he massaged his forehead.

"We still have a deal, don't we?" Sarah asked.

"Of course."

244

She smiled and stopped just short of giving him a grateful hug. "Good, then let's go."

"Go? Mitchell raised his eyebrows inquisitively.

"To the past, Mitchell, to the past once again."

23

It was the uncertainty of it all, Sarah reasoned, that made her feel as though she'd lost her bearings. What could they possibly know about Obee? There was Margaret, after all, living proof of his disposition. Wasn't a person either this or that? Weren't these kinds of things mutually exclusive? In this area, Sarah had always thought so. She looked at the journal still in her hands and wondered. Maybe these items had an order after all. An order that couldn't be easily categorized, but an order nonetheless. One that perhaps had begun to reveal itself the first day she had come to Obee's study, when she witnessed those two opened books.

I am not what you supposed, but far different.

The words returned to her with force. Just because these articles weren't bound didn't mean they lacked a logic. Here possibly was a genre all its own, one that was just not rigidly drawn. Sarah thumbed through them again. The dangers of the nickel picture shows, the refusal to go swimming—what was that other line from Whitman? *Was it doubted that those who corrupt their own bodies conceal themselves?* The warning about things "unnatural." And now, this letter.

Our good friend, Danny Nolan, may throw some light on this matter.

The echo sounded again, prompting her to remember something strangely coincidental. The reason Conan Doyle ultimately failed in his attempt to save Sir Roger Casement's life was because of a diary that was found detailing the man's homosexuality, a crime that to many was far more despicable than being a traitor. Doyle had refused to condemn such behavior, an action that purportedly cost him a seat in the House of Lords. At the time Sarah had read about it, she had admired him greatly for not abandoning his friend, for supporting him until the end. Now, in a twist of what Doyle himself might call metaphysical fate, she was being put to a similar task. Once more she heard the echo. But this time, having applied the kind of reason even Holmes might have admired, she was willing to listen to its message: walk through the fog, it said, and follow me to my source.

The official objective of the organization to which Danny Nolan belonged was "to promote and to protect the interests of people who by reasons of mental and physical abnormalities are abused and hindered in the legal pursuit of happiness which is guaranteed them by the Declaration of Independence, and to combat the public prejudices against them by dissemination of facts according to modern science among intellectuals of mature age." The Reverend John T. Graves, president of the group, read that line from their 1924 charter to Mitchell and the other reporters covering their convention in Chicago. After Graves left, Danny Nolan remained to answer their questions.

"Mr. Nolan, how can it be that a reverend is the president of your group? His behavior . . . it is an affront to God, is it not? An abomination?"

"I know some find it so," Nolan replied in a voice that was deeper than everyone expected. "But," he added evenly, "Reverend Graves believes he was created in God's image as well. God loves all his children, or so the Bible says."

Mitchell was one of the few who smiled at this quick response. He liked Nolan's verve. A man of about fifty. Well-dressed, but not foppish in the least. Tall, of medium build, he appeared altogether average in his dark blue suit. Altogether masculine, too. That, in fact, may have been why Mitchell's learned colleagues seemed so on edge.

"Just how are you folks so abused, Mr. Nolan? You have your streets, your clubs, the baths. Everyone knows about them. Why do you need more?"

"Well, sir," Nolan replied rubbing his cleft chin, "I'll give you an example. An engineering student I knew was arrested for doing what came naturally to him. He was a smart boy, a kind person, the son of a college professor. But at the police station he shot himself. Why? Because he knew the contempt he would receive from his fellow students, the shame he would bring to his family, simply for being himself. On this topic gentlemen," Nolan said making eye contact with every member of the squirming crowd, "society is unforgiving."

"Aren't there treatments, as in any other disease?"

"Treatments? Oh yes. There are bromides, malted cereals, predigested food diets."

Mitchell thought he detected the slightest hint of a brogue. First-generation Irish, too? If so, he was no doubt used to such ignorant remarks. One had to admire his patience.

He continued, "Dr. Sigmund Freud's psychoanalysis has been tried. People have even taken to surgery. But most of these methods don't work. The problem is categorizing our behavior as a disease in the first place."

"Well, even in your charter, you acknowledge that it is abnormal."

"True, but that doesn't mean it's a curable ailment, like a broken leg. We think of abnormal as something more like a variation on a theme. I even believe that one day it won't be viewed as abnormal at all. We've been around a long time, you know, at least since the Greeks."

"Mr. Nolan, you believe in science, don't you sir?"

"Of course."

"Well then, how do you think the species will survive if this behavior is condoned through, what you call, *rights*?"

"There are all kinds of people. Women, for example, who are unable to bear children. The species seems to accommodate them just fine. Sex organs are not just for procreation, you know."

"That's disgusting!" a young reporter from *The Bee* exclaimed. "Tell me, Mr. Nolan. Just how many of your breed are there, anyway?"

"How many are there of *yours*?" Nolan snapped back. He'd apparently finally had enough.

"Most of the world, I'd say."

"Really? That's a pity," he said only barely under his breath. "But if you mean how many are in our organization, more than you'd think, I imagine. You know," he added with obvious relish, "I have a tip that might help you come up with a preliminary number."

"Oh?"

"Yes. One of the ways *our breed* recognizes each other is through our neckties. When we go out, we always wear a red one."

At this remark, everyone in the room simultaneously checked their ties and then glanced nervously at their neighbors. Several were as red as a ripe tomato. Mitchell, who was wearing no tie at all, laughed aloud.

"I'll take one more question."

"Mr. Nolan, can't you fellows just abstain, exhibit some self-control?"

"I might pose the same question to you, sir. But I suggest you read Dr. Magnus Hirschfeld, if you are truly interested in an educated answer. Now, I really must go. Thank you everyone."

Yes indeed, Mitchell thought as he listened to his indignant brethren huff and puff at Nolan's abrupt departure, you had to admire this guy.

One of the main reasons Mitchell had earned respect as a reporter was because he always did his homework. Covering the human rights convention was no exception. Before writing the story, he researched everything he could find on the subject of homosexuality. He discovered that attitudes toward the condition were historically and culturally varied; from despised to tolerated to even condoned. That is, except for here in America, where since the country's inception, the condition seemed to be held in universal contempt.

"The first governor of the Massachusetts Bay Colony, John Winthrop," Mitchell wrote in the article that eventually made its way to print, "called homosexuals 'monsters in human shape.' Based on the vitriol expressed by outsiders toward the human rights convention," he concluded with editorial flourish, "it seems we have not yet shed our Puritanical roots."

The medical community in this country had in recent years made matters worse, Mitchell surmised, by turning a centuries-old practice into a dangerous pathology, prescribing treatments that were often brutally inhumane. A few dissenting voices spoke, however, one of which was Dr. Hirschfeld, the man to whom Danny Nolan referred. A German physician and sexologist, Hirschfeld infuriated the establishment by stating that homosexuality was an innate condition, unchangeable, and therefore unjustly criminalized. Arguing for "Adjustment Therapy," which essentially was acceptance of one's condition, he boldly asserted that homosexuality was not a disease.

Mitchell tended to agree, but based on the reaction of his fellow reporters and the silence of the usually loquacious reformers, he didn't think the country was ready for such an idea. When he read that the poet Robert Frost had urged the dismissal of a popular homosexual teacher at Amherst College, he was certain of this assessment. If an enlightened American such as Frost felt this way, well, what could one expect from the average citizen? As for Mitchell, he believed in the policy of live and let live. After all, it had never bothered him that some of the photographers he admired most were of this persuasion. Why, if it made him take better pictures, he might even give it a try himself. He walked up the cobblestone steps of Michaelangelo's, the Italian restaurant on the outskirts of town where Danny Nolan had suggested they have a late lunch, and thought of Sarah. Well, he said to himself, perhaps not quite yet.

TOLEDO DAILY BLADE   STERILIZING WOMA

E. P. BRECKENRIDGE, PRES.   GRAFF W. ACKLIN, SEC'Y, TREAS.& GEN. MGR.
HENRY J. HINDE, VICE-PRES. & WORKS MGR.

The Toledo Machine and Tool Co.

MANUFACTURERS OF

Presses, Dies, Punches, Shears

and other Sheet Metal Tools.

1736, 1738, 1740, 1742, 1744 DORR STREET
1302 TO 1326 HASTINGS STREET

CABLE ADDRESS "TOMATOOL" TOLEDO

TOLEDO, OHIO, U. S. A.   Mch. 14/10

Hon. Judge O'Brien O'Donnell,

City.

My dear friend:-

It is with the greatest regret that I am, because
of my desire to maintain the old family prestige forced to take exceptions to the statements made in the brief sketch given in Sunday's Times of your family history.

My Father was a direct (?) descendent of one of the
first and foremost so-called Irish Kings from the Galway Section in
the county of the same name Ireland. A well known fact was stated
in the sketch referred to that the power of the different factions
was maintained by their aptness and ability to wield a shillalah ;
both my brother and myself know from actual experience that it
would not be possible to excel the way my Father handled this
weapon. The memory is one that will remain long with us.

I expect and presume that you will on receipt of
this immediately recognize that there was at least one other Kingly
family in Ireland besides the O'Briens and O'Donnells.

Thinking it possible that you might not know to
what sketch I refer , I enclose the clipping .

I agree with the historian in one part and that is
the absolute mystery of the facts as to why you remain a bachelor.

Our mutual friend Danny Nolan however may throw some light on this
subject.
                          Yours very truly,

Gathering Containers and An-   Two Boys Arraigned for Alleged
                                Bootlegger—Another Admits

24

Henry Hinde lived in a modest neighborhood in East Toledo
on the border of Collins Park. He was retired, and by the eager sound
of his voice when Sarah called, in need of company.

"Thank you for seeing me at such short notice," she said to Hinde, who opened the door just as she touched the bell.

"Not at all. Come and sit down. I've just made some fresh coffee and have some delicious cookies from the bakery. Chocolate macaroons," he whispered slyly, as if they were a vintage bootlegged wine.

"I appreciate your hospitality sir, but this is rather urgent. Do you mind if I get to the point?"

Hinde, a pleasant, butterball of a man, frowned. He evidently had a longer visit in mind.

Sarah sighed as she saw his jolly, pug-nosed face drop precipitously. "Well, maybe just one of those cookies," she said.

The remark perked the man up considerably, and he started talking volubly about everything from the last war to the Charleston, a dance he thought must have been invented to humiliate the uncoordinated. He had obviously been much deprived of conversation. When he finally slowed down a half hour later, Sarah somberly handed him the letter from her purse.

He fingered it with fond recognition and nodded. "That's from my company, all right. It's been five years since we closed our doors." For a moment he stood wistfully lost in thought. Then his gaze started to move curiously across the page. "This is my stationary, but it's not my signature, ma'am."

"Are you sure?"

"Of course, I'm sure. I'll agree it's a pretty good imitation. But it ain't mine. Just a minute. I'll be right back," he said, and quickly returned with various documents bearing his signature.

"Look here. It's close, but see, my H doesn't curve like that."

Sarah agreed. The H's were different. She observed him carefully and believed he was telling the truth.

"Well then, do you know who might have written it?"

"No idea."

Hinde started nervously shuffling the magazines on the coffee table, which, as she had noticed earlier, all bore the same title: *Friendship and Freedom*. Their eyes met knowingly. Hinde swallowed hard. "Ma'am, I lead a quiet life. If you don't mind, I'd like it to stay that way."

"Look, Mr. Hinde. Believe me. I'm only interested in who wrote this. Do you mind telling me how well you knew Judge O'Donnell?"

Hinde shrugged. "Not very well. We did some work for him now and then. He had quite a knack for mechanical things you know. Down to earth for such an important fellow. And, he's done great things for the city. But, really, that's all I can tell you. Now, if you'll excuse me."

"All right," she said, sensing it would be counterproductive to persist. "But if you think of anything, could you please call me at the courthouse? This is very important. Judge O'Donnell is seriously ill, and the author of this letter may be responsible."

"Of course," he replied slowly.

"Goodbye then sir," Sarah said turning to leave, "but please remember, you could be the key to a cure for a person, who, by your own admission, is one of Toledo's best."

The comment was manipulative, but guilt often worked when all else failed. Particularly when a person possessed a highly developed conscience, which Sarah rightly presumed Mr. Hinde did. Before she had even gotten halfway down the sidewalk, she heard him call out.

"Miss Kaufman? Miss Kaufman, I could get you a list of my former employees, if you wish."

"That would be wonderful, Mr. Hinde."

"Come back later then, about five. I'll see what I can do. After that though, I want no further part in this."

"Certainly. And thank you . . . thank you very much Mr. Hinde," she said, hurrying away before he could change his mind.

Mitchell told Danny Nolan that he would prefer to explain in person why he wished to see him. "Name the place and lunch is on me," he added as an inducement. Danny was already seated when he arrived.

"Nice place," Mitchell said.

"And the food is superb," Danny proclaimed, extending his well-manicured hand. "Please, sit down Mr. Dobrinski."

Mr. Nolan was again dressed conservatively. Grey suit, white shirt. Not even the hint of red in his tie.

"That was an excellent piece of writing," Danny said. "I'll bet you're the only reporter who bothered to look up Hirschfeld. For that alone, I commend you."

"Ah, you mustn't judge my colleagues too harshly, Mr. Nolan. They're really a tolerant bunch of guys, considering they were raised on war and football."

"If that's tolerance, our cause is surely lost. But you, Mr. Dobrinski. I suspect you had the same kind of upbringing. Who taught you to be so accepting, and, I might add, so insightful?"

Mitchell lit a cigarette. He knew the answer. But he surprised himself by feeling proud rather than angry at the thought of her.

"My mother," he finally said. "She was a very progressive woman."

"You were lucky."

"Yes, I'd never thought of it that way, but I suppose on that accord I was."

After ordering lunch, Danny began talking without any prompting about the human rights convention. It was only a start, he conceded, they still had a long way to go. Indeed, it looked as though their organization was going to be ruled unconstitutional.

"Mr. Nolan—"

"Please . . . Danny."

"Danny. I have to be honest with you. I would be more than happy to conduct a follow-up interview at some future date. But I didn't ask you here for that."

"Oh?" he said reddening. "Oh, I am sorry. I just assumed you'd want to know how things went."

"Well, yes, of course. That would be a logical assumption. But actually I contacted you for a more personal reason."

"Personal?" Danny eyed Mitchell without blinking. Mitchell politely ignored the suggestion and got to the point.

"I'm wondering what sort of relationship you've had with Judge O'Brien O'Donnell."

"Who?" Danny asked. Mitchell was familiar with that kind of automatic response. It allowed one a moment to digest the question. His mother used to chide him for doing the same thing himself. ("I think we should get your hearing checked," she would say dryly.)

"Why do you ask?" he said, stiffening.

Then Mitchell told him about the letter. "It says 'our good friend Danny Nolan may throw some light on this subject.' And so that's what I'm here to ask you, Danny. Can you? Can you throw light on this subject?"

For several moments Danny didn't respond. By turns his almond shaped eyes widened and narrowed, his full, etched lips opened and locked. He mumbled something under his breath, nodded vigorously, and then offered Mitchell a smile that would put the Mona Lisa to shame.

"Mr. Dobrinski, would you be interested in taking a little trip?"

"A trip? Where to?"

"I'd rather not say just yet, if you don't mind. I believe there may be someone there, however, who can help you."

Well. Nolan had trusted him, now he must return the favor. "When?"

"Right now."

Mitchell glanced at his uneaten ravioli. When this is all over, I'll bring Sarah here, he thought. "After you," he said rising.

Danny stood up. He matched Mitchell in height and surpassed him by at least twenty pounds in weight.

"Before we start, Mr. Dobrinski, I must warn you. Where we're going, it may make you feel a bit . . . uncomfortable."

"If a reporter isn't uncomfortable now and then, he should quit," Mitchell said with more apprehension than he let on.

"All right then. This way."

The commanding tone inspired confidence. Nolan was a man—a different sort of man—but a man nonetheless. Strong, intelligent, a leader. With one shuffle of the deck, he could have ruled an army. So, like a private with his captain, Mitchell obeyed without further question, following Danny as he led the way toward the train that would take them to their mysterious destination.

It was now 4:30. A five minute walk to the storage room for some carbon paper had caused Sarah to miss Mitchell's call at 3. It was her secretary that informed her that he would be detained.

"Mr. Dobrinski told me to tell you that, and I quote, 'something encouraging pertaining to our business has come up.' He said that he would call you tonight at your home."

Sarah generally understood the message, but she wished for the details. Something encouraging. But what? She also wished she had been there to pass on her own news, although, hopefully, there would be even more to tell him later. She would know soon enough. The taxi she had splurged on to avoid the crowded evening streetcar was at this very moment carrying her back to Henry Hinde's.

Hinde was waiting at the door again, but this time he invited her in much more officiously. He offered no refreshment, the coffee table had been emptied, and he was dressed as if he were going out. A black jacket, striped blue shirt, and a bright red bow tie.

"Here they are, Miss Kaufman. They go back quite a ways. You may take them with you, if you like. Just mail them to me as soon as you're finished. And remember what I said. From here on out, you don't know me."

Hinde showed her to the door and that was that. Fine with Sarah. She couldn't wait to get at the list. The streetcar home from this direction was nearly full, but she took it anyway, seating herself in the only vacant spot near a window. Ripping open the sealed packet, she began scanning the names, about eighty in all. Clerks, salesmen, mechanics. All Toledoans at one time or another. Amazing, she only recognized one of them. Only one, who worked there in 1910 as a mechanic. "Huh, I didn't know that," she said aloud. "What luck!"

"Excuse me?" the young mother sitting in front of her said, turning her bunned head around.

"What? Oh, nothing. I'm sorry." Sarah smiled to convince the apprehensive woman that she and her child had nothing to fear before returning to the list.

Sarah couldn't believe her good fortune. The only familiar name belonged to a man who would undoubtedly know something. She didn't have the time to ponder the wisdom of including him in this mess. But, if it had to be anyone, how fortunate that it was a friend. She got off at the next stop and changed directions, remembering that he had recently moved to the Angelo Hotel. She reached her stop at 6 p.m., nearly dark in this season of progressively shorter days. She walked two blocks and stood before the modern edifice. He must be doing quite well, to be able to take permanent residence here.

Sarah entered the spare, elegant hotel lobby and approached the desk clerk.

"That way ma'am. He's on the second floor."

At his door, she pulled up on the brass door knocker and let it fall. Once, twice, three times. She waited and repeated the process. Damn. Not home. Of course, Friday night. A single man, he'd probably be out until midnight.

She considered for a moment. The only thing to do was return later. Tillie could light the candles without her, and the courthouse was close. She'd go there . . . this time more cautiously. She touched the scab that had started to form on her forehead. She'd even spring for a cab again and have the driver watch her until she was safely in the building. Mitchell was going to be late anyway. She left the hotel with her hope revived, delayed but not foiled.

They were headed for Detroit, sixty miles north on a course that paralleled the Dixie Highway. The train ride took about an hour.

Detroit and Toledo had shared a mutually beneficial, if illegal, past. Michigan had gone dry before Ohio, and for a time, Toledo had supplied smugglers with all the liquor they could carry in their camouflaged flasks, false-bottomed shopping baskets, and hidden compartments. When Ohio ratified Volstead, Detroit took its business to Canada, from which goods were easily smuggled along the Detroit and St. Clair Rivers. The result was a thriving illegal liquor trade, an industry second only to that of the automobile manufacturers. Detroit had almost as many speakeasies as cars.

To one of these establishments, about ten minutes into the journey, Danny finally admitted to Mitchell was their destination.

"Yep, we're going to a 'blind pig,'" he said, and then added with amusement, "perhaps doubly blind is more accurate. But enough of that now. You know, Mr. Dobrinski, I've found that people generally like to talk about themselves. Would you?"

"It's Mitchell, and I would if there were something worth talking about. I could recite the whole boring tale before that conductor over there comes to collect our tickets. I'm sure you've had a much more interesting life."

"Well interesting and difficult, as you might imagine."

The train rolled on, but instead of either of them relaying their private histories, they—or rather Danny—just talked. About everything. His knowledge was impressive, speaking as confidently of Judith Anderson's performance in *Cobra* as he did of Lou Gehrig leading the minor leagues in batting. He was fascinated by the Prince of Wales' visit to the states, adored Gloria Swanson's latest picture and had tried many of the recipes in Fanny Farmer's cookbook. He was as appalled by Coolidge's denouncement of the Senate's inquiry into tax returns as he was by the turning of a national tragedy into a commercial enterprise: by that he meant the recent auction in which the clothing Abe Lincoln had worn when he was assassinated had been sold for six thousand five hundred dollars. He had already read with little pleasure *In Our Time*, Ernest Hemingway's recently published collection of short stories, and with great pleasure Zane Grey's *The Call of the Canyon*. The only personal detail he divulged regarded his finances. "I live on an inheritance, Mitchell, and I use it well: for the good of others, but also to educate and amuse myself."

"You're a true Renaissance man," Mitchell said as they disembarked the train.

Danny smiled. "Yes, with the heart of a woman. Come on, let's go." And he laughed heartily as he led an embarrassed Mitchell toward the exit.

25

By 1924, speakeasies occupied hidden spaces in nearly every kind of building imaginable. Restaurants, drugstores, penthouses, mansions, tenements, hardware stores. The one they stood before now was called "The Valentine Club," a plain-looking two-story structure

262

that at certain hours was a legitimate meeting place for so-called lonely hearts: "normal" men and women seeking the companionship of the opposite sex. Illegitimately, it was something else entirely.

Danny expertly carried out the speakeasy's intricate rites. First, he pressed the doorbell five times, using quick staccato strokes. After a few moments, a man slid a panel behind an iron grill and peered out. Mitchell couldn't distinguish the man's features, but he could tell that the expression was meant to intimidate. He didn't say a word, just stood behind the door and waited. A moment later, Danny showed him a yellow card and whispered the magic words: "My heart is pure." The door miraculously opened, and they were quickly ushered inside.

After they entered a small foyer, proudly lined with pictures of members of the "legitimate" club who had married, the still silent man directed them through a labyrinth of dark rooms toward a long spiral staircase. As they descended, Mitchell thought of the time he toured a submarine for *The Blade*, and had to stop himself from hyperventilating. He wasn't prone to claustrophobia, but on that one occasion he'd had an attack of the most extreme sort. When they'd reached what seemed like the center of the earth, the man guided them through the final passage: a narrow, tunnel-like hall. Once they arrived on the other end, he refined his simile. It wasn't like the earth at all. It was like another world.

Out of the darkness, the sudden appearance of people mingling, laughing, and drinking was jolting enough. But this particular crowd made the experience seem unreal. Their guide was obviously affected by the transition, too. Turning around he grinned widely, and slapped Danny familiarly on the back. "Hey Danny boy, they're playing your song. What timing!"

He meant that literally. A large, ebony woman was at the piano belting out a jazzy rendition of "Danny Boy" to a visibly moved crowd. The irregular beat and emphasis of the minor key had transformed the quaint ballad into a peculiarly seductive melody. The woman's emerald green, sequined gown shimmered against the dim lights as she played, and that, coupled with the room's dreamy smoke and tinkling glass was intoxicating, even without a drink.

Everyone Danny encountered greeted him warmly.

"Danny! Long time no see, buddy."

"Dan, my love!"

"Hey, Danny. Who ya got there with you, honey?"

Danny waved with a gesture that must have meant "he's not one of us," for after that, although they were still friendly, the cat-calls ceased.

The bar, referred to as the "Merry-Go-Round," was not restricted to any one type. Some of the patrons were heterosexual couples, and a few women appeared to be looking for a date. Even the obvious sightseers were treated congenially provided they bought drinks and didn't harass anyone. The overwhelming population, however, was homosexual. Some men were hand in hand, others were dancing, a few in highly provocative positions.

The whole scene would require some getting used to. Acceptance from afar was one thing. Up close one had to work a bit harder. However, far more threatening to Mitchell was the proximity of all that booze, the holy grail for those who knew the password. Except for that one binge after Pamela left, Mitchell hadn't touched the stuff in years. But a bar atmosphere, no matter who the clientele, was dangerous. He needed to get his business over quickly. He glanced at Danny, who appeared to read his mind.

"You're quite a good sport," Danny said. "But I'm sure you could think of other things to do with your time."

"Well, as a matter of fact—"

"Hey Jim," he called out to the bartender. "Could you come here for a minute?"

The man responded immediately, confirming Mitchell's assessment of the respect Danny commanded in this community. "Yeah, Dan?"

"I'm wondering if you might be able to help my friend here. Could you spare a few minutes . . . in your office?"

Jim summoned one of his employees and asked him to take over. "What can I get you to drink," he asked the two men.

"I'll have the usual," Danny said, which turned out to be an Irish Whiskey. Gin and tonic was Mitchell's drink of choice, and his throat grew parched at the thought of it. Nevertheless, he ordered a ginger ale.

The office was a tiny broom closet of a room in the back of the bar. After some brief introductions, Mitchell seated himself in a chair and lit a cigarette. One vice at a time, he thought. He was, after all, only human.

Mitchell had to look up to meet Jim's heavily hooded eyes. The man was at least six feet five. And very thin, thinner than Mitchell himself. With his craggy face and tan leathery skin, he appeared to be about sixty, but something in his demeanor made Mitchell think he was younger. Even at twenty, the man probably had not been handsome by anybody's definition. Still, he possessed some ineffable quality that made one instantly like him. People either had that or they didn't. Mitchell himself did not.

Danny was an adept facilitator. He quickly defined the terms of their discussion, shifting his gaze from one man to the other.

"Mitchell, Jim here has owned this place for years. He knows everyone who comes through his doors. Jim, Mitchell has some questions for you about Judge O'Brien O'Donnell."

Jim glanced at Mitchell and then back at Danny.

"He's all right, Jim."

"Okay, sir. What can I do for you?"

Mitchell sipped his ginger ale and lit another cigarette. "I don't really know what I'm suppose to ask."

"Ask him if the judge has ever been here," Danny prompted.

"All right. Has Judge O'Donnell ever been here?"

"Yes, yes he has. But not for quite some time."

"By himself?"

"No, not that I can recall."

"No?"

Mitchell turned to Danny for assistance, his reporter's instincts temporarily abandoning him.

"Tell him who the judge came here with Jim."

Jim took his empty glass and expertly spun it around. He waited until it came to a stop. "With Ken. Kenny Ballard."

"Kenny Ballard? Who's that?" Mitchell asked.

"A regular here."

"What's he do?"

"He's an engineer for Ohio Gas. Used to be the judge's roommate."

"Roommate?" Mitchell could hear his mother asking him if he was a parrot. "How often did they come here?"

"Oh, not very often. And it wasn't exactly here. It was in the days just before Volstead, when things were still legal. I owned another place then, down the street. I remember because that was when Ken did some consulting work for the Pilliod Brewery."

Mitchell sat upright. "Do you know exactly when he worked there?"

"Hmm . . . let me think. It was . . . I don't know . . . about seven or eight years ago, I guess. Nineteen fifteen, sixteen, some time around then."

Mitchell felt his chest tighten. "Does that mean O'Donnell and Ballard were . . . well, whatever you call them?"

"Lovers? Can't say. I was never sure about that. All I know is that they were close. But I'll tell you this. The judge is a great man."

"Yes, so I've heard," Mitchell said.

Danny now spoke. He had set the stage, and presumably Jim had performed exactly according to plan. "I have a feeling Ballard's your man, Mitchell. I'm not sure why he wrote that letter. But I do know he never liked me. I always assumed it was because I had talked to O'Donnell about the human rights platform. Ballard despised the idea. Wanted nothing to do with it. He was one of those self-loathing types. Hadn't come to terms with what he was. Exemplary case of the need for adjustment therapy." Danny licked the rim of his glass.

"But why did we have to come here, then, if you already knew this?" Mitchell asked with some annoyance. "It could have saved time."

"I'm sorry for that, but I wanted you to hear Ken's name from an objective source. You might have questioned my motives, seeing that the man implicated me somewhat."

Mitchell nodded. Jesus Christ. This Ballard guy had been O'Brien's roommate. Sarah must know him. He drained his glass and handed it to Jim. If ever he needed a drink.

"Danny, we've gotta get back . . . immediately."

"All right," Danny said, pulling out his watch from his pocket. He flipped open the scrolled gold cap. "Unfortunately, we just missed the eight o'clock. The next train isn't until eleven."

"Shit." Mitchell bit his lip and considered his options. There weren't many at this time of night. "Well, I'd like to go now anyway," he said. "Just in case. Who knows, the train might be late. Besides, I've got a couple of calls to make. I can do that at the station."

The urgency in Mitchell's voice caused all three men to simultaneously rise. Single-file, they marched back to the bar, where Mitchell took a final look around. Really, except for that one difference, these people were just like anyone else. All they wanted was friendship, love, and a little fun. Considering how they were treated by society, it seemed to Mitchell that they were more entitled than most to break the law to have it, too.

The man who had led them in now led them back toward the entrance with his inscrutable expression returned. As they began their ascent up the stairs, Mitchell could hear a cacophony of mostly male voices singing along to the wildly popular tune "Lady be Good." He smiled briefly at the irony, but he was focused on another lady, on Sarah. In the dark, narrow maze through which they were being directed, he found himself thinking particularly of her dream. He'd almost forgotten it completely, but now the memory of it struck him so acutely that behind each door they passed through, he half expected to see the images that had frightened her so come to life. Perhaps it was the lack of clear boundaries here. In such a topsy-turvy environment, it was easy to get spooked, to consider the possibility of the supernatural. But even when they reached the open air, where the stars and moon greeted them reassuringly, where all of nature appeared to be in its rightful place, there was no escaping it. That dream had been prophetic on at least one account: there was an ominous presence seeking to do harm. The only difference was that now his identity was almost certainly known.

26

Sarah twisted her neck to loosen the muscles that hours of
work had tightened into a knot. When she looked at the clock, she
couldn't believe the time: 10:40. Well, if he wasn't home by now, he

should be soon. She only hoped he didn't have company or, worse, that he had gone out of town.

Sarah couldn't have asked for a more accommodating cab driver. Not only did he wait until she was in the courthouse, but he offered to pick her up when she was done.

"Just ask for Pete Mulligan when you call, ma'am. I'm on duty all night."

Pete was a crusty, talkative old guy who told Sarah that he didn't see "many fellas these days which know'd a thing about how to treat a woman. There just ain't no chiffery anymore," he said with disgust. Pete himself welcomed the opportunity to help a "damezel in destress." He also prided himself on his punctuality. And he demonstrated that such pride was justified. He arrived at the courthouse five minutes after Sarah called and delivered her to her destination with equal speed. By 11:15, she was back at the Angelo Hotel.

Sarah asked Pete to wait while she went inside to make sure her friend was home. "Do you know if Mr. Ballard has come in yet?" she asked the sleepy desk clerk.

"Yeah, 'bout an hour ago, I think," the man said, yawning.

Thank God. She went outside to pay Pete.

"I'll recommend you to everyone I know," she said. "Thanks so much. I'll be okay now."

Pete tipped his hat. "T'were a pleasure, ma'am. You know what to do if you need me later," he said, waving as he drove off.

In a few moments, Sarah found herself again in front of room 201. This time when she dropped the knocker, a familiar, though unusually hostile sounding voice responded. "Who is it!"

"Ken? Ken, it's Sarah, Sarah Kaufman."

A long silence followed.

"Ken? Did you hear me? I'm sorry. I know it's late, but I desperately need to talk to you."

Again, silence.

"Ken?"

"Are you alone, Sarah?"

"Yes, I am."

"Just a minute. Let me get my robe."

She breathed a bit. Many people were grumpy when awakened suddenly. According to Tillie, she herself was one of them.

The door soon opened, and behind it stood Kenneth in a floor-length, maroon silk robe. For a moment he glared at Sarah icily. "Hello Sarah. Come in," he said, as he checked the hall. By the time he turned around, his expression had softened a bit.

"Ken. I'm so sorry. You look exhausted."

"Well, it is almost midnight, Sarah."

"I know."

"So, what's so important?"

"May I?" Sarah asked, pointing to a sofa in the corner of the room.

"Of course. Can I get you a drink?"

"Just some water."

"Have a seat. I'll be right back."

Kenneth returned with a glass of water and a whiskey. Sarah took a few sips of water and then quickly explained why she had come. This was no time to mince words. Obee's suicide attempt, the blackmail note, the letter from Toledo Machine and Tool. Now Ken, too, would know. When she finished, she showed him the employee list Hinde had given her.

"Yeah, I worked there briefly," Ken said with a blank expression. "It was while I was looking for an engineering job."

"Ken, please take a look at these names, and tell me if any of them strike a chord, someone who might have something against Obee."

Kenneth gave the list a cursory examination. "No. Why?"

Sarah took the letter from her purse and handed it to him. "Mr. Hinde didn't write this letter, Ken. I believe the person who wrote the blackmail note wrote the letter as well."

Kenneth fingered the letter and laughed, somewhat maliciously. "Oh . . . I see," he said. "So you're a detective now, are you?"

Kenneth sounded strange. He was obviously irritated, mocking her in this way.

"Sarah, I'm curious. Why didn't you tell me anything about this before? I suppose it was because Obee didn't want me to know."

"Obee was in no position to make such a request. It was I who decided not to tell anyone."

"Well, then, why tell me now?"

"Honestly Ken, I thought I was doing the right thing. If I've offended you, I apologize. But this isn't the time to pout. Obee has been blackmailed. He tried to kill himself because of it. I thought you of all people would do anything to help him."

"Of course I would, my love."

"Well, then. Why don't you look at the list again. Take your time. I need to freshen up anyway."

"All right. The bath is down the hall."

"Thanks. And Ken, look at the letter, too. It's a long shot, but maybe you'll recognize something in the handwriting."

Sarah turned on the faucet, washed her hands with a shriveled bar of musky smelling soap, and threw some water on her face. Perhaps she should have anticipated Ken's reaction. He felt left out. After all, he was Obee's friend before she was. As she reached for a towel, she caught a glimpse of herself in the mirror above the sink. "It's a wonder he didn't say anything about these bruises. God, I look dreadful." She took out some powder from her purse and applied it to dull the redness.

Then she pinned a few strands of loose hair back into place. "That will have to do," she said, with her hand ready to twist the doorknob.

What made her take one last look in the mirror she wasn't sure. But when she did, she saw something that gave her pause. She probably wouldn't have even noticed it had she not just seen the same style of print at Henry Hinde's. Not a fancy style, but one that had caused the man no small degree of distress. She turned around to make sure the reverse image wasn't deceiving her. By the bathtub was a magazine embossed with the words *Friendship and Freedom*. She picked it up and thumbed through its provocative pages. Funny. What would Ken be doing with . . . but there were more. Many more. Next to the tub was a rack full of them.

Unfortunately, the precise moment when truth presents itself isn't subject to choice. A revelation occurs in its own time, frequently when one is least expecting it. Like a bolt of lightening, as it is commonly said. To Sarah, this particular one felt more like an earthquake. An overall trembling, followed by a sickening, undulating wave slowly creeping over her was how she would have described it. Luckily she was near the toilet. When the wave reached her stomach, she might need it.

Her vision blurred, her chest tightened, her legs grew weak. Thought was temporarily suspended. Then finally, the wave made its way to her feet, "Oh my God. No." She grabbed the magazine and rapidly leafed through it again. "No. No. How could this be?" How, she asked herself, still waiting for her mind to fully catch up with her body, could she not have even considered the possibility? The air reeked of musk. She could barely breathe as she fought to think.

Above her was a small window recessed within a wooden casement. Instinctively she tried to open it. It didn't move. A careless paint job had petrified it into place. It was a ridiculous idea anyway. No fire escape offered rescue, only a cement alley. The fall would surely kill her. Illogically she searched for another means of escape. She found none of course, but her frantic actions caused the magazine rack to topple over, sending the contents clattering onto the floor.

"You all right, Sarah?"

Now it was she who was silent.

"Sarah?"

"Yes, yes, I'm fine . . . I'll be right out."

Sarah looked around the tiny room once more. Get out of here as soon as possible. Figure out the rest later. She replaced the magazines, straightened herself and turned the knob.

Kenneth was standing in the doorway with a fixed gaze and a firmly clenched jaw, barring her exit.

"Find something interesting, my dear?"

"No, Ken, what do mean?"

"Why so nervous?"

"I'm not nervous, you just startled me."

"Oh, come now, Sarah," Kenneth said. "You can do better than that. Jews have mastered the art of deception."

The venomous tone was devastatingly familiar. He had masked his voice well.

"You know I can't let you have this letter back, Sarah," he said waving the now rumpled blue paper in the air. "Nor, I'm afraid, can I let you leave."

Sarah eyed the front door.

"Don't try it, my dear. Now, be a good girl and move back into the bathroom."

He shoved her hard. "I said get back!" he shouted as he locked the door from the outside.

"I gave you fair warning, Sarah," he said through the closed door. "More warning than you deserved. You didn't listen."

"Kenneth, please, can't we talk about this?"

"Talk? Obee used to say that, too. Let's talk about this Ken. Let's talk about this. So patronizing."

"But Ken, why? Please tell me why." Sarah was leaning against the door, her lips touching its surface. She could hear him sucking air through his teeth.

"I suppose," he said, "that in your final hours you're entitled to an explanation."

Sarah slid down against the wall onto to the cold tile floor.

"Ken, you don't mean that."

"Do you want to know or not?"

"Yes. But wouldn't it be easier to open the door? I promise I'll stay put. You won't have to raise your voice—"

"Shut up! Shut up and listen."

Kenneth was quiet for a moment. She could hear him shifting positions and breathing deeply, as if waiting for the curtain to rise. When he spoke, however, it was more in the manner of a confession than a studied performance. The words poured forth hypnotically, relentlessly.

"You know, Sarah, from the very first day I met you, I sensed you'd be trouble. Remember? That day Obee brought you to the apartment? A woman invading our private little world. We were doing so well without you. It would have only been a matter of time until he gave himself to me fully. Oh, he fought it. Sure. He told me that he didn't feel that way about me, that he couldn't feel that way about any man. But I knew differently. I saw his conflict. I knew that he took dope to deal with his confusion. Why else would he go out with me? He knew what was going on in those places. Are you listening, Sarah?"

"Yes."

"A few months after your visit, I touched him, ever so gently. And you know what he did? He removed my hand, looked at me kindly with those sorrowful eyes of his and shook his head.

275

"'I'm sorry, Ken,' he said. 'You're a great friend; my best friend. But I can't. Please, let's talk about this. Let's talk.'

"So I talked. I asked him why he'd never had a woman. Why he loved to be around men. What was his obsession with the Newsies, Big Brothers, even baseball anyway if it didn't have something to do with his feeling for the male sex. I'd seen him look at men on the street. I recognized that look. I asked him about his passion for music and art, his love of fashion. You know what he said? That he'd just never met the right woman. He loved the friendship of men, that was true.

"'But, Ken,' he said, 'your idea of relationships is too narrow. Why, if you went to France, you'd see men walk arm and arm, even kiss. But that doesn't mean they love each other romantically. And, Ken,' he added with a condescending smile, 'all kinds of people appreciate beauty. It's part of being human.'

"Narrow idea of relationships. France. What bullshit! I'll take him off that pedestal he uses to rationalize his feelings, I said to myself. So I asked him about that Jew boy, Nate Greenberg, the one who'd come over and read poetry. The one who I saw Obee put his arm around.

"'Nate is just a good friend, Ken,' he said. 'A friend, the same as Sarah, the same as Kate was to you. You know, everyone considered you and Kate a couple, too.'"

Yes, Sarah thought, I certainly did. There was a pause, so she ventured a comment. "Ken, you know that nothing ever happened between Obee and me, don't you?"

"Maybe not, Sarah. But you opened him up to the idea of women. Of that I'm sure. And then he married that status-seeking little bitch. I loved him. She wanted only his name."

"I used to think that, too, Ken. But I'm not so sure anymore. Whatever Winifred's shortcomings, she seems to genuinely love him. You know, at one time I felt as betrayed as you."

"You could *never* feel like me!"

"No, of course not."

"I suppose you'd like to know about the note, now," he continued, not waiting for a response. "It was ingenious really. And if you hadn't stepped in, the matter would be done. When you held that first press conference I knew Obee had told you about it. After that I kept tabs on you. You and that obnoxious Dobrinski fellow. It was very unwise to let him in on this. But it was easy to follow you nonetheless."

Sarah closed her eyes and forced down another wave of nausea.

"Sarah, do you know what it's like to be an engineer? Confined by facts and figures. Pumps, machinery, valves. A real man's job, my father used to say. So I did it, to please him and because God saw it fit to bless me with mechanical aptitude. Just one of His cruel tricks, no doubt. For the work was like death to me. I desperately wanted out. And then, for the first time in my life it seemed that my prayers might be answered. John O'Dwyer . . . you know, Sarah, I don't know what kind of spell you cast over men. First Obee and then John. Seeing him cozy up to you at the ballpark; how can a man of such taste stomach a woman like you, anyway?"

Kenneth stopped for a minute, apparently ruminating on this thought. Sarah said nothing. His revulsion of her chilled her to the bone.

"O'Dwyer approached me to do some troubleshooting at the brewery," he finally said. "I jumped at the offer because of the money— triple what was I was making at the gas company. If I was careful, with both jobs in a couple years time, I could quit. But then Frank Westfall died. With prohibition on the horizon, whoever filled his position could make or break the breweries. O'Dwyer wanted me to convince Obee to go with them. If I succeeded, he would give me a hefty bonus. Ah, yes. I could get out even sooner. I readily accepted, and not only for the money. Are you still listening, Sarah?"

"Yes," Sarah said, her ear firmly against the wall. Ken's voice had diminished significantly in volume, but in this position she could still hear well enough.

"Obee had hurt me. I wanted to hurt him back."

Kenneth laughed, and then was quiet.

"I knew Obee better than anyone, Sarah. Better than even you. I knew how he revered this backward little town, how much the people mattered to him. He was committed to them all right . . . committed to a fault. I knew just how superstitious he was, too. And, I knew about the drugs. It was hard not to living with him. So I came up a with plan. I told him the drowning was no accident, that the O'Dwyer machine was behind it. I never told O'Dwyer of course, but he never asked. All he cared about were results anyway. I told Obee that Westfall had been dangerous to the breweries and that if he, himself, didn't vote with them, or if he told the police, they'd ruin his career . . . or worse. That he could end up like Westfall. I knew Obee would believe this. He trusted me, and he knew first hand about O'Dwyer's tactics. But just to be sure I added something.

"'Obee,' I said, 'somehow, they've found out about your addiction.' Obee hated that word. I saw the fear on his face, and I took advantage of it.

"'They'd ruin you, my friend,' I said, sympathetically. 'You've got to think of yourself . . . and the city. What would the people do without you? You can't leave them in the hands of the machine. You're their only hope.'

"It worked, too. Without his job, Obee knew he would be lost. And besides, he wasn't sure which way he was going to vote anyway. The Poles were a loyal bunch, but he was worried about all those jobs at the breweries. Always thinking of others . . . all except me. So he voted with O'Dwyer. Not, of course, without consequences. My little story catapulted him into drugs again. But I didn't care. When he returned from the sanitarium, I felt I had some power over him. We continued to live together, but his rejection of my advances didn't bother me as much. I even started to have hope again that he might come around."

Kenneth then spat loudly, as if his mouth had suddenly filled with bile.

"And then Winifred appeared," he said. "A new clerk. Another woman. Every day she'd roll her eyes and shake her backside at Obee. It made me sick. One day she asked him to help her move a painting in the lobby. After that, Obee started to regularly leave the apartment and not return until morning. The little tramp. She seduced him. She knew what she was doing. And he was so naive. The pregnancy was inevitable. He tried to hide it from me, but I overheard. This time, however, his talking would be his undoing."

"So there was no murder," Sarah said, ecstatic despite her desperate state.

Kenneth laughed again. "No, of course not."

"Ken," Sarah said gingerly, "you started to tell me about the blackmail note."

"What? Oh, it's very simple really. I used up my money. I knew how much the Klan wanted him to lose. So I offered my services. If I could keep him from winning, they would pay me enough to retire. That's why I sent it. And I'll not let you interfere with my plans. I'll get paid, and get out of this hell hole yet."

"The Klan! Ken, do you really hate that much?"

"Ha! You're so naive, Sarah. Do I have hate? A person feels as much hate as they receive."

"That's not true for me," she said honestly.

"Well, you must be the exception, then."

"If you feel that way, why not work to change people's attitudes, Ken? There are groups, Progressive groups. How do you think the Klan would feel if they knew you were—"

"Stop it! Stop it! Stop with your reform gibberish. It's meaningless. I don't care what they think anyway . . . as long as they pay me. And they will pay me, Sarah. At your expense, I'm afraid. I didn't want it to go this far, but you've given me no choice. Westfall's death was an accident. Yours will have to be made to look like one. I think the bottom of the Maumee might be the best place for a Jew anyway."

Sarah shuddered. How was one supposed to respond to such a horrifying remark? She could start screaming, hoping someone would hear her. But that might only inflame him more. Before anyone would have time to react, he could be done with her then and there.

Instead, she asked a question that she would have wanted him to answer even if her own survival wasn't at stake.

"Kenneth, I never suspected you were truly antisemitic. I always thought you were joking when you made those remarks. Why single out the Jews?"

"Well, it's not religiously motivated if that's what you're wondering. I couldn't care less if they killed Christ. He abandoned me a long time ago, too. No, it's because Jews are the worst kind of hypocrites. They profess to be so open-minded, so liberal and compassionate. Yet, do you know that it was a Jew who first rejected me? I just wanted some affection, and he called me a sick pervert.

"But surely you don't think all Jews are like that, Ken? How can you, you, of all people, generalize so? Surely you must know that there are homosexual Jews!"

"That's enough, Sarah! Enough! He beat his fist on the door. I've talked enough. Be grateful. You'll die smarter than you were. Now, no more talking!"

Sarah heard him rummaging about the apartment as if looking for something. Terror rippled her body, but this was no time to panic. Think. She had been with dangerous people before. What did she do then? Reason. She had calmed them down with reason.

"Ken, Ken please." She raised her voice but tried to keep the tone even. "Ken, listen. Be logical. What do you hope to accomplish? You have not yet committed a serious crime, and I promise not to press charges. I'm sure I can convince Obee not to as well. But if you go through with this, you'll be a hunted man. You won't get away with it."

For a moment, Kenneth's frenetic movements halted, his footsteps thudded back toward the bathroom. Sarah held her breath. Yes, he was inserting the key. He opened the door and gazed at her with glassy eyes, then lowered his head.

"That's right," she said, smiling nervously. "You see my point, don't you, Ken? You're being very rational. We can get you some help and—"

Suddenly he grabbed her by the neck and turned the bathtub faucet on to maximum. His grasp tightened as the tub started to fill. What was he going to do? Drown her here then drop her in the river? She struggled, but he was too strong.

Everything was spinning; spinning, blurring and changing shape. So this is how it will end. Death by murder. God, God.

Just as the world started to fade, there was a series of heavy knocks. Her blood pounding against her skull? Ken instantly loosened his grip. She looked up, coughing, gasping for air. He shut off the water, grabbed a towel and with super-human strength, ripped it into three pieces. The first he tied around her mouth, the second around her wrists, the third her feet. He shut the door and locked it.

"Who is it?"

"Mitchell Dobrinski. I'm a reporter from *The Blade*."

"I know who you are. What do you want?"

"I want to talk to you," Mitchell said.

"You have no manners, sir. It's very late."

"It's important."

"Sorry. I'm not talking to anyone at this hour."

"All right, that's enough with the games. I know what you're up to, Ballard. Open up!"

"Who the hell are you to tell me that! I want you to leave, now!"

Mitchell banged on the door.

"Stop it," Kenneth shouted. "I mean it, Dobrinski. Get out of here or I'll call the police!"

"Go ahead," came another voice. "You can call the police, but you'd be much smarter to open the door, Ken."

"What? Who?"

"Come on, Ken."

Silence.

"Ken."

Sarah heard Kenneth drop to his knees and break into sobs.

When Mitchell burst through the bathroom door Sarah was, of course, relieved. But she also couldn't help but think of a dime novel hero, coming to the rescue in the proverbial nick of time, saving, as Pete Mulligan had put it, the "damezel in destress."

She could barely walk, and for a moment, she and Mitchell just stared at each other with the tacit understanding that neither would ever view things the same again. He quickly untied her then simply helped her out of the room where she had come close to taking her last breath.

"I'm glad you took me up on my offer, Mitch," O'Dwyer said.

"So am I," Mitchell said, gazing at Sarah more reverentially than he no doubt intended.

O'Dwyer looked over at Sarah. "No hard feelings, I hope," he said apologetically.

Sarah smiled weakly. "I don't agree with much of what you do Mr. O'Dwyer, but you seemed to have redeemed yourself in this matter," she said.

With Kenneth slumped on the couch, Mitchell and Sarah then shared their stories, one by one supplying the pieces that finally completed the puzzle. The last question came from Sarah.

"How did you know O'Dywer would have that kind of effect on Ken?" she asked.

"I didn't. It was a last ditch effort. When I discovered Ballard had worked for him, I called him immediately. It was John who suggested coming along."

O'Dywer nodded. "Yes, Miss Kaufman. You see, when Kenneth came to work for me, he observed my tactics and tried to copy them. He told me that he liked the way I could bend people to my will. O'Dwyer reddened slightly but continued speaking. "Over a couple of drinks, he even confessed to me about his own skirting of the law. He wanted to show me we were cut out of the same mold.

"That's why I think he fell apart when he heard my voice. He knew I was aware that he had taken a few liberties with the boiler codes. All I'd have to do was mention the explosion at the shoe factory in Massachusetts, and the engineering board would expel him for life.

And I knew, too, about his embezzling of funds. Just a small amount from a company he left years ago, but enough to get him locked up. Perhaps he surmised I knew other things as well."

"Thank God you were home," Sarah said.

O'Dwyer then walked over to Kenneth, put his arm on his shoulder, and glanced back at Mitchell and Sarah. "Now, Ken," he said, "let's pay a visit to the judge, shall we?"

THE TOLEDO

ONLY MORNING AND SUNDAY NEWSPAPER IN

Times

TOLEDO, FRIDAY, DECEMBER 18, 1925

**PLAYS SANTA FOR 16 YEARS
BUT IS REAL ONE THIS TIME**

Judge O'Brien O'Donnell.   Peggy O'Donnell.

ONE week from this morning a little 21-month-old miss will awaken, scamper from her bed at her home on Bancroft street and Pemberton drive and then rub her eyes in wonderment at the array of things Santa Claus has left her, all of which has been promised her for months by Judge O'Brien O'Donnell.

That morning will perhaps mean more to Judge O'Donnell than any during the 16 years he presided over the juvenile court of Lucas county and listened to the Christmas hopes of hundreds of children. The little girl he is going to make so happy this year is his own daughter, Peggy, whose real name is Margaret Louise. Last year she was too small to appreciate a visit from Old Saint Nick, so the visit was deferred.

Judge O'Donnell forsook other bachelors about three years ago. Peggy is his and Mrs. O'Donnell's only child.

27

Dr. Miller asked Sarah to talk to O'Brien first. "He may think he's having visions if you all go in at once," he said. "In fact," he added with a perplexed expression, I feel like I'm having them myself. Are you sure about this, Sarah?"

Sarah stared at the three men. At one time or another she had misjudged them all. Misjudged their ability to love, to hate, to do the right thing. It was her actions that brought this unlikely trio together, and now it was up to her to decide if, when they parted ways, they would keep the experience they had shared to themselves.

That was really the question that Dr. Miller was asking. Was she sure? About O'Dwyer, who she had never trusted; Kenneth, who she had always trusted; and Mitchell, who she had just begun to trust.

"Yes, I'm sure," she said.

When she entered his room, O'Brien was in the same listless state she had left him in a week ago. He opened his eyes briefly and turned away, shriveled and dejected. She spoke anyway, and kept speaking until she noted a flicker of a response. When she explained about Westfall, he turned over and stared at her. A light appeared in his vacant eyes.

"No, Obee," she repeated. "There was no murder."

It took several minutes for the words to settle in, but finally, O'Brien reached up and embraced Sarah. She then called in O'Dywer.

"I'll tell them to warm the bench for you, Judge," O'Dwyer said.

"John."

"You'll be yourself in no time, my man."

For several minutes, neither man said anything. Both were weak and raw, meeting at a psychological crossroads, one ascending from the depths of an emotional hell, the other on his way down. Kenneth spoke first.

"Well, I guess she's told you everything."

"Is it really true, Ken?"

Kenneth's bloodshot eyes narrowed. The muscles of his jaw contracted. "Yes it's true! But now I have a question." Kenneth turned to the others. "Please, can you give us some privacy?"

After they were all out of the room, Kenneth turned to O'Brien.

"Search your soul, Obee. Did you ever want me, desire me, as a man does a woman?"

O'Brien thought for a moment and then looked away. When he turned back his eyes were filled with tears.

"All right. I'll tell you. Honestly, I don't know. Perhaps there was a moment. These things are confused in my mind. I believe they always will be. But, you know, Ken, I don't care anymore. I have a family now, a family to which, thanks to Sarah, I can return. I've made many mistakes. But I've made my choices. And, you've made yours, too, Ken. I know you don't understand me, but I, too, can't understand. No matter what, I always considered you my friend. I accepted you as you were. Loved you. To have done this to me. I am a man of forgiveness, but I fear this exceeds my capacity."

O'Brien turned away.

"Thank you for the truth," Kenneth said, and he walked out into the hall where Dr. Miller was waiting. Everyone, especially O'Brien, had agreed that prison would do the man no good.

In one week's time O'Brien was resting at home. A week later he was back on the campaign trail, performing for the press as usual, particularly for Mitchell, who, with the promise of a hefty raise, had finally agreed to Steven Marks' obsequious pleas to resume his job. The story he eventually told about the judge included only the details of his reelection. The headline simply read: *On November 8th, 1924,*

Judge O'Donnell gave his acceptance speech for his sixth term in office to a roaring crowd with his wife and daughter, Margaret, by his side. Later that evening, Miss Sarah Kaufman hosted a party for him in her home.

After dinner, Sarah went to find Obee. He was off by himself in the hallway, holding the baby. He looked better than she'd seen him in years.

"Judge," she said, "to celebrate your victory, I brought you a small gift. It's the latest thing. They say it calms the nerves."

"What nerves?" he said, holding out a steady hand.

"Well, they're fun anyway."

"Ah, a crossword puzzle! I've wanted one of these." He examined it with an enthusiasm that recalled earlier days. "Let's see. Ten across: a six-letter word that means one joined to another in mutual benevolence." He looked at Sarah. "Friend. Yes. That's it. F-r-i-e-n-d. Margaret, my little one, some day I'll teach you how to do these," he said, looking down at the baby in his arms. "I think you'll like them."

Epilogue

Margaret endured an unconscious week of tubes and needles before pneumonia officially claimed her life. An aneurysm started it all, sending her into a coma from which she never emerged. Occasionally, during the first few days, she would seem to respond. A slight movement in the hand, a twitch of the mouth. But then, nothing. On the seventh night, she spiked a fever. Her three children were there to say their farewells, whether she could hear them or not. The death of a beloved mother. A mother who always had a kind word. Who cooked and cleaned and read. Who performed her daily tasks with grace, who tap danced a week before she died. A mother who had held fast to a secret.

When her children saw the admission papers, they at first assumed it was a mistake. A distortion of time brought on by the illness. Their mother's birthday was in March, not November. March 4, 1924.

Then came the painful task of going through her belongings. So many things. Rings, receipts, to-do lists. Unsmoked cigarettes, half-used lipstick, a talking stuffed animal. Crossword puzzles. When they came across her passport, they saw again what they still half believed was an error. November 23, 1923. But there next to it was her birth certificate, bearing the same date. Surely, that was no mistake.

They looked at each other with shocked expressions. The whole thing was unsettling, and slightly exciting. What did this mean? Had

289

their happy childhood been an illusion? Of course, they were still related, but somehow their identity felt at stake. They would gaze at pictures of their mother and behind the familiar, open face was now a hint of the enigmatic. It was there, in the eyes. Why she had kept this from them they could only speculate. They each had their ideas. For weeks it occupied their thoughts. But in the end, did it really matter? There might never be a way to know for sure. They had loved her and she them, that was the important thing.

When it came to dividing her property, it was her youngest son who was lucky enough to get the old pull-top desk. He was happy about this not only because he'd always admired the piece, but because his mother had cherished it so. Perhaps, he thought, it might tell him something of the part of her she refused to reveal. The empty drawers and hidden compartment that had fascinated him as a child symbolized the mystery waiting to be solved, the past that he imagined with the coolness of the wood on his fingers.

Author's Note

Writers who claim that their book "wrote itself" imply some mystical force at work in the creative process. A skeptic at heart, I have always attributed such a view to an unwillingness to accept criticism. If the book wrote itself, then the author is not really to blame for whatever goes wrong. But the writing of this book has made me wonder.

My doctoral work was in nineteenth-century American literature, and so when my mother-in-law, Margaret, gave me the scrapbooks to review, I initially saw in them a potential scholarly article; something about judicial authority and the press. But then she died, and with her death came the revelation about her birth. Instinctively, I turned back to the scrapbooks, and the rest, as they say, is history or, more precisely, historical fiction. For, fight it as I may, a story emerged in those documents, telling itself in words too strong to resist; a story in which each of my questions seemed anticipated, if not predetermined.

Wouldn't it be interesting, I thought, if the judge had a female colleague? And then I encountered Sarah Kaufman. What if there were a mystery, perhaps involving a murder? Frank Westfall's drowning and O'Brien's illness, side by side on the same page. What if there were some evidence to corroborate my growing sense of the judge? As if by magic, the letter. And on it went.

Truth really is sometimes stranger than fiction, but fiction is often a more compelling way to illuminate truth. This story is thus a fiction comprised of real people and events. The achievements of the central characters are entirely factual, however. O'Brien O'Donnell was a genuinely remarkable historical figure. He lived long enough to fill two further scrapbooks with articles that, even after he retired, continued to chronicle his every move. I thank him particularly for hiring Sarah Kaufman, who, in large part due to his enlightened attitudes, was allowed to become a distinctive figure in her own right.

A few names referred to only briefly in the book deserve further mention. Suffragette and education reformer, Pauline Steinem, was the grandmother of noted feminist, Gloria Steinem. Roger Bresnahan, the "Duke of Tralee," was a Hall of Fame baseball player whose invention of the shin guard was adopted by major league baseball. Moe Berg, shortstop for the Mud Hens and later catcher for the Brooklyn Dodgers, became a celebrated spy for the Allies in World War II.

Acknowledgments

Without the assistance of the following individuals, the dream of this book would have never become a reality. Frank Lehmann of Lehmann Bindery, who allowed the process to begin by unbinding the scrapbooks with precision and care. Harry R. Ilman, whose colorful work, *Unholy Toledo,* provided crucial background material. John Husman, for his help with Mud Hens history. John L. Keefer of Ohio Pioneer Pathways, who responded to my numerous requests fully and promptly. Keith McCrea of the Lucas County Probate Court. His generous, voluntary research helped enormously to fill in the missing pieces. History professor and writer, David Kuchta. His thoughtful critique helped me complicate the characterizations and deepen the plot. My daughter, Brooke Fruchtman, a fine editor whose wicked red pen prodded me to cut out the schmaltz. My son, Benjamin, whose refusal to read the manuscript until it was in print spurred me on. My parents, Rhoda and Marvin Kantor. Had I written *War and Peace* their confidence in me couldn't have been greater. Editor extraordinaire, Susan Mary Malone. Quite simply, she helped me see what I needed to do. My cousin and graphic artist, Lauren Kahn. Her cover design captured visually the essence of the story. President of Sunstone Press, Jim Smith, a consummate professional who gave me the opportunity of a lifetime. My husband Dean. Impossible to thank enough; for emotional support, technical expertise, honest critique and reading,

reading and more reading. I thank them all, but none more than my mother-in-law, Margaret, who shortly before her death, handed me some family scrapbooks she thought I might enjoy.